The Sage

Witch's Ambitions Trilogy Book Three

Kayla Krantz

Cover by Laura Callender and James Price
Edited by Kat Hutson

ISBN: 9781732423084
First Edition: August 2019
Library of Congress Control Number: 2019900199

https://authorkaylakrantz.com/

Always let your voice be heard.

Witch's Ambitions Trilogy

Book One: The Council

Book Two: The Elemental Coven

Book Three: The Sage

Chapter One
All is Fair

love you.

Those three words are the cure-all, end-all of pain. For some people, the world stops when they hear that phrase from their favorite person; for others, it's a reason to keep going, to keep fighting when they've lost all other hope. Love is a magical element, and even we magical beings don't quite fully understand it.

This especially applies to me. I've never been the overly affectionate type, but Clio had been the death of that. Long before he confessed his feelings, I had always felt he was special in a way no other person was. Talking with him is easy. In those early days of Ignis, we'd dive deep into a conversation, and the world would disappear around us, like we were the only people in existence. We had a lot of moments like that—insignificant to everyone but us. Those moments built our relationship, solidified our friendship. They were an anchor holding us in place while the world raged around us.

When I suffered with my healing and Clio lost his parents, we were there for each other.

But things change—not always for the worst.

I've discovered different aspects of humanity in the

Elemental Coven, my newest lesson being that love can be expressed in more ways than just words. Now, cradled in Clio's arms, I focus only on him, what he means to me, and how lost I'd be without him. If that focus slips away, everything will end. I look up, staring deep into Clio's eyes, wishing those three magic words would fall from his lips so I can ignore the new pit of agony rising in me. I can't walk.

My mother abandoned me to certain death.

My legs had been rendered useless in the battle.

One by one, the pieces fall into place, and I don't like the picture they form.

Love should make none of this matter, but that's not how it works, and I can't wish away the pain.

"Stay with me," he says, his hand cupping my cheek.

I barely hear him as my eyelids flutter, and a second later, the blackness reclaims me.

Chapter Two
Reunion

WHEN MY EYES open again, the whiteness of the room comes to me in spots—just small, bright flecks breaking through the darkness. Then the pain follows, thoroughly gripping and by far stronger than anything I've felt in a long time. My fingers tense, clutching the fabric beneath me as I wait for the wave to pass.

My left leg hurts, but that's nothing new. But the pain wiggling into my right leg is definitely a first. With that thought, the memory comes rushing back—icicles spearing both my legs; Grail; the battle. I scream out in a mix of physical and emotional agony. My shaky fingers try to reach out, to touch the bandages wrapped around my legs, but I can't do it.

I'm so afraid of what I'll find there—to see how bad the damage really is.

"Lilith! Lilith, look at me!" Fingers press gently into my shoulder.

I tear my eyes away from the bandages the second I realize I'm not alone. Clio is beside me, black hair disheveled and eyes bloodshot. I recognize that look; he hasn't slept. Most likely, he's stayed by my side since they brought me in. I wonder

3

how long ago that was. The bandages on my legs look clean and dry. There's no telling how many times my dressings have been changed since we returned.

"Are you in pain?" Ambrossi asks. "Where does it hurt?" My Healer stands on the other side of my bed, and I swivel my head toward him.

"Everywhere," I manage and rest my head on the pillow again. Even those small movements drain me of what little energy I have.

I hear footsteps; Ambrossi is on the move. I don't look at him. Clio strokes my hair and the side of my face, but I don't look at him, either. It's been a long time since I've seen him—I spent weeks thinking he was dead—so I should be overjoyed that he's here now, that he's still *alive*. But I feel numb. I stare up at the ceiling, then it all comes back to me and I recognize where we are.

This is the hospital wing in the Community Villa of the Elemental Coven. I think of my sister Willow and wonder where she is right now. I'm both surprised and hurt that she's not already in here at my side.

Someone offers a glass of water, and I turn my head enough to see Clio. He smiles, thin lips barely moving on his pale face as he extends the cup to me. It feels like we've been apart so much longer than it's actually been, but I can't deny that he looks different. His varying scars and the haunted shadow in his eyes make him look older, somehow.

I force myself to smile back and take the cup, swigging down the water. It makes me cough once.

"*Careful*," Clio warns, but I don't look at him until the cup is empty.

He raises his eyebrow, like he's certain I'll be sick after drinking too much too fast. But I don't feel nauseous; I feel more focused, sharper. Again, that leaves me to wonder how long I've been in this bed. How long I've been unconscious.

"How do you feel now?" Ambrossi asks as he pries the

empty glass from my fingers.

"Better." I cough so hard again, a mouthful of water sprays out of me.

Clio reaches out to gently rub my back as I catch my bearings. I have to ask these next questions, and I can't bring myself to look at anything but the bandages on my legs. Two of the people I love are in this room, but there are still far too many out there, and I don't even know if they're okay.

"Where's Helena?" I'm still not sure I really want to know the answer, but I close my eyes and wait for a reply. Crowe's words rise in the back of my mind—his mention of a dead witch when I asked about my mother and best friend, right as I was captured by the Council.

No one speaks for so long that eventually, I open my eyes, and I see her—Helena, ethereal glow making her more beautiful than I've ever seen her before. She stands just inside the door, a smile growing on her porcelain face as she gazes back at me.

In situations like this, I've found myself thinking less and less and instead relying on reflex. I regret that instantly when I end up flinging myself off the table to get to her. My chin cracks against the hard white floor, and my teeth snap together, sending an ache all the way up into my brain. I hardly notice the pain when she rushes to my side.

I heard Clio yell my name, and now he's on the floor beside me too, but I don't look at him. Helena pulls me into her arms. I grab her as tightly as I can and bury my face in her shoulder, bawling my eyes out.

"How'd you get out?" I ask, needing the answer more than I've needed anything in my life. For a time, I assumed she was the dead witch Crowe mentioned. When she projects her thoughts to me in the form of her memories, I realize now that she was. She *played* dead when the Council came, and they believed it.

'It's okay. I'm okay,' Helena reassures me.

I squeeze her tighter, still not quite able to believe her. It seems as if every time someone tells me things are okay, the complete opposite is true.

Helena turns her head, and I realize Clio has shifted closer. He reaches out a tentative hand and settles it on my shoulder. "Let's get you back in bed."

He doesn't move until I bob my head in consent. Then his arms wrap around me, slowly taking Helena's place, and he lifts me easily to set me back down on the hard mattress. The smallest hint of a smile appears on his lips, but the concern in his eyes is hard to miss. I don't like that concern, but amid the fray in my mind right now, it's a lower priority.

"Where's Ivy?" I don't have to say it out loud for Helena to hear me, but I do.

Clio's face scrunches in confusion, but he follows my gaze to Helena, trying to read her expression for clues of what I'm talking about. Uncomfortable in the spotlight, Helena drops her head to break the connection, and I know why before she says a word. I won't want to hear this, she doesn't want to *say* this, but because I asked, she'll tell me.

"She's gone."

The way she says it, I know Ivy isn't dead—it's worse. She ran away again, once more thinking of herself over me, over Willow, and I don't know what to say. So I say nothing. I sit still, blinking rapidly to keep my tears from falling.

"Give us a moment, please," Clio says, looking first at Ambrossi then Helena.

"Of course," Ambrossi says and places his hand on Helena's back, guiding her out the door.

When the door clicks closed, I look at him, at the exhaustion on his face, most prominent in his eyes.

"Who's Ivy?" he asks, reaching up to swipe a fat tear off my cheek with his thumb.

I sniffle, lift the blanket to my face to wipe away all the signs of my weakness, and think about how to answer him.

There isn't a good way to tell the story, and the more I think about it, the more I realize I don't really want to.

"That's… something I'll tell you another time."

Maybe Clio sees the fresh tears rolling down my cheeks or senses that I'm close to a breaking point I don't normally reach. "Okay."

I blink back more tears and reach out to grab one of his hands. They're so much larger than mine. The scars dappling his neck are here as well. His palms are darker than the rest of his hands—a side effect of being a true Ignis Equipped. I lace my fingers through his, fearing he'll pull away at any minute and I've only imagined how close we really are, before I let myself look into his strong green eyes.

"I really missed you," I tell him.

"I missed you too," he says and smiles. That smile disappears when his eyes drift back to my bandaged legs. He rests a hand on my knee, and I can *see* the thoughts flying through his head.

"That's dangerous," I say.

He quirks an eyebrow and looks at me from the corner of his eye. "What is?"

"Thinking that intensely."

He licks his lips and sighs. "I can't help it. This… this was my fault."

The response catches me off guard, and I struggle to sit up. Instantly, he lifts his hands to try easing me back down, but I don't obey. I'm mystified by his words, grasping for understanding I can't reach on my own. "How in the world is this *your* fault?"

"I got there too late… I didn't…" He stops, visibly pained. "I didn't protect you like I said I would."

I don't like this. It doesn't sound like something Clio would ever say, and I can't believe I'm hearing him say them now. I frown. "Really, Clio? I'm a big girl. I can take care of myself."

His eyes move to my legs again.

The shift in focus angers me, and I jut out my chin. "Think what you will, but I'm grateful it happened."

He purses his lips and looks at me as if I've completely lost my mind. "You're grateful you were kidnapped? Grateful you've been secluded from everyone you've ever loved? That you can't walk?"

I breathe in slowly. "It sounds bad when you put it like that, but you don't know the entire story, Clio. There's a lot of things I wouldn't have known without having come here. I would've been a different person if the Council still had me in their clutches. I don't regret the path my life has taken. I mean, we've saved so many witches and found out the truth behind the war. I never would've done any of that if Willow's people had never saved me."

"Maybe, but it's not fair for you to have to sacrifice so much," he says.

"Who said anything about fair?" I blink and think of Willow. At one time, she had given her life for this war. Then I think of Iris and Chastity, who'd sacrificed themselves too. "There are witches who have given more than I have and witches who have given less."

"Who?" he demands.

I let go of his hand, and he clutches it into a fist. I trace my finger over his knuckles, studying the way they turn white from the pressure. "Clio, the point is we've *all* made sacrifices for the greater good… That's one of the milestones that come with war."

His eyes glaze over, but he doesn't look up from the edge of my blanket. He's made sacrifices too, whether or not he's willing to admit it. One look at him, at the scars on his neck and face, makes that much apparent. If I could see the scars on his heart, I would bet good money it would look the same way. He doesn't argue the point further, but I don't know if that's because I've truly won or if he's too lost in his own memories to even try anymore.

Clio remembers things about this war that I can't even imagine. I told myself I wouldn't push him, I wouldn't *force* him to talk, but now that we've reached this part of the conversation, it's all I want to do.

"Clio... where have you been?" The dryness of my throat only exacerbates the raspy croak of my voice.

"I was... away," he says, reaching up to finger the ugly scar on the side of his neck. He looks away, as if looking for an escape, but there is none.

"*Where?*" I ask breathlessly. Where could he have gone that the Council wouldn't have found him and recruited him to take my old place? "I... I thought you were dead and..." I can't finish that thought. Even though he's right here in front of me, it still hurts to remember that uncertain period of my life when I had no idea *what* happened to him.

"I don't know." He swallows, and his face contorts. "Fern saved me. I would've been dead if she hadn't protected me, *healed* me. She watched over me until I was well enough to take care of myself."

I look at all his scars again, imagining them fresh and raw, bleeding, and Clio's life seeping away with the blood. "You got all those wounds in the Battle of Ignis?"

"No," he says quickly. *Too* quickly, and it confirms what I'd already guessed. Clio almost died trying to save me.

"You don't have to lie to me," I reply. "What you did was noble. You can't help what happened any more than I can."

"I should've been a better fighter. For you, for Helena, for myself. And I failed when it really mattered."

There's a reason Clio and I get along as well as we do; we understand each other in ways we will never understand other witches.

"But you did fight, Clio. You fought your way back to health and found me." I pause before adding, "*How* did you find me?"

"Fern... knew you were there. I don't know how. I thought the Council had saved you from the Elemental Coven, but Fern said you were in handcuffs, and... well, I just had to see for myself. I'm glad I did."

"So if Fern knew about the battle, where is she now?" I ask emotionlessly, very aware of the fact that I have still not seen her since I left Ignis for good. The thought that she never stopped looking after me warms what little bit of a heart I have left.

"I don't know," he admits. "She disappeared when we reached the Grove and saw the battle."

My stomach clenches. *Not this, again.* Suddenly, I wish I'd stayed unconscious. I'm grateful to have Clio back in my life, but the uncertainty of Fern's situation leaves me uneasy again.

"If Fern knew where I was, why wouldn't she tell me you were okay? I thought you were *dead.*"

"I almost was... You have no idea how much I hate myself for leaving you there like that. Maybe Fern knew that if she said anything, I'd go after you. It was my fault you were captured."

He's right, I know, but I've become so adjusted to people doing me wrong that the thought doesn't hurt as much as it might've at one time. "But that turned out to be a good thing," I say.

THE SAGE

Chapter Three
Sickness

THE BEST THING about Willow is how high she holds
her head. I've always bled self-confidence, but she is the
embodiment of it. It's hard for me to imagine her ever
feeling hesitant to charge into a difficult situation, and in this
case, I'm right. As Clio and I sit staring at one another, the door
bursts open, hitting the wall so hard that it bangs with an echo.
Before I can even make sense of what's happening, she pulls me
into her arms, Kado yipping at her heels. I'm so happy to see
both of them that the tears I managed to blink back only a
minute before come pouring out in torrents.

I grab onto her, and she runs her hand down my short
hair, flattening it to my scalp. I never want her to let me go.
Before the war, and the knowledge of Willow and the Elemental
Coven, I used to think about running away, to a brand new
place, and starting over just to see what it would be like to be
someone else. Now that I'm here, in the thick of it, I can't
imagine *ever* wanting to be anyone else.

Willow pulls back and swipes a lock of hair from my
eyes. Her black eyes are wide, unnerving in their anxiety. "I'm so
glad to see you're okay," she says and hugs me again. This time,
she squeezes me so tightly, I squeak, desperate for breath.

"Uh, hi?" Clio says, and I hear the chair scrape the floor

11

as he stands. "Should I give you two a minute alone?"

Willow pulls away and looks from me to him and back to me again. Slowly, her eyebrows rise, and the finest smile appears on her face. "Is this him? You found Clio?" she says. Heat fills my cheeks, and she doesn't wait for the answer before she throws her arms around him. "Thank you for bringing my sister back to me."

He peers at me with wide eyes over her shoulder. He's still trying to figure out who she is and how he should react to her. I could help him, but mentally, I'm somewhere else. I'm busy adjusting. Seeing the two of them together in the same room leaves an odd feeling deep in the pit of my stomach, like my old life and new life are clashing, and I'm not sure which one I want to win.

"It's good to finally meet you," she says, extending her hand when they break away. "I'm Willow. Lily's sister."

Clio blinks and slowly returns the handshake. "I'm Clio." He turns to me. "Lily? I thought you hated that name."

Willow turns to me, the smile still there. "You hate your nickname?"

I shake my head. "It just always felt weird. I guess, deep down, I associated it with you, and I didn't understand that."

Clio pulls his hand back from Willow and takes the smallest step backward. "I... I have so many questions."

"I can imagine," she says, bobbing her head. "And don't worry, you'll learn everything in time. For now, though, you need to spend all the time you can with her."

He reaches out to clutch my hand. "I intend to."

Willow smiles, and I know it's because a fierce blush has appeared on my face. "You two are such a cute couple."

Despite everything I've been through, I can't find the courage to meet Clio's gaze and see how he reacts to her statement. Even though he's never given me a reason to think differently, I don't know what I'll do if he disagrees. What if he says it was all just a joke?

THE SAGE

So, I disengage myself from the situation. "Hey, boy!" I call to Kado, reaching my fingers toward him.

Excited yips burst from the dead dog, and his tongue laps over my palm before he sets his front paws on the bed, prepared to jump up with me.

"No, no," Willow says and taps him on the head.

Kado's enthusiasm fades as he looks up at her, the excited barks fading into concerned whines. He sniffs loudly and nuzzles my hand. Clio takes another step away.

"What's wrong?" I ask, my own smile faltering.

"This dog…" He gestures toward Kado.

Then I remember how jarring everything must be to him. I've gotten used to Willow and her resurgence, as well as her collection of reanimated animals and people. I've grown so used to death that I barely notice the massive scar across Kado's torso—the one that had originally killed him.

"He's dead," Willow says with a shrug. "I am too."

Clio's eyes go wider than I've ever seen them.

"He's harmless," I assure him. He's gone as white as Kado's fur, and I'm a little worried this is all too much for him to accept.

Kado, sensing the sudden tension, takes the opportunity to lick Clio's hand. Some of the panic visibly leaves Clio's shoulders. "I have a lot to learn," he says at last, running his fingers through the soft puff of fur on the top of Kado's head.

I bob my head, and a new flash of memories hits me— Crowe and the file. He saved my life at Headquarters, but the last image I can remember of him is Crowe running through the thick of the battle beside Katrina. "Where's Crowe?"

"With Katrina, I'd imagine," Willow says.

That drains all my concern at once. Even though Crowe was on the Council's side before the Battle of the Grove, I hear no disdain in Willow's voice. For saving me, he's welcome here. Not to mention the fact that Katrina wouldn't have it any other way. In the face of everything, it's nice to think *something* positive has happened.

"I'll go get him, if you want," Clio offers.

I shake my head. "It can wait." I don't want to say out loud that I was worried Willow had turned him away. I'll give Crowe his time to settle in, to be with the love of his life. For everything he's done for me, it's the least I can do for him.

"Okay. Whatever you need," Clio says, squeezes my hand, and sits down again.

I smile back at him, but it feels a little forced when I look at Willow. Now that my initial feelings of the situation have settled, my brain is diving deep. When I look at Willow, I see Ivy, and then I remember what Helena said—how she abandoned us once again. *I was a fool for thinking that a snake emerging from its skin would be reborn as anything other than a snake.*

As far as I know, Willow didn't see Ivy in Ignis. Helena and I were the only witnesses to the fact that, for years, she was Helena's pet cat, hiding from the threat of execution rather than letting either of her daughters know she was still alive. I wonder if Helena had already told Willow about, or if she thought it would be better coming from my mouth.

Just as I make the decision to ask, the door once again slams open. Clio hops to his feet, he and Willow forming a protective wall between whoever is entering and me. Annoyed, I glance around them as Ambrossi runs inside.

"I need everyone out now!" he demands, panting. When he catches sight of Willow, he gives her an apologetic blink.

"What's happening?" she asks. Helena appears in the room, pushing a bed ahead of her. There's a witch curled up on it, but I can't tell who it is under all the blankets.

"Food poisoning," Helena says, and the end of the sentence is punctuated by the sound of the witch vomiting.

Clio crinkles his nose before he turns to look at me. "I'll come back as soon as I can, okay?"

I nod but don't look at him. Willow and Clio hesitate a moment longer before another warning look from Ambrossi sends them on their way. They know better than to argue with such a dedicated Healer in the presence of a sick witch.

Chapter Four

Answers

'M NOT SURE which is worse, listening to the thoughts inside my head or the witch in the other bed puking their guts out. I stare down at my bandaged legs and experience a moment of pure envy for the other witch in the room. Whoever it is will get better.

I will not.

Helena checks in on me and the other witch a few times, but other than that, I'm alone, and that's dangerous. My mind is in a constant state of wondering, of straying away from what I should be focused on. I need to talk to Crowe, to see if he still has the file. I have no idea what's inside, what it could tell me about Ivy, or if it has anything to do with why she's abandoned us again. I could see, but I can't work up the nerve to summon Crowe.

Instead, I torture myself with other aspects of my life until I think I'm going to scream. Just for the Hell of it, I try to move my legs—both the one injured at childhood and the one just recently destroyed. They hurt the same. It shouldn't be possible, and yet it is. I'm curious what they look like under all the gauze and bandages. I picture deep holes and frayed tissue.

It's hard to believe *icicles* are behind this. I reach down, gently fingering the edge of my bandages.

As if Helena sensed me about to do something I shouldn't, she appears in the room and approaches my bed, orange eyebrow raised curiously. "What are—"

I grab her collar so tightly that I nearly choke her. "Where's Crowe?" I ask, fairly certain that I'm scaring her but also unable to release my manic grip.

She blinks, black eyes stretched wide. *'I'll get him for you, but first, we need to move you to a new room.'* She projects the thought to me, and I release my death grip, feeling guilty.

I narrow my eyes, not liking the answer but at the same time wanting to see him too desperately to argue. "Thank you." Then I pause. "Why do I need to change rooms? What's wrong with this one?"

The other witch hurls again, and I grimace. Helena gives me the same look in return. She gently helps me up into her arms. At first, I assume she'll drop me—that I'm far too heavy for someone delicate like her to carry—but she manages me just fine. As she approaches the door, I send a last glance back at my old bed and the sick witch beside it.

"Get better soon," I call, but there's no response.

I didn't expect one.

I look at Helena's long red hair as we move easily down the hallway. It seems longer than the last time I saw her, and I wonder if it'll continue to grow even though she's technically dead. "That witch must be pretty sick if you're moving me."

She shrugs. "Not particularly. I could put you back in there, if you want. I just felt maybe you didn't want to listen to another witch puking half the night."

"See? This is why you'll always be my best friend. You just *know* things."

She smiles, and if she were still alive, I imagine a fierce blush would've overtaken her cheeks. Not out of embarrassment but out of pride for the fact that we know one another like the backs of our own hands. The room she takes me to is across the hall from the last one but a ways down—hopefully far enough away to not hear the vomiting echoing down the hall.

The new room is small, comfier, designed more as a bedroom than part of the hospital wing. The bed isn't a tiny one with silver railings at the edges; it's fluffy and comfortable, and I sink right into it.

"This is much better, Helena. Thank you." I hadn't realized how badly I needed the change of scenery until it was forced on me.

"You're very welcome, Li," she replies and reaches out to swipe my hair out of my eyes. "Did you need anything else before I go get Crowe?"

I shake my head, feeling that twinge of nervousness all over again, and pull Helena into a hug so tight that she'd be winded if she still needed to breathe. There really are no words to describe how much I love this girl.

"How's your pain?" she asks. She pulls away as if she fears she might hurt me with her affection. Her fingers trail my bandages so lightly, I barely feel it.

I smile or put what I think appears to be a smile on my face. That is one question she doesn't want me to put into words, and it's one I don't want to even attempt. I know it will end with me in tears. If I'm going to see Crowe in a minute, that is the last thing I want to do.

"Not too bad," I force myself to say.

Helena narrows her eyes. "Really?"

"Yeah, yeah. I just want to talk to Crowe."

"Be back in a minute," she assures me, and she does not lie.

I count the seconds, and exactly sixty later, she's back with Crowe in tow. I sit up when our eyes meet. His hair is windblown, cheeks still covered in ash and soot, and I know he's given no time to himself since we arrived—not even to sleep or bathe. He's been at Katrina's side, and this is most likely the first time he's been asked to leave it.

Love is a hell of a drug.

"Thank you," I tell Helena.

She nods and curtsies. "Let me know if you need anything else."

I've been stubborn in the past about asking for help, and she knows I haven't changed that much. She'll be better off reading my mind if she wants to know my true thoughts, and by the way she narrows her eyes before slipping out of the room, I have a feeling she's come to the same conclusion.

Crowe doesn't greet me or ask how I am. He slips a bundle of papers out from the folds of his cloak and hands them to me before swiping the strands of messy red hair from his eyes. The exhaustion as he plops down in the chair makes him look ten years older at least.

"Have you slept?" I ask him.

He smiles and lifts a hand to his face, wipes his eyes, and looks at me carefully. "Haven't had the time. And I'm guessing you haven't had much of it, either."

"You'd guess correctly," I say and yawn, as if his acknowledgment of my exhaustion finally makes it real.

"There's a lot here to take in," he admits.

"Katrina give you a tour?"

Crowe bobs his head. "It's a lot different from the Land of Five."

That's the truth. "How's Dawn?" I ask, wondering if Crowe has even taken the time to inquire about her.

"She's... well..." His face twists into an undecided grimace.

"She's what?"

"She's not handling things as well as you," he admits, and the corner of his lip twitches. "She hasn't even been kind to the Healers. She told Ambrossi to never talk to her again. I don't think she meant it, but she's struggling with the idea of... well..." His gaze drops to my legs.

Her struggle is mine.

"She'll be okay," I say at once.

I don't know how I know it, but I do. I remember the very first time I saw her, her bouncy walk as she climbed the hill during the Arcane Ceremony. She was a powerful witch then, and that kind of strength doesn't go away because of one tragic event. "It might be years from now," I admit, reaching down to brush my fingers against my originally damaged leg, "but she'll adjust."

Crowe smirks at the gesture.

I jerk my hand away. "What's so funny?"

"You... being *optimistic*. I'm not sure what to do with that."

"I'm allowed to be from time to time."

"Of course you are. It's just strange. I haven't seen it much." He shrugs, but the irritating smirk remains on his face.

"Fair enough." The very first time I met him, I *had* tried to hit him in the face. I've never truly been kind to him, just civil at best. It's hard to believe we became friends through that.

Biting his lip, he eyes my legs again. "You play it down, but how are you, really?"

I look down at the folder, not wanting to see the pity on his face—if there *is* any. There was a second ago, and I ignored it with the laughter, but now, it's not so easy. Crowe's always been a strange one when it comes to emotions, going from hot to cold and back within five minutes. But I can't handle that kind of uncertainty right now.

"Have you had a chance to read it yet?"

Crowe shakes his head. "It... uh... didn't seem right without you. It's *your* mother in there."

My mouth is dry as I stare down at the manila folder. This is the moment I've waited my entire life to reach—the minute I would learn the truth of my parents, my leg, *everything*. Slowly, I open it, and the first thing I see is a picture of my mother. But she looks young, too young, and I wonder when

20

this was taken. I lift it with shaking fingers and turn it over, but there's no writing on the back.

My eyebrows pull together, and I hear the creak of Crowe's chair as he shifts closer, but he doesn't speak, either. He's giving me time, as he promised he would. I set the picture aside and pick up the front paper.

Name: Ivy Paradox
Eye Color: Blue
Hair Color: Black
Mother of two daughters: Willow and Lilith
Coven of Origin: Mentis
Power: Shapeshifting

Tears build in the corners of my eyes. Until now, it was easy enough to think the encounter with my mother was nothing but a figment of my imagination. This proves it was real, that *she's* real, and that leaves me torn.

I set the paper next to the picture and turn to the next page. Willow's name is at the top, followed by a brief description and the word *Deceased* after the date and time of her execution. Below that, I see my name, and my breath catches in my throat. The first word after my name is a giant red *Missing*, and I wonder who took the time to write that down. Had it been the Sage or someone else? Someone I've never met?

I think of the extensive bunker of witches housing all the old members of the Council before the Headquarters were destroyed. There's no telling who it was, but they didn't forget about me after I disappeared in the Battle of Ignis. The Council kept me in their thoughts right up to my capture, just as I suspected they would.

Swallowing, I push the thought away and force myself to keep reading.

Original Coven of Origin: Mentis

Last known Coven of Residence: Ignis
Powers: Many
First appearance in Mentis, Lilith is believed to have been born outside the Land of Five. Briefly, she was raised in Mentis until Ivy was lost. Lilith was then passed along to foster parents Regina and Howard, UnEquipped Ignis residents, to monitor her for signs of further magic development. While her original abilities are unknown, she was corrupted with Ignis magic at the age of three when Howard disobeyed orders. Her childhood passed without signs of ability until shortly before her Arcane Ceremony. Her results were unlike those we have seen before.

A drop of water hits the paper, and I realize I'm crying. I'm not sure which is the hardest part to comprehend—the fact that I was born *outside* the Land of Five or the fact that Regina and Howard always knew the truth about me. Yet instead of doing what the Council wanted and throwing me to the wolves at the first sign of magic—to be stripped of powers or executed—they disobeyed orders and kept me hidden for as long as they could.

A sickening jolt of realization flares through me. The Elemental Coven weren't responsible for killing my adopted mother and father. That was the Council. And the worst part? They did it right under my nose, and I stupidly believed them.

Eyes burning with tears, I look up and meet Crowe's gaze. His face is pale, and he glances from me to the paper before asking, "What's it say?"

I can only pass the paper to him. He reads it quietly, and I watch the curiosity behind his eyes morph first to confusion, then horror. Finally, he peers at me over the edge. "I don't understand. If the Council wanted to strip you of your powers, why did they nominate you to take Tarj's place?"

"I don't know," I say softly, staring at the picture of Ivy again. "I don't understand any of it."

THE SAGE

I've been passed from home to home to home my entire life. It's no wonder I have no clear idea of who I am. I'm a mixed creation, holding pieces of all the different witches and homes that I've come into contact with over the years.

Crowe brushes the hair from his eyes again and blows out a breath. It's hard to read his face, and I don't like it. I wait to see if he says anything, but he doesn't, so I try prodding into his thoughts, a thousand questions at the front of my mind. Who wrote this file, and how deep does the information go? Surely, Crowe must have *some* idea.

"What is it?" he asks as soon as he feels the intrusion in his head. He lifts a hand to cover the space between his eyebrows and blocks the connection.

"Did you know?" My voice trembles with so much uncertainty, it's almost impossible to understand the words.

"About this?" he retorts, smacking the paper with the back of his hand. "No, I... I never read the files."

"What about the others? Rayna, Hyacinth, Lynx... Tarj? Anyone?"

Crowe shakes his head slowly. "We didn't... they didn't tell us anything like that."

"Like what?" I ask, wondering exactly what kinds of things he *does* know.

"Details." He stops to rub a thumb over his lips. "We were all like you. We... didn't know much, in the grand scheme of things. We were like pawns, just moving where we were told without really knowing why."

"You knew more than me," I point out. "You knew about the bunker, about the files, about the *prison*. The Sage said I was her apprentice, and she didn't bother to tell me *any* of that."

"I was also with the Council for longer than you."

That answer doesn't make me feel better, but I can understand it. Almost. "And you never got curious. Never wondered about the files? Never even tried to see if they had one on you?"

Crowe swallows with an embarrassed frown. "No. With Sable around, I did what I could to obey orders. The Security Wing wasn't exactly the easiest place to get in and out of."

"But not completely," I point out. "Sable knew you by name."

Crowe frowns. "Yeah, well, let's just say the Sage tested me differently than she tested you."

I'm not sure what to say to that. I remember her telling me about the extremes they'd put Crowe through, testing his body to the physical limits of survival. I drop my gaze to the folder, studying the dull cover. "We'll never know the whole story, will we?"

Crowe shakes his head. "It's doubtful. The only one who knows it all is the Sage."

"And her mind is a fortress."

Chapter Five

Another Coven

CROWE LEAVES NOT long after that, and I'm alone, staring at the walls. I'd thought my sickly roommate was bad, but no roommate at all is worse. I used to do everything alone, dreading the times when I had company. It's hard to believe I'm the same person. As I stare off into space, my fingers run over the empty half of the bed. I wish Kado were here, or even Clio.

Normal witches sleep. I can't help but chastise myself for the fact that I'm just not *normal*.

I blink slowly and look at my legs again. The thought of sleeping reminds me of my newest power—astral projection. Compared to the others, it's my strongest ability. Possibly because it's the newest, but I can't help but wonder if the reason goes deeper than that. It's also becoming my favorite. When I project, I can move without my disability to slow me.

That's the only way I'll ever walk again, and I start crying.

I should be grateful that I'm still alive—a lot of witches did *not* make it through the Battle of the Grove—but I keep thinking maybe it would've been easier to die. If I had died and

Willow used her powers to bring me back, would I come back with both legs healed?

I let out a huge sigh. I'll never know.

Forcing myself out of this despairing pit, I look down at the manila folder on my lap. I insisted Crowe take it with him before he left, but he didn't. Now, I'm stuck with it—my demons in physical form. Part of me is grateful. This is all information that Willow should know, and I have the feeling that without proof, she wouldn't believe me, wouldn't even take time out of her day to listen.

I think about the other Coven outside the Land of Five—the one in which I was apparently born. What's it like? Then I contemplate Clio's seemingly magic return. Since coming to the Elemental Coven, I haven't had much time to ask him for the details of his life when he was away. I'm willing to bet he hasn't been in Aquais or Aens this entire time. Willow's people would've been able to find him if that were the case. She told me he was nowhere in the Land of Five, and at the time, it was a concept I couldn't grasp.

The Council had always warned us about venturing beyond the borders of the Land of Five, claiming the landscapes had been so devastated by war that it was too dangerous. Was it really? Or was it dangerous to the *Council* if we were to find that other Coven? More witches?

I'm dumbfounded by the fact that the thought never crossed my mind before. There have always been witches who oppose the Council, witches who disagree with the way things are run. Border skirmishes were common events in the Land of Five when I was a kid, but the more I think about it, the more curious that information becomes. There haven't been any border fights in recent years, and I wonder if there were ever any, or if that was the Council's way of covering it up, using their brainwashing witch Tabitha to ensure all loose ends were tied up when witches turned up missing or dead.

'Our mother did it because she loved us so much.' Willow's

words drift into my mind again.

"Ivy's got a lot to explain," I whisper to the folder. "If she ever comes back."

"What's that, now?" Clio's voice drifts from the doorway, and I jump. He laughs and sits down in the empty seat beside my bed. "Sorry. I didn't mean to spook you."

"It's all right," I say, trying to hide the file. But his eyes are already on it.

"What's that?"

I look down at it, turn it over, and wish again that Crowe would've held onto it for me. I don't like the story in these pieces of paper, even if it's a part of me. I want to burn them, but then Willow would never get to read it. At least no one else would know.

Then I look up into Clio's green eyes. If there's one witch I can trust to keep a secret, it's him. Letting out a slow breath, I push the folder toward him.

"It's a file Crowe helped me steal from the Council. It's about my mother." Clio just stares at me. "My *birth* mother."

"What's it say?" he asks, eyes stretching wide with curiosity.

"Here." I hand it to him. Saying any of it out loud would make it all too real somehow, and I'm still trying to process it myself.

Clio shrugs, scanning every page, before he looks up at me. "That's terrible. I'm sorry, Li. Why would he give this to you right now? You're already dealing with so much."

"Don't blame him. It was my idea. I needed to know what it said. It hurts—it does—but there's another Coven. Somewhere out there. Have you ever heard of it?"

His face is entirely blank. He's always been able to keep his feelings under lock and key, and right now, that's not what I want to read. I need raw, terrible emotion—something fierce. But I'm gradually beginning to learn that I can work with *anything*. His silence gives me an idea.

"Clio… what happened to you after the Battle of Ignis? Where did Fern take you? I had Willow try to find you, but she said you were missing, that you weren't in the Land of Five… So, what…" I wanted to ask him what he did to survive, but I can't finish the question.

He smiles and grabs my hand. "Fern took me from the battlefield and somewhere with beautiful plants and flowers. There was water and animals and life. There weren't any other witches there, and I think it was a place special to fairies. I was so out of my mind between guilt and healing that I never stopped to ask. Either way, she healed me, and when I started to get better, she showed me how much the Council had distorted the world. I didn't believe her at first, but… well, when I was healed, she… did something that was hard to ignore."

My eyes widen, and I lean forward, trying to offer comfort that way.

"She took me to the Coven where you were born."

I grip his hand even tighter, fighting against my useless body to sit up straighter. "So it's real? It… exists?"

Clio nods. "It's real, but… it's nothing like the Land of Five. The witches there are kind but different."

I've come to learn that 'different' comes in the good version and the bad version. If this Coven is my real birthplace, I hope it's a good place. But it seems more like that it's the opposite, just because it's tied to me. I raise an eyebrow. "Different how?"

"Over ninety percent of their witches are UnEquipped. They're a lot like Mentis used to be except, they don't care about magic. Not really."

My mouth hangs open. "How?"

"Our ancestors weren't all witches, remember? The Land of Five was formed because of the split between Magical and Non-Magical humans, so it makes sense that somewhere, the non-magic people made their new home. It makes sense that so many generations of UnEquipped witches would eventually stop being born with any magic in their blood at all."

"If most of them can't even use magic, why would the Council lie about them?" I ask. "They're not a threat." They can't be.

Clio scoffs. "Isn't it obvious? Magic or not, they *are* a threat. To the Council's authority. Admitting that they're out there, living beyond the boundaries, would mean admitting to a lot of their lies. The Land of Five would've turned on them if they knew."

I take in a shaky breath. I want to see the Coven, to know where I really come from. Then I remember that Willow was in her teen years when I was an infant. She must have some idea of the Coven, and if she doesn't, she needs to.

"Willow needs to know," I blurt out.

"I agree," Clio says. "And you need to be the one to tell her."

"What if she doesn't believe me?"

He looks down at the stack of papers in his hand. "This is pretty hard to ignore, Li."

I nod. "You're right. Can you do me a favor?"

"Anything."

"Take that folder away from me for now so I can get some sleep?"

He smiles and leans forward to kiss me on the forehead. "Consider it done. Anything else?"

"Can you get my dog?"

Chapter Six
Reality

*T*HOUGH THE HOSPITAL bed is far less comfortable than the one in the impressive room Willow had given me, it's easy enough to imagine I'm in my own room when I wake the next morning with Kado lying sprawled out beside me. His hot breath fans over my face, and I slowly open my eyes. When I see him just an inch away, I smile and reach up to poke his nose. He opens his eyes almost instantly and yips, running his tongue along my chin.

"Good morning, Kado," I say, reaching up to stroke the side of his muzzle.

He sits up and barks again before leaping from the bed and landing on the floor with amazing stealth. He yips at me, spinning in excited circles, and my happiness fades as soon as it appeared. I've seen that dance before.

"Are you hungry?" I ask.

He barks in agreement and twirls again.

I try to smile, but it's hard. Usually, I'd climb out of bed with him and walk him to get something, but now, all I can do is call out, "Helena! Ambrossi!"

Kado stops and cocks his head, sensing the shift in my

mood. Whining, he brings his forepaws down on the edge of the bed and stares at my legs, lapping gently at the bandages in a desperate attempt to fix me.

Helena steps into the room. "What's wrong?" she asks before glancing down at Kado. "Time for breakfast?"

Kado looks at her but stays stubbornly beside my bed before I tell him, "I'm okay."

He licks my hand and whines again before finally padding to Helena's side.

"Good morning, Lilith," Ambrossi calls, entering the room just as Helena and Kado leave.

"Is it?" I ask, embittered by his optimism.

"You're alive, aren't you?"

"Depends on what you consider alive," I reply and shift around until I'm sitting up.

Ambrossi smiles at the foot of my bed. "How's your pain today?"

"Emotional or physical?" I retort, raising an eyebrow.

He sighs, pressing his lips together. "This is hard. I know that, but I need you to cooperate. I don't know what it is with you and healing, but I'm only trying to help. You used to accept it."

I know he's thinking about the amethyst pendant he gave me as a child—the one that supposedly lessened the pain in my leg. I carried it but not for medical purposes. It served more as a medicine for my anxiety. Thinking of it now, I wish I had it for the sake of having *something* in my hand, anything to distract me from this conversation.

"Well, maybe not *accept* it," he adds, "but you didn't fight as hard."

"So what do you want me to do?" I ask, even more petulant now for his comments.

"Relax and let me work. It's the only way I'll be able to make you better."

I raise an eyebrow, curious to know how deeply his

confidence runs. "You really think there's a way to make this better?"

Ambrossi frowns down at my bandages. "Honestly? I don't know. The damage is severe, but I'm going to do my best, as I always have. I'm hopeful that none of Grail's magic directly affected you and that the wounds he caused will heal normally with proper treatment. As for the emotional damage, I'll see if Laura can make a visit."

I doubt that will make a difference. The last time Laura cleansed my aura, I didn't feel much better, but I'll let him believe whatever he needs to believe in order to be happy. I opt for silence and watch Ambrossi carefully pull the bandages off my legs. I tell myself that I'm going to look; I'm going to see just how bad it really is so I can stop torturing myself with my imagination. For all my promises, though, I can't bring myself to do it. I stare at the ceiling, listening to him whisper a few spells for the pain. A cold chill soaks into my legs, and I cringe as he rubs a slimy poultice over the wounds. Even then, I don't look. I wait until I feel the tight pressure of new bandages before I release my gaze from the ceiling.

"There, now. That wasn't so bad, was it?"

I snort. "You don't have to talk to me like that, Ambrossi. I'm not a child. But yes, I appreciate you. You know that."

"Chin up. I'll be back to check on you in a little bit. Do you need anything?"

"No," I say automatically.

I expect him to walk away, but he stands there, watching me, as if he expects me to change my mind. I don't, and eventually, he takes his leave. I exhale, not realizing I had been holding my breath, and stare down at the fresh bandages—every detail perfect. I wish I had just a fraction of his confidence sometimes. I comb my fingers through my hair, feeling the tangles, and would have loved a hairbrush—or better yet, a bath. I could've asked him, of course, but just the thought of it is awkward.

I decide to wait for Helena.

Though I've only been in this room for a day, it feels like eternity. Cheryl, one of the Reanimates from the attack on Alchemy, has helped me to the bathroom a few times, but other than that, I haven't left this bed. I considered asking her for a bath, but the five-minute bathroom treks bring enough awkward silence that I almost miss the solitude.

I stare at the wall. This must be what prison's like.

Looking at the door, I wonder where Kado is. I thought he'd be back after breakfast, but that was hours ago. Maybe even he was tired of being cooped up in this room. Can't say I blame him.

Every passing hour makes the room feel just the slightest bit smaller, as if the walls are closing in around me.

This mind-numbing sadness is a punishment; it has to be, for letting down everyone dear to me. Maybe if I was quicker, or smarter, I wouldn't have ended up in this position in the first place.

The door opens, and I glance up, hoping to see Helena.

Clio stands in the doorway instead, and I feel the slightest sting of disappointment. Odd. Never before would I have thought I'd be *sad* to see Clio.

He senses none of my emotional turmoil. He smiles at me, the expression not one I'm used to on his mostly expressionless face. "I got you a present," he says.

I struggle to prop myself up on my elbows and grin at him. It feels so strange on my face. "You're wonderful, my dear, but your presence doesn't actually count as a gift."

Clio chuckles. "Just you wait." He darts out to the hallway and comes back in. When I catch sight of what he's pushing toward me, what little bit of good cheer I had leaves my body.

It's a wheelchair.

"I figured you could use a change of scenery," Clio says

as soon as he catches my expression. "Being cooped up in here all day isn't good for you. This way, you won't have to wait on anyone to go anywhere."

My nose twitches, but I don't react more than that. I wish the floor would open up and swallow us whole. The idea of a walking stick was itself too much to bear, but this? I don't know if I can do this. I'm dangerously close to seeing how I manage dragging myself across the floor instead.

"It's not so bad. You'll see." Clio pats one of the wheelchair's armrests.

I raise an eyebrow. "How would you know?"

He sighs and reaches up to scratch the back of his neck, taking the opportunity to train his gaze on the floor. "I don't know. Not exactly. But I have to imagine anything is better than being bedridden."

I wouldn't be bedridden if Helena came back, and I'm immediately mad at myself for thinking it.

Since when am I dependent on other people? Especially Helena. It's not her fault I'm like this. Why should I have to burden her? I can't find my way out of my own thought spiral, so I don't speak.

"Just try it first, and if you don't like it, I'll make it disappear, okay?" Clio says, tilting his head.

I clench my teeth and stare at the chair. Yes? No? I don't know what to decide. Clio takes my silence as a cue to pick me up. I don't protest. I enjoy his warmth against me and wrap my arms around his neck, letting myself revel in the moment. He's gotten stronger since the Battle of Ignis; that much is apparent. He doesn't even bat an eye as he crosses the room with me and lowers me into the contraption.

I feel like a different person when I look up at him—broken, defeated, and helpless. I don't remember why it's supposed to make me feel better.

"Look," he says, moving behind me to grasp the handles. He starts to push it, and I lift my dead legs onto the footrest so they don't drag across the floor. We go out into the labyrinthine halls before he says, "Doesn't it feel nice to be out of that room?"

I don't want to admit it, but it does. The slight breeze and even this little movement is a welcome change from the four white walls at which I've been staring. My fingers clutch the armrests, and I refuse to speak. I don't want to fuel his ego by admitting he was right. I glance up at Clio from the corners of my eyes. There's the smallest hint of a smile on his face, and I know he sees through my façade.

He always does, and that's why we get along so well. He understands that even the strongest friends can be broken on the inside.

"Out of the way!" Maverick commands, dashing down the hallway with Willow and Ambrossi.

Clio pulls the chair against the wall, and we watch the witches run with wide eyes.

"That can't be good," Clio says.

It's not. Whenever Willow is summoned to the hospital wing, it isn't good. They disappear into the room with the newly sick witch, and I look up at Clio. Willow wouldn't need to be here if it was just food poisoning.

Mustering all my authority, I say, "Take me in there."

He raises an eyebrow. "I'm not sure that's such a good idea."

Something is wrong; I can hear the panicked thoughts of every witch in the room, even this far down the hall. I breathe in slowly, trying to calm my irritation. "Let me make it clear, Clio. *I'm* going in there. Either you push this chair, or I'll crawl."

He sighs, and the corners of his lips lift into a frustrated smirk. "Always so stubborn."

"Ignis pride," I counter.

He doesn't argue any more but pushes me down the hall, albeit far slower than I would've liked. He doesn't want to go, to see what's happening, but he'll do it for me.

Eventually, we enter the room and the commotion. I see only one bed. The other was moved to make room. Willow stands beside the bed, enveloped in the purple cloak of her magic, and I catch Maverick's eye.

He's not one to lie—not through his words, emotions, or expressions. So when I see his grimly set lips, I know. This Sickness is far worse than Ambrossi thought.

Chapter Seven

Emergency

WHEN WILLOW COLLAPSES to the floor, I look at the bed, expecting to hear a gasp or see movement from the revived witch. I can't see anything from the chair. I turn to study Ambrossi's face for clues instead.

He's gone deathly pale, and I feel like I've been here before. In my memory, all I see now is Flora lying in that bed, the Alchemy Adept, and the devastation that gripped Willow when she realized her powers hadn't worked. As far as I know, that's the only time she's suffered like that. Maverick cradles Willow as she regains consciousness, braced for what's to come. The next second, she's staring at Ambrossi. He still hasn't moved, every muscle of his face unchanged. Just like I did, she knows what it means.

"No," she moans, low and heartbreaking. Then she buries her sobs against Maverick's chest.

With a hand on the back of Willow's head, he looks up at Ambrossi. "What is this sickness?"

Ambrossi looks back through shining eyes. "I don't know. I've never seen anything like it before."

"You have to let me try again," Willow says, standing on

wobbling legs, as if they don't want to support her weight.

Maverick wraps an arm around her waist and pulls her toward him again. "You're going to exhaust yourself."

"But—"

He turns her face gently until she's forced to look at him. "But nothing. You've done your best. I'm sorry, Willow."

"No!" She tries to push him away, to rush back to the witch's bedside, and Maverick looks at Ambrossi. When the healer nods, Maverick scoops Willow into his arms. She screams the entire way to the door, but Maverick doesn't stop. He takes her from the room and down the hall, her cries eventually fading into echoes.

My heart breaks for her. I can't imagine her pain right now. I tried to understand it when this happened with Flora, but I couldn't then, and I still can't now. Ambrossi looks down at the witch on the bed and sighs, lifting the sheet to cover the witch's face.

"You'd best be on your way," he says. "I need to gather the Healers and let them know what's happened."

"What exactly *has* happened?" Clio asks.

Ambrossi sighs again, eyes trained on the shape under the sheet. "I wish I knew."

Clio swallows and pushes me out into the hallway. We're both quiet, as if the mood in the room wormed its way into our blood.

"I think you should go see Willow," he eventually says.

Her screams echo in my head, and I frown. "I think she just needs time with Maverick right now."

"It'll do her good to have both of you, I think." He doesn't listen to any of my further protests. Outside the Community Villa, we catch a glimpse of Maverick moving through the purple plants. I don't hear Willow anymore, but I don't know if it's because she's so far away or if she's finally stopped crying. We catch up to Maverick just as he reaches Willow's mansion. Kado is flanked by two of Willow's

38

Reanimated tigers, all of them greeting us at the door. One of the tigers growls at Maverick when it sees Willow in his arms, but she reaches out to stroke its muzzle, and the deep rumble stops.

Clio shivers, and the other tiger turns to look at him. No one says a thing as we enter Willow's room. Gently, Maverick sets her on the bed, and she stares straight ahead, her face carved with so much grief, it's difficult to look at her. Kado and the tigers stand at the doorway, as if they don't want to come too close when Willow's like this.

"This is the second time in a month I couldn't save someone," she mutters.

"It's not your fault," I say immediately. "We know why it happened with Flora."

She turns to me with clouded eyes. "But why today? A normal illness should not have done something like this."

"We can't rule anything out at the moment," Maverick says. "Obviously, there's more to this than we thought. The Healers will figure it out."

"Maybe," she says, staring at the wall. She clearly doesn't feel any better. I don't either, but I draw some comfort from the fact that we have some of the best Healers in the Land of Five. If any witch can figure out what the illness is, Lazarus and Ambrossi can. "And what of the second witch with the same symptoms?"

I don't want to think of the next witch in line. Whoever it is has probably already heard what became of the first, and I do not envy the fear that would bring. Clio is thinking the same. Judging by Willow's pained frown, she's guessed it, too.

"Whatever it is," she says, "it's capable of spreading. If the Healers find no cure..." She nearly chokes on the words.

We all know what she would have said anyway. If this disease has no cure and cannot be reversed by even Willow's magic, it'll be disastrous. The look of absolute defeat on her face kills me, but I can't think of a thing that would relieve her. I think of Crowe, of the information in that folder. Would it cheer her up to let her in on what I know, or would it only make her feel worse?

A distraction *is* a distraction, no matter its form.

I crane my neck up to look at Clio. "Clio, do you still have that file?" I whisper.

His green eyes meet mine, and he looks confused, as if he's asking, 'Are you sure?' I don't back down from the stare. Eventually, understanding replaces his confusion, and he slips the file out from beneath his cloak.

When I take the file, Clio looks at Maverick. "Let's give them a minute alone," he says.

Maverick glances at the papers in my hand, then his attention returns to Willow. She meets his gaze and nods. Both men leave her room, hesitate for a moment in the hallway, then finally exit her house altogether.

"You have something to tell me?" Willow sits up, dangling her legs over the edge of the bed.

"Yeah, uh… I don't know how to begin."

"Does it have to do with the illness?" she asks, her black eyes wide.

I shake my head. "No, and I don't know if this is really the best time to tell you this. But I figure you need to know. There's something I didn't tell you about Ignis… about what happened before I was captured."

She raises an eyebrow, then drops her gaze to the folder in my hand.

"Our mother is alive." I force out the words, and I can almost *see* them, suspended in the air between us.

She blinks, then looks back up at me. The dark pits of her pupils seem to deepen with her shock. "That's not possible."

"It… it is, Willow. She faked her death so no one would look for her and lived as a cat for years." I pass her the file.

She opens it instantly, her hands clutching the paper with Ivy's information on it. The red word *Missing* is hard to ignore.

"I can't believe this," she says and closes the folder. Her eyes are distant, as if she's gazing into a memory, but her face hardens before she looks at me once more time. "If you met her, where is she now? Why was she not at the battle?"

I bite my lip. I don't often catch my sister in a vulnerable moment—after all, she's a beacon of strength and hope for our entire Coven—but she looks so innocent right now that I find myself regretting the decision to tell her. Because this will destroy her, just as it destroyed me.

You made your bed... Grief's voice lilts through my mind.

As always, I scowl at his intrusion and push him away. "She ran again."

Crying without the tears is even worse, I learn. That's the only thing I can think as I hold my sister. I can't tell what's killing her more quickly or painfully—the discovery of the Sickness or the news of our mother. When a knock sounds on the door, I'm actually feel relieved. We both look up to see a small group of Healers, Lazarus in the lead.

"May we come in for just a moment?" he asks in his ancient voice.

Willow wipes at her face and regains her composure, pulling on a mask of strength with shocking speed and efficiency. If I saw her now for the first time, I wouldn't have guessed she'd completely broken just five seconds ago.

"Of course. Did you find anything?"

Ambrossi, Helena, Alpine, and a few other Healers enter the room.

"The Sickness... does not appear to be natural," Lazarus says. "I performed several tests, and the herbs did not respond."

"Don't tell me she was poisoned," Willow says, thinking of the hordes of poisoned Healers we saw in Alchemy.

Lazarus shakes his head, and I grimace. "What other options are there?" I ask.

"It's a magical Sickness," Ambrossi admits with a sigh.

If Willow didn't look concerned before, she definitely

does now. "A *magical* Sickness? As in someone's actively causing it?"

"That's what I believe," Lazarus says.

"Considering what we know of Flora," Ambrossi adds, "and how certain magic can affect resurgence, it certainly makes sense."

"One of our own?" Willow asks.

"None of our witches can do that," Maverick reminds her.

"Doesn't mean they can't learn it." I see her already compiling a mental list of possible suspects.

"The Council, then," Clio adds.

"In my time, I can't remember a witch ever being capable of such a thing," Lazarus says.

Willow and I exchange a glance, thinking of Tabitha.

"Memory isn't always reliable," Willow replies. "Just because you don't remember doesn't mean it didn't happen."

"Especially with the Council housing so many witches," I point out with a scoff. "There's no telling what kind of magic they have at their disposal."

"What do we do now?" Helena asks.

"Keep an eye on the other witch," Willow says. "Try every possible cure you can think of, and if none of those work, invent some new ones. I want all our herbs exhausted and all the spellbooks ransacked. Leave no stone unturned. And keep a watch for any other potentially sick witches. If this is another witch's doing, it makes sense that they would want it to spread. That's the last thing we need."

The Healers bow their heads in acknowledgment and make their way from the room to carry out her orders. Willow gives me a look that's particularly hard to decipher before she turns to Maverick.

"I could use a drink."

Clio reluctantly leaves my side, and Willow takes charge of the wheelchair. We head to her throne room, the tigers looking up at us in curiosity as we stop beside the giant pit in the middle of the room. With a sigh, Willow lowers herself onto the edge of the pit, swinging her legs over the side, and wraps her arms around one of the cats when it approaches to rasp its tongue across her cheek.

Maverick appears a few minutes later, hands a drink to both Willow and me, then departs once again. I watch him go before studying a tiny bead of water running down the side of my glass. Willow's mood must be something fierce if she doesn't want *Maverick's* company. It seems as if every time something bad happens, he's the one she leans on—her constant source of strength.

Willow downs half her drink in one breath, and as I wait for her to finish, I take the smallest drink of my own. It tastes sweet, but there's an underlying burn of alcohol. Willow sighs and sniffles. I take another sip.

"His name was Alfred," she says at last. "He was a good witch."

"I'm sorry I never got to know him."

She shrugs. "Not everyone liked him, but he was strong. Loyal." She pauses to wipe her mouth before her eyes drift toward my lap. "Where did that file come from?"

"The Council's file room," I reply. "Before I escaped, Crowe helped me get it."

"Why would he do that?" She knocks back the rest of her drink and sighs. "He could've been killed for helping you."

"Katrina's here," I remind her. "People do insane things for the ones they love."

"I suppose," she says and sets her glass down on the stones around the pit. The loud clang echoes through the throne room. "Makes me wonder what Mom's motives were, then."

"I don't know," I say. My interaction with Ivy was so short, so odd, and so unexpected that I hadn't had much time to gather my own thoughts, let alone any information that may be useful.

"I really thought she loved us," Willow continues. "When I was a little girl, I adored her. She used to be my role model, you know. I always looked up to her."

I can hear the pain in her voice, and I want to intervene, to make that sound go away. But if I speak now, my voice will most likely sound the same as hers.

"Then she started to disappear. There were days when she wouldn't come back, and when she did, it was like she had changed. Then she brought you home one day, and I loved you so much. It killed me when she took you away again, but she told me how much she loved me and you, and that she was working on something special."

"Something special? What was that?"

Willow shrugs. "She was killed before I ever found out. Or, at least that was what I believed." She gazes longingly at her cup, as if she wishes she had the power to refill it with her mind. Then she turns toward me with a frown. "What did she say to you?"

"Not much, honestly. She basically said she hid because she would be killed if anyone knew she was close. She told me that my adopted parents knew who I really was and that they had orders to kill her. So she lived as a cat to watch over me."

Willow laughs and picks up her cup, tipping it fully upside down against her lips, as if to drain every possible drop it can offer. This time, she throws it to the ground, and though the tiger next to her flattens its ears at the sound, it doesn't stop or growl. It paces toward her, sniffing her hair before nudging her gently.

She reaches out to pet it and says, "It seems kind of funny that she appears and now, when we have sick witches."

The suspicion in her tone is new. "What are you saying, Willow? You think Mom is responsible?"

Willow shrugs. "I'm not ruling out the possibility."

I frown, not sure why I feel so defensive of Ivy, but I do. "I think you'd remember if she could do something like that.

Don't you?"

Willow bobs her head. "Yes, but you know just as well as I do that memory is not reliable. As long as Tabitha is still alive, there's no telling just what we've forgotten."

"Fair enough," I say.

"Mom was a wanted woman, even back then. There had to be reasons."

I bite my lip, not wanting to argue with Willow but at the same time wanting to be heard. "Not necessarily true. I'm wanted too. My only crime is being born."

She looks at me sympathetically. "Don't you get it? It all starts with her. The entire reason you were with Regina and Howard was because of her. Because you were born into her danger."

Another fair point on her part. "So, what should we do?"

She shrugs and pulls her knees to her chest, looking so defeated that I don't expect her to answer. "Nothing we can do now but wait."

Chapter Eight
Doubts and Fears

WHEN THE HEALERS do their sweep of the building, they find a handful of other sick witches with similar symptoms. In almost no time at all, the Community Villa is filled to the brim with witches puking their guts out. Willow floats through it like a ghost, at all hours of the day, constantly checking on the new faces admitted and trying her best to comfort those who have been there longer.

When I'm finally brought in for my exam, Ambrossi keeps me away from the others, but I wonder why he bothers. Since I already shared a room with the first sick witch, no one would be surprised if I came down with the Sickness. As he pokes and prods, I hold my breath, expecting concern to fill his eyes and to be assigned to a room. Instead, I pass the exam.

"You're sure?" I ask him.

He nods, looking just as surprised as I feel. "Yes, but it's tricky. Let me know if anything at all doesn't feel right."

"I will," I promise.

Ambrossi squints at me. "*Will* you?"

I roll my eyes. "I'm stubborn, but I'm not a fool."

"Okay," he says, and with, that I'm sent on to Laura to

have my aura cleansed and evaluated as well.

Feeling only slightly better, I hold my breath as Clio gets his exam too. From my place in the hall, I try to peer into the room, but I can't see much. Ambrossi insisted I wait outside, just in case, so I do. When Clio appears in the doorway, I stare at him with wide eyes.

"I passed," he says.

I let out a massive sigh. "Good. Let's go back to Willow's."

Clio raises an eyebrow. "Ambrossi told me you're supposed to stay here for the night."

Frowning, I narrow my eyes. "What? Since when?"

"He says that he's worried you'll take a turn for the worse. He thinks you should stay here one more day, just in case."

"You're joking."

He shakes his head. "I don't blame him."

"His rationale is to keep a healthy witch near the sick witches?"

"He's worried you're already sick but not showing signs."

Sounds like Ambrossi, all right. I open my mouth, considering trying to trick Clio again, and all the willpower leaves my body. Ambrossi is stubborn, and Clio is too. I may be able to outwit one of them, but I can't challenge them both. I'll lose, and I have too much pride to admit it.

"Fine. Take me to my assigned room, then," I say and cross my arms over my chest, exaggerating a pout the best I can.

"I don't like this either, you know," he says, pushing me down the hall. "It's like we can finally spend time together again, but we can't. Life isn't fond of us."

"No, it's not."

Clio pushes me through a door. The room is one of the cushier ones but still noticeably a hospital room with an uncomfortable bed to boot.

"Can't you just lie and *tell* Ambrossi I'm staying here?" I ask as he wheels me toward the bed.

Clio shakes his head. "No. If you really *are* sick, that would put everyone at risk. Do you really want to do that?"

I close my eyes for a long time. I don't want to make anyone suffer for my decisions, but in this moment, it's hard to admit that.

"I'll see you later, okay?" he says. "Try to get some rest. Morning will be here before you know it."

"Doubt it," I say and cuddle under the blankets.

Clio leans forward to kiss my forehead. "Try it and let me know."

I make a face at him, and he laughs but doesn't say anything else as he departs. The door clicks shut behind him, and I'm alone again, staring up at the ceiling and thinking through my day.

Poor Willow. I press my hands over my eyes and imagine again and again how hurt she was after being unable to revive Alfred. What if her magic is weakening? I have to stomp out the horrible thought.

I hate being here, in this room so far away from my loved ones who may be able to comfort me. I expect Ambrossi to pay me another visit, since it was his idea to make me stay here, but even he keeps his distance. I consider leaving on my own, but when I try to move, I'm once again reminded that I'm stuck here. The wheelchair is in the room, of course, in the corner of the room where Clio left it, but seeing it doesn't make me feel better. The work to get to it on my own would leave me exhausted.

My mind swirls, and I feel so weak, so small, as everything inside me swells larger and larger with panic, worry, and anxiety. I know the worst thing I could possibly do right now is seclude myself, but knowledge and actions are two very different things. I can't imagine reaching out to other witches when I'm feeling like this. Part of me wishes Willow would just seal my door shut for good so I'd never have to see the light of day again. Desperately, I glance around the room—at the chair Clio was so excited to show me.

The thought that he's so dedicated to cheering me up should lift my spirits, but I can't help my sour mood. I wonder if maybe his concerns and effort would be better placed in someone else—someone with a true hope of one day being happy again. Self-loathing is not a new concept to me, but I feel like I'm drowning in it.

Then, as if someone senses my need for a lifesaver, there's a knock on the door.

"Go away!" I call, not caring whose feelings I may hurt. I squeeze my eyes shut, part of me hoping against myself that they *don't* go away.

"I know my dear sister isn't allowing herself to wallow." Willow's voice comes through the cracked door, her words slightly slurred. She must've drank even more after I went to my exam.

"No…" I say, frowning. Willow won't leave easily, and deep down, I know I'd rather have her company than none at all. "You're not really one to talk, you know."

"Maybe not, but I can tell when you're lying a mile away," she says and pushes open the door.

I glance up at her before my gaze falls to the chair. "You have something to do with this?" I ask. "I didn't get the chance to ask you earlier."

Willow sighs, her pink lips pouting ever so slightly, before she smiles and clamps her hands together in front of her chest. "It's going to be an adjustment, but I think it'll do you some good."

I tilt my head, knowing with sudden clarity that I *don't* want her company. "Yes, and no matter what you say, it won't make this any easier. It'd be like me saying the Sickness is just something we need to get used to."

Her face twists, and I'm almost afraid I crossed a line. When she speaks, though, she isn't angry. "I was afraid of that, but I understand. You'll come to terms eventually when this becomes your new normal." She pats my foot, sporting a hopeful smile.

What a terrible sentence she just gave me. For all the times I hated her frowns, now I've come to hate her smile as well. "And what if I never do? What if this never feels normal to me, and I can't accept it?"

Her smile drops, and I'm sure she's thinking of Ivy and the woman still being alive after all this time.

"No matter what, just remember that you're surrounded by witches who love you and want nothing but the best."

That brings to mind Clio's obvious excitement when he showed me the chair, and my toughness melts away. "That's the only fact I know I can depend on. You know the same goes for you, right? These witches hated me when I arrived, and that gave me the most accurate picture of this Coven. No matter what, they're going to support you. They don't know how to survive any other way. You're their mother. Their queen. Their everything."

"So you'll stop wallowing?" she asks.

"I didn't say that." I fold my arms across my chest.

"Come on. It can't be that bad. You haven't even let me see how you look in it."

I bit my lip and tilt my head. "It's a *wheelchair*, Willow. Not a dress."

"Either way, it's going to be part of you," she replies. "Might as well get used to it."

I lift an eyebrow, hating that she's trying so hard. It's *too* hard, and the longer this goes on, the more annoying it becomes. "You're not making me like it any more, you know."

"I figured as much, but I think it's also important for you to realize that I can be just as stubborn as you. If not more so."

We stare at each other. I can already tell that she's not going to leave me alone until she gets her way, and I don't have it in me to fight as much as I'd need to in order to get out of this. "Okay, put me in it. But I want back out immediately."

Willow flips her hair over her shoulder before she approaches me with a smile. Though she's not much larger than I am, she scoops me up with unnatural ease and plops me down in the chair. She takes two steps back and tilts her head, studying me with such intensity that goosebumps break out across my arms.

"Well?" I ask, slowly blinking at her.

"It works," she says with a nod.

"Uh-huh. That's what I told you." I reach out for her to pick me up again.

"And you were right." She lifts me out of the chair, and in a few seconds, I'm back on the bed.

When she all but drops me there, I grunt, Willow smiles briefly, then she plops down next to me. Her eyes glitter with the onset of tears. Please don't cry. If there's one thing I don't like, it's being the shoulder someone else cries on. "What is it?" I ask, trying to sound calm. "What's wrong?"

"The Sickness." Her gaze drops to the floor. "If we can't find a cure…"

I feel bad for her, now. I really do. Willow is strong—there's no doubt about that—but when I *really* look at her, I see the child inside her. She was executed when she wasn't much older than I am now. Though she's technically older, she *looks* the same age as me, and right now, her personality mirrors it. She's worried, scared, not sure what to do, like a lost child looking for her mother.

"I know you're worried, Willow. So am I. But there's a cure. There has to be, and we'll find it."

She purses her lips. "Do you know anything about… Healing or Alchemy?" She wipes her eyes with the back of her hand.

I shake my head. "Astral projection is all I've picked up from that Coven. I've spent a lot of time watching Ambrossi and Katrina"—it feels as if I'm in the hospital wing for something every other day—"and I don't think I could ever grasp the magic they perform."

She sighs and rakes her fingers through her hair. "I know. I just… wondered what Lazarus told you of the poison in Alchemy."

"I don't think this is the same as that," I say. "You brought Alpine back, remember?"

Willow nods and bites her lip. Her eyes are distant, searching, and I can tell how hard she's working to figure out a plan. "I do, but I figured it was worth asking what you thought."

"I can try to pick up the skill if anyone is willing to teach it," I offer but cringe as soon as the words are out. Healing takes a certain patience and dedication that I don't have. I don't see myself as a caretaker, but right now, I'd be willing to do anything if it meant making Willow smile again.

She shakes her head, immediately horrified by the suggestion. "It's not a good idea. I don't even like you being *here*, this close to the Sickness. But it's necessary." She stands up, hands clenching into fists as she glances at my legs. When she looks away just as quickly, I realize I wasn't supposed to catch her doing that.

"Have you talked to Malcolm?" I ask. "Fairies have better healing abilities than we can ever dream." I stare at my legs too now, not only because it's easier than looking into Willow's big, scared eyes but because it helps me remember the truth of my own words.

Shortly after joining the Council, Crowe introduced me to the Advisory Council of Fairies—two tiny women with vastly different personalities. A fight between Crowe and me had concerned Callista, and she used her magic to make the pain in my bad leg disappear for a while. Sure, when it came back, it came back fiercely, but the point is, she did what no other Healer could do. She gave me *peace*.

Willow shakes her head. "Not yet, but it's worth a try." She crosses the room to the door and stops to look over her shoulder. "I love you, Lily. I hope you know that."

The words bring a surge of warmth through my chest. It's not often that someone tells me they love me, and when it comes to my sister, I can only remember her telling me a handful of times my entire life. She pauses, as if the same realization floated across her mind as well.

I don't let her dwell on it. "I love you too," I tell her, confident in the fact that for once I can express myself without worrying it'll backfire.

Her eyes are still sad, but there's the smallest hint of a smile on her lips now. "Good night," she says and lets the door click shut.

Chapter Nine
Demons

I WISH I could sleep. It's lonely in the depths of this room again, and I find myself wondering why I didn't try to make Willow stay for just a few more minutes. As strange as it seems, I can't stop thinking about the way she looked at me in that chair, and it makes me think of Dawn. I wonder how she's doing—if she's coping with the no-walking thing better than I am.

When I remember Crowe's reaction, though, I doubt Dawn's improved more than I have. Beyond my direct question, no one else has mentioned her. Why? Are they so worried about her anger that they fear even speaking her name? It seems silly, but I have the inkling to visit her, to try cheering her up, even if it's for just a few minutes. I don't make an attempt to move, though, because I can't, first of all. Second, what would I even say if I went through all that effort?

I've got nothing.

Somehow, in the middle of my plotting, I fall asleep.

THE NEXT MORNING, Ambrossi wakes me. He looks more exhausted than I've seen him in a long time. There are darkened half circles under his eyes and a sickly pallor to his skin. His steps look uncertain and wobbly, but he's somehow still standing.

"You haven't slept," I say as he turns away to gather the ingredients for his poultice.

"No, I have not." He turns to look at me with a weak smile.

"It's really bad, isn't it? This Sickness."

He breathes sharply through his nose and studies his handful of green leaves. Obviously, he's contemplating the best way to answer that. He stalls as long as he can, seeking out a bowl and a pestle for crushing it all up. Only when he's created his liquid concoction does he answer. "Yes, it is."

"What are you going to do?" I ask.

He's quiet again as he unwinds my bandages, his face drawn so tight with concentration that I wait for him to speak, convinced he'll eventually say something inspiring. "Honestly?" he asks as the last of the beige strips slips from my skin.

I nod. "Of course. What good would it do to lie?" I don't add that Ambrossi and I don't lie to each other, but it's always been implied.

He meets my gaze. "I'm looking to Lazarus and hoping he knows what the hell to do."

Frowning, I look down at the floor, desperate to break away from his stare before he sees my true feelings. That wasn't the response I wanted to hear. Then again, I'm not sure anything would've been right.

"It was an unfair question," I say at last.

Ambrossi shakes his head. "No, you had every right to ask. I just hate that I can't answer it in a capacity that'll make you feel better."

"Who cares if it makes me feel better?" I reply. "I'm not the one who's sick."

Ambrossi's features tighten, and I wince as he paints the cold poultice onto my legs. I know why he's not speaking; he's still worried that I'll turn up with symptoms. I expect it too, but I won't tell him that. This entire situation is already uncomfortable as it is. Ambrossi is a capable Healer—he always has been—but it's unnerving to see him so upset about an illness.

Willow too.

When this Sickness hit, it seemed to pull the rug out from under both of them. I wonder how I'm still sane, which makes me contemplate the validity of my own sanity. The more I think about it, the more likely it seems that I may be the only not taking this seriously. Though it's only been a couple days since the Sickness hit the Coven, I haven't tried to do anything differently—besides comfort Willow and Ambrossi, of course. In my heart, I believe there's a cure and that one of these witches will be dedicated enough to find it before it gets out of hand. Maybe it's foolish to hope, but I don't know what else to do.

"Lazarus will figure something out," I say, surprising us both.

I worry a lot about Karma, about balancing the negative and positive energy I put out into the world. Usually, it's negative, which may be part of why my luck is so bad now. Still, I'm not sure how I feel about releasing my hope into the world. It feels like a betrayal to myself to let anyone know I'm vulnerable at all.

"I hope so," Ambrossi says and picks up a rag to smear some of the extra green liquid off my legs. "If I can't depend on him, I don't know who I can."

The mentor-apprentice bond has always and will always be a complicated concept in the Land of Five. No matter how old witches get, how long they've been in their practice, or how far they drift, they will always feel a closeness to their mentor they can't explain. Ambrossi feels it for Lazarus, and I feel it for Crowe.

This feels like one more betrayal, too—to trust *and* hope in the same ten minutes. Ambrossi secures my new bandages in place. His dark eyes focus on his shaking fingers, but I have a feeling my words are still running through his head. He's hoping I'm not wrong, that Lazarus *will* find something to save us. Because if I *am* wrong ... well, imminent threats don't quite need to be explained in depth.

Ambrossi pats down the end of the bandage and grabs my foot, pushing my leg slightly upward. "How's that feel? Too tight?"

I shake my head. The bandages are perfect, as they usually are when Ambrossi puts his best foot forward.

He nods, satisfied, and lets my leg rest back on the bed. "You'll be going back to your own room tonight. I don't want you this close to the Sickness for much longer."

"Good," I say, grateful that at least tonight, I'll be back in my bed with my dog. At least I'll have someone beside me when my mind starts up again with torturing me.

"I'm going to have Katrina take you to get something to eat," Ambrossi says. I nod, but he narrows his eyes, unconvinced. "You *will* eat something, right?"

"Yes, mother," I reply, then wince as my own joke bites me coming out.

Sometimes, silence is fine.

Ambrossi gives me an odd look but doesn't comment on my outburst before he leaves the room to track down Katrina. When he returns, the petite, blue-haired girl has joined him. She smiles and greets me. Ambrossi gives her a brief rundown of what's expected of me once we get to the cafeteria; I'm to eat a meal—*any* meal—as long I put something in my stomach. Then we're heading through the halls of the Community Villa.

She's silent today, and I don't press her to talk. She waits until we enter the bustling cafeteria before asking, "You going to be okay?"

I nod, knowing my answer won't make a difference. "You can go if you need to."

"It's not that. I—"

I raise a hand with a patient smile. "You're fine,

Katrina."

She smiles apologetically and disappears into the hall again. I wonder what's on her mind, but not for very long. The cafeteria is rough. It feels like as soon as my wheels cross over the threshold, every witch turns to look at me. Now I wish I'd made Katrina stay, at least for a minute longer. Her intensity would've kept their gazes away. Heat blooms across my cheeks, and I hate myself for it. I'm not a shy witch—certainly not the type to care what others think of me—so why am I so bothered now?

Something about accepting help just really gets to me, I suppose. I scan the room, looking for at least one friendly face.

The Reanimates, with Helena at the head, are always friendly toward any outside witch. Having been the objects of prejudice in the Coven for longer than I can imagine, they know what it is to feel like an outsider. I consider joining them, then I find Dawn instead. She's in a wheelchair too, seated at the very end of a table in the back corner of the cafeteria. There are no other witches at the table, and I wonder if that's because no one wants to sit with her or because she's scared off everyone who's tried.

What the hell. I maneuver toward her, realizing I've never seen a more perfect opportunity in my life.

She doesn't look up as I stop beside the table. Her fork stabs into her food, metal grinding against ceramic; she's clearly annoyed by my presence despite never looking at me.

"Hey, Dawn," I say, folding my hands together, setting them on the table, and preparing for a barbed comment. I prefer a greeting, but judging by the tension in her shoulders, I don't think I'll get one.

She sets down her fork, moving slowly, and when she looks up, her eyes glisten, as if she's on the verge of tears. Without meaning to, I cringe. I expected anger, not sadness. I stare at her, less prepared for whatever happens next.

"Hey?" she asks finally. "Hey?"

I swallow, frown, and bob my head, unsure what line I've crossed but also feeling slightly eager to find out.

"How can you say, 'Hey,' and talk to me like everything is normal? It's not!"

"It seems normal to me." It was a reflexive response, and I slap my hand over my mouth, not sure why I ever let the words escape.

Everyone has a period of adjustment when they come here. I've experienced it firsthand and watched a few witches I love go through the same. Even Clio, who is dedicated to me through thick and thin, still struggles to find his place here. For Dawn, who had no other choice but death, this is bound to be difficult.

I definitely hadn't said anything to cheer her up.

Instead of growing anger, her face softens. Now I'm confused again. Dawn is full of unpredictable energy.

"Lilith, how do you do this?" she asks with a rude gesture toward what's left of her lower half. I can't see her very well beneath the rim of the table, but I remember Crowe and I pulling her out of her cell. Bombs destroyed one of her legs, and fresh bandages are wrapped around the stump at the middle of her thigh, hiding the gory remains from sight.

I shrug. "I've never had a choice. I didn't think about it as something I couldn't do. Just something I would do."

She frowns, as if she expected some life-altering lesson from my mouth only to now be disappointed. Swiping her long, ratty hair from her face, she dips her head sideways to get a good look at me and my bandages. "Huh."

"It'll be okay," I tell her with a confidence I do not have.

"That's easy for you to say, Lilith," she says. "There's a possibility that one day, they can fix the damage done to you. There's no re-growing my leg. It's me and this chair for the rest of my life."

I stare at her. What can I say? Things really can always be worse. It's all about perspective.

As if he senses my distress, Clio enters the cafeteria. He smiles at me from across the room before grabbing two plates and bringing them toward the table. Dawn is seething now and shoots him a glare before she backs away from her meal—maneuvering the wheelchair with her telekinesis—and leaves the room.

Clio blinks, watching her without a word. When she disappears into the hall, he sets a plate in front of me and says, "Well, then."

"Don't take it personally," I say, thinking of the shining emotion in Dawn's eyes. "She's going through a lot."

Clio's lips twitch sideways, but I see no sympathy in him. *'Aren't we all?'* I hear him think it as clearly as if he said it aloud. He takes a bite of his food and asks, "How are you feeling today?"

"Better," I reply. "Ambrossi said I can go back to my own room tonight."

"Good. I didn't like the idea of you staying there any longer."

"Me neither," I say and take a swig of juice.

He falls into silence as he devours his food, but I barely pick at mine. It's flavorless and bland. My next bite feels soggy, and I regret it. I drain my cup to wash down the feeling and push away my plate, waiting for Clio to finish. As soon as the last of his food is gone, he wipes his face with a napkin and frowns at me. "You're not hungry?" he asks.

"Not really."

"Hmm. It's probably because you've been cooped up for a while." He takes a huge gulp of water and stands. "I think you should get outside for a bit."

"No. I don't want to." Now, I suddenly miss the prison cell of the hospital wing. Having no human interaction is miserable, but somehow, so is being around people.

I can't win.

"And that's the problem," he says, pushing away from

the table and stepping up beside me. "A little fresh air will do you some good."

"Fine," I say and stare at the floor. I can't argue with Clio.

I may be surrounded by witches who love me, but they are *all* as stubborn as I am.

Clio smiles and lightly presses his fingers against the underside of my chin until I look up. He bends down to kiss me, and I feel my face flushing again. From the corner of my eye, I see Helena smiling at us. It's the first time she's seen any affection between Clio and me, but she expects it. That much I can hear in her mind. That makes me smile too, and when Clio pulls back, he raises a questioning eyebrow before turning around to see Helena. The same kind of smile blooms on his face too.

"Having a quiet conversation?" he asks, then chuckles as he steps behind my wheelchair.

"The less you know, the better," I say, beaming at every witch we pass on our way out of the cafeteria—even those who glare at me. Right now, nothing can get me down, neither their hostility nor my own.

Outside, I breathe in the warm air, staring at the beautiful, towering purple plants. Now, at midday, their shadows seem to shine with an air of mystery. I've always admired the beauty of the Land of New Life, but there's something about the moment that makes it all perfect. Clio leads us toward the plants, then into them, and I glance at him over my shoulder.

"Are we going anywhere in particular?" I ask, wondering how well he knows this place. He hasn't been here long, but he seems perfectly confident, weaving stealthily and with ease through the first line of purple stalks.

He shakes his head. "There's no harm in exploring a little."

I smile. When I first came here, I had the same thought. Even now, I don't know my way around this Coven as well as I probably should. I stop talking, enjoying the silence as we go for our version of a walk. Poking slightly into Clio's brain, I feel the happiness radiating from his core, and I bask in it. It's a good feeling—not one I often experience.

"No, Mom, you gotta remember how you used to do it," someone says through the plants.

Clio freezes, and we both pause to look at one another. "That's Crowe," I say.

He nods, and without me having to ask, he moves toward the speaker. We hear footsteps and more protests, followed by angry growls. I swallow, unsure of what we'll find. Through the plants, I see Crowe and Rena in a clearing up ahead. Clio stops before we can interrupt them, and I'm glad he does. I'm not sure this is something I want Crowe to know I've seen.

Frowning, Crowe steps back, and Rena just looks at him. She's a tiny woman, petite and lithe. Crowe has a small build too, but even he seems large compared to his mother.

"I'm not sure I can do it anymore, Alexander," the tiny woman says.

"Nonsense." He rubs the bridge of his nose before looking back at her. "Try again."

Rena takes a deep breath, lets it out, and steps forward. She tries to twirl with her next step but stumbles over her own foot and falls, landing on her knees. Crowe rushes to her side, but Rena lifts a hand. "It's okay. Maybe I'm never meant to dance again," she says, staring at the purple mesh of plants beneath her knees.

"No, no, no. You don't have to give up anything you love just because... because." Crowe growls and pulls her to her feet again. "All you can do is try."

"Exactly, Alexander. And I'm failing." Rena slumps to the ground again without another attempt to move.

Crowe just stands there, staring at her. He grasps his chin, as if he doesn't know what to do, and I feel a twinge of sadness for both of them. Rena looks so small crumpled on the ground, and I can't help but picture her the way she looked when she was alive. She was so full of life—rosy cheeks and slender body. Now, she looks just like a corpse, and I guess that's appropriate, considering the fact that she is one.

"What's his issue?" Clio whispers in complete confusion.

"He's sad." I don't know how to sum it up better than that. I saw it when Crowe gave me the file, but this is an entirely different level of pain for him—a level of pain I'm grateful for not having experienced in a while.

"I don't understand what he has to be sad about," Clio says, shaking his head. "If my Mom were still alive in *any* way, I would be head over heels... even if she *was* a little different."

I swallow and look at the new sprouts of purple plants peeking through the soil. It's impossible to not feel the pain pulsing off Clio in waves. I know very little about his parents. When we were young, I met his mom a handful of times. That much I know, though it was so long ago, the details are hazy. The only other thing I know about his parents is that they're dead now. But I don't know how or why, and neither does Clio.

When I worked up the nerve years ago to ask him, he only told me, "They never came back."

He'd simply gone on living, as if his parents had never existed, and I was too confused by it all to bother asking questions. Looking into Clio's eyes now, I see the sparkle of tears, the guilt he refused to acknowledge when it was appropriate. I reach out to him, my fingers trailing along the shirt over his stomach. He pulls away quickly, wipes his eyes, and forces a smile.

"I'm fine. I was just saying."

I look up into his eyes. It's a lie, and he's a fool if he thinks I don't know that. I do have to admit, though, that he's strong—stronger than I'll ever be. When my adopted parents died in battle, I sobbed all night, not caring who saw. Clio won't even let *me* see what he feels.

"Remember, I understand your pain," I tell him and reach up to put my hand over his heart.

He doesn't smile, but I have the feeling my gesture makes him feel better all the same.

"Come on. Let's give them their privacy," he says and spins my chair around to head back the way we came.

I take one more glance over my shoulder and see the devastation on Crowe's face before the plants sway behind me and block him from sight.

Chapter Ten
Family Feud

E DON'T SPEAK again for a while as we head around the Elemental Coven for what seems like hours. I both appreciate and resent the silence. What started as a stroll turns into a fast walk for Clio, and I have the feeling he's in the same state of mind. The longer we're out, the worse I feel. I nearly scream with relief when he decides it's time to go back to Willow's mansion.

The scene with Crowe and his mother replays in my mind, and I wish I could understand why. Maybe it's because I always felt a rift between my adopted mother Regina and me, like Crowe seems to feel with his mother now. Or maybe it's because I've never been that close to my real mother—and most likely never will be. Whatever the case, it stays with me.

At dinner in the cafeteria, the witches who glared at me during lunch are poisonous now. They're unhappy about the limited information they've been given regarding the Sickness, and they're beyond holding in their feelings. They stand in a group, yelling and throwing plates of food around the cafeteria. Maverick is quick to end the riots with a pulse of his magic, but it doesn't wipe out their rage. At the end of the it, everyone is just left feeling more bitter as the perpetrators are taken away to face punishment.

If the Sickness continues, I know it'll only get worse. I see the heartbreak in Willow's eyes again, when she realized her magic wasn't enough to counter whatever brought this Sickness to us. Maybe she already knows just how riled up her Coven is, and that's why she's been silent and absent since last night. At the same time, the show these disgruntled witches just put on was completely unfair. These witches know Willow, that she'll do *anything* for them, so rioting against her makes no sense.

Then I remind myself that people always do the wrong thing in fear.

As true as it is, it doesn't make me feel any better.

Clio does not slow in his journey through Willow's mansion. At the entrance, one of the tigers sniffs at his pantleg, but Clio pretends not to notice. The cat loses interest quickly, and we weave through the labyrinthine halls and into my old room at last. Kado is happy to see me, his broad tongue sweeping over my cheek as he tries to crawl into my lap. Clio hardly looks at the dog as he moves me from my chair to my bed. Then he pushes my black hair away from my eyes and stares down at me.

"This feels familiar," I tell him, thinking of the night I fell asleep at his place after the first of my powers developed.

"Except this time, I'm not leaving," he says and sits beside me on the bed, easily burrowing his way under the sheets and blankets.

It's an intimate feeling, being so close to Clio. While I've been in his bed before, it was never *with* him. Until now, the closest I've ever been to another witch was the handful of kisses we'd shared. This is intense, overwhelming, and I almost consider telling him that maybe he should get a room of his own.

Then I meet his eyes, see the warmth and compassion in their depths, and wonder why I'm being such a child. This is *Clio*. He's been a huge part of my life for years. I trust him, and I love him.

I stiffen at the thought. It's an odd time to realize how true it really is. *I love him.*

I smile at him, and he smiles back. Somehow, I wonder if it's possible for him to read the thought in my head. He bends forward to kiss me, and when he pulls away, confusion floods across Kado's undead face. He sniffs at Clio, then looks at me before deciding to leap up onto the bed anyway. Clio groans under the dog's paws sinking into his chest and stomach, but less than two seconds later, Kado's curled up in his usual place by my side.

"That dog really loves you," Clio says, reaching out a hesitant hand to pet Kado's face.

Kado licks his fingers before resting his head on my chest, and I say, "I love him too."

Clio smiles at that and pulls his hand away. "So, how did your talk with Willow go?"

"Worse than I hoped," I say. "I guess I didn't realize how much our mother meant to her. I mean, Willow has memories with her, and I never did until recently. I should have realized she would take it harder than me, but it was like she turned into a different person." I pause. "Should I have just kept it to myself?"

Clio shakes his head. "Hell no. Yes, it hurts, but in the end, Willow deserves to know. She'll be okay."

"Yeah maybe. You didn't see the look on her face."

"Get some rest," Clio says and bends over to press his lips against mine—a soft brush of skin to skin.

Another surge of happiness surges through my body at the contact, and I kiss him back, savoring every second. No matter what, I will always count my blessings that he's part of my life.

***

I FALL ASLEEP as close to happiness as I think I've been in a while. It's a deep, dreamless sleep, and when I roll over halfway through the night, I'm still tucked in Clio's arms. I rest my ear against his chest, listening to the soft beating of his heart. I like to imagine Kado and Clio are sleeping just as well as I am. The rhythm of his heartbeat lures me back into sweet sleep until someone whispers in my ear.

"Lilith. Lilith," the lilting voice continues, breath puffing against my cheek.

I groan, irritated for being woken up, for being pulled away from this bliss. The noise stops, and a hand shakes my arm. The sleepiness starts to give way to anger, and I crack open an eye, wondering what's so important that I have to get up *now*. I catch sight of green hair and wings, but it's all still blurry. The thought of what I could've seen makes me pause, and I rub my eyes and blink again.

It's Fern.

For a minute, I assume I'm still asleep. I turn over, Kado whines, and my eyes slide closed again. It's all a dream.

"Lilith," the tiny voice repeats.

Now, I'm not so sure. I open my eyes again and see her, the tiny fairy, hovering in the air an inch away from my nose. A smile crosses her lips, and she reaches out a finger to tap me. Then I realize I'm awake—she's really here.

I sit up, and that's when I see she's not alone. Huddled in the corner is Ivy, her body wrapped in Helena's cloak. Her face is streaked with dirt, and her curly black hair is a wicked, wild mess. I open my mouth, whether to scream, cry, or talk, I don't know. Instead, an eerie noise escapes—something between a scream and a laugh.

Now Clio's awake too, and when he realizes we aren't alone, he sits bolt upright in bed. He moves to grab me, to protect me from the strange witch in the room, but I'm in such a trance, I try to get up off the bed. I fall to the floor with a thump, pain radiating through my ribs, and them I'm surrounded by all of them.

Clio reaches me first to scoop me up in his arms and deposit me back onto the bed, his gaze darting between Fern and Ivy. "Good to see you again, Fern," he finally says.

The fairy flutters toward us and lands on Clio's shoulder, but now he's studying Ivy. He doesn't say anything to her, because he doesn't want to; he recognizes her from the picture, from the information he read in the file. Anything he has to say to her is *not* kind.

I take Clio's lead and ignore her as well to look at Fern. It's been ages since I've seen her, and it's good to displace all the gruesome images my mind had conjured with this one—an updated picture of Fern in all her health. Carefully, I grab the tiny, delicate woman from the air and hug her the best I can. "You have no idea how happy I am to see you."

She smiles at me, but it drops when she looks toward Ivy. My mother has taken the smallest step forward, shivering under the cloak. I sigh, glancing at my dresser.

Clio hurries to grab one of my dresses from the top drawer. He tosses it to her, and she offers a silent thank you before she goes to work pulling on the dress under the privacy of the cloak.

"Why are you here?" I snarl, trying to keep eye contact, but it's harder than I expected. I glance at the floor; she looks so rugged, so tired, that it's hard to imagine anything good happened to her in her time away.

"I needed to see you again… I—"

Clio tilts his head, ready to offer an acidic comment. He doesn't feel the tiny hint of compassion I still harbor.

"I'm so sorry, Lilith," she continues and sobs, lifting a hand to her mouth to stifle it.

At one time, this scene might've broken my heart, but it does nothing now. It's strange to hear her apology; my automatic response is to accept it, to play down how hurt I was—a reflex that in no way mirrors how I truly feel. There are miles of subconscious aches within me, deep canyons radiating with hurt, and as much as I would love to just forgive her and move on, the pain of her betrayal will never fully leave. There are too many places for it to hide, and it's been hiding for so long, it's part of the landscape.

I remember the look on Willow's face and am entirely certain she feels the same.

"Go get cleaned up," Fern tells her.

Ivy takes another step forward, then I lift my hand. "Wait." She freezes. Her wide eyes study me—a mix of hope and fear. "Before she does anything, Willow needs to know she's here."

"Li…" Fern says.

"This is Willow's Coven," I say. "She deserves to know. Don't you think?" I ask Ivy this directly. "If you're going to ask for a favor, the person granting it should know that's what's happening." Then I look at Kado still nestled on the bed. His head rests on his paws, black eyes peering uncertainly over the blankets at the scene unveiling before him. He doesn't know whether Fern and Ivy are friend or foe, and I'm beginning to feel just as uncertain.

"Kado," I call, and he sits up. "Go get Willow."

He's gone before anyone can stop him.

"Li, do you really think that's the best idea?" Clio asks.

I look down at the bandages on my legs, the wound I suffered for Ivy's selfishness, and feel a sharp righteousness in my defense. I don't expect Clio or Fern to understand. I look at Ivy, part of me expecting to see her run again, but her face is a calm veneer. I think she understands this decision—at least more than Clio and Fern do.

Kado yips to announce his return, and Willow's just a moment behind him, her long brown hair windswept from the run. "Is everyone al—" She stops when she catches sight of Fern and then Ivy. "Lily, who is this woman?"

Her voice is high, too high, the kind of pitch squeezed

by contained emotions—pain or sorrow. There's no telling. I swallow, unable to say the words, to answer her question. So I stare at her instead, pouring every emotion I can manage into the act. Willow's black eyes sharpen before she looks away.

I hardly know what to think, watching my sister and mother eye each other like cats before a brawl. I can *see* the tension in Willow's entire frame, and Ivy looks too uncertain of herself to ever be considered the adult in this conversation.

"Mom," Willow says coldly.

Ivy helplessly reaches out, then drops her arms again, as if she just assumes any attempts to hug her daughter would be futile. I feel bad for her, but I understand where Willow stands just the same. My original damaged leg reminds me of that. This isn't an easy situation—for anyone.

"You've grown so beautiful," Ivy says, trying to defuse the tension.

Willow sneers. "I haven't 'grown' into anything. I've been dead for almost two decades."

Ivy visibly struggles for words. "D-dead?" She stares at Willow, studying her—the eeriness of her black eyes and pallor of her skin.

"Yeah. When you decided to run away and hide," Willow snaps. "To save yourself instead of your own children. I *died* for that. But unlike Dad, I came back. Unless you can think of an apology stronger than my resurgence, I don't want to hear a word you have to say."

Even I cringe at the raw hatred in her words. I can only imagine how Ivy feels.

Then Willow turns toward me, her black eyes still blazing with fury. "And you! What the hell is wrong with you for bringing her here? What were you thinking?"

"What's wrong with me?" I ask with a laugh. "Not the parade of assholes who made me this way."

Willow jerks her head away with a disgusted scoff.

I hold out my palms. "Look, she needed a place, and you

needed to see her."

"I need her gone," Willow snarls. "I need to have people I can depend on in my Coven."

Ivy opens her mouth. "I—" But Willow's burning gaze fires toward her, and Ivy closes her mouth instantly.

Willow scoffs again and turns away, not even bothering to look back once.

"I've failed you…" Ivy says, staring down at the ground. "Both of you."

I have no idea what I to say—what I *can* say. She's right. As a parent, she failed in her most important responsibility—keeping us safe at all costs.

Fern, ever the problem-solver, hovers toward Ivy and lands on her shoulder. "Let's get you settled in." Then she looks at me. "Li, we'll talk later." I nod.

"I'll see if someone can find me a bed," Ivy says before striding out of the room.

I watch her go before thinking of Willow, unsure who I should follow. In the end, I decide to let them be. They both need time, and my begging can't possibly relieve all the pain in the depths of their hearts.

Chapter Eleven
Permanent Death

"**T**HAT WAS A disaster," Clio says, exaggerating each word.

Kado whines in agreement.

I tilt my head to look at him through the corner of my eye. "Yeah, but it needed to be done. Maybe now that everything's out in the open, they can start to heal."

Clio's upper lip twitches. I can tell he doesn't believe me, but he doesn't say it. "What about you?"

"I have *different* healing to worry about," I remind him and gesture at my legs. Whatever emotional hurdles I might have to face in the imminent future don't concern me nearly as much as my physical body.

Clio looks even more serious now. He reaches out to brush his fingers over the bandages on my lower thigh. "How are you today?"

I shrug. "No better."

"But no worse, right?" He lifts me in his arms again and sets me in my chair. I look up at him. Concern isn't something I'm used to hearing in his voice. "We need to have Helena or Ambrossi look at you again." He starts to move around the chair but stops to look down at me when I grasp his shirt. "What's wrong?"

"What's the point?" I ask, loosening my grip. "We all know what Ambrossi won't say. This, these wounds, are more magical damage, Clio. Fire and Ice. Ambrossi can't heal it. Lazarus can't even touch it. If I had my guess, I'd say Lynx is the only one who could possibly come close, and if I'm being completely honest, I don't think I'd want him to try. That kind of magic... it's a curse."

The image of Flora's dead body wrapped in the pit of her grave flashes through my mind. Clio's lip twitches again, and I can tell he doesn't know what to do with the information I've just given him. He's used to me breaking down, to his role in being the one who builds me up again. When that's not necessary, he doesn't know *what* to do.

His large hand rests on the back of my chair, then he pats it once. "You've gotten so strong."

I smile at him. That's the closest thing to a compliment he'll give, and I'll take it. Back in our home Coven of Ignis, I used to admire everything about him. He was our class Adept, after all, the witch proven most capable of their magic. It was a high honor, and yet he never rubbed it in my face. Instead, he chose to help me, to train me.

"If anyone's strong, it's you," I whisper, reaching up with a finger to trace the thick, ugly scar up the side of his neck. My lip trembles.

"It's okay," he says, capturing my hand in his, then his lips are on mine. "I'm here now. With you. It's in the past."

I look away, an argument bubbling inside me that I can't put into words.

Clio must see it. "I'm still going to take you to Helena, just to make sure you're healing properly."

I sigh and let him have his way. This time. "Okay."

He smiles at the minor victory and pushes me out of the room. Kado follows us out into the hall, and Clio looks at him uneasily, as if he thinks something bad will happen if Kado gets a little too close. "Uh, is he allowed out here?"

I nod. "He's allowed to go anywhere I want him to."

Kado lifts his head at my words and barks—a happy yip—before he trots faster to keep up at my side.

"VIP privilege, huh?" Clio teases as we round a corner and pass one of Willow's tigers.

I laugh with him and reach out to stroke Kado's fur. He nuzzles my palm, making it easier for me to reach him, and leads the way outside. He barks at one of the tigers by the door to move. The huge cat gives him a dirty look before its massive amber eyes sweep over Clio and me. Then it steps back. Kado proudly guides us outside. The puff of fur on the top of his head serves as a beacon while we travel into the purple plants and make our way to the Community Villa.

Clio hesitates outside the building. Even Kado stops to look at him.

"Are you okay?" I ask, studying his sudden, statuesque stillness.

He bobs his head, a lock of his black hair falling into his eyes. "Yeah. I just can't imagine it's a good thing to keep going in there. Where the Sickness is."

I shrug. "Where else would we take them? The Healers were already set up in here, and that kind of equipment can't be moved very easily."

"I guess not," he says, and despite the tightness around his eyes, he pushes me inside the building.

The second we enter the hospital wing, I know something is wrong. There's a crowd gathered at the entrance, and the fact that most of them are Reanimates does not escape me.

"Excuse me. Pardon me. Coming through!" Clio calls out as he maneuvers my chair this way and that, desperate to get to the front to see what's happening. Most of them oblige, but a few stay put, shooting Clio scathing looks as he pushes past them anyway. When we finally make it through, I see a purple glow radiating from the room at the end of the hall—Willow's resurgence.

Clio and I don't speak, but he hurries us forward, leaving screaming witches behind us and bumping others just to get to the light. We emerge into a scene very like one we've already witnessed. Another witch has died, and not even Willow's magic is enough to heal her.

Worst of all? I know this witch.

It's Fleur.

***

A DAY THAT began chaotically ends in very much the same manner. Willow didn't want to waste time holding a meeting first. She moved on Fleur's funeral, and the witch was buried within an hour of her death right next to Alfred. Willow's motive came from fear of contamination.

I'm numb down to the core. I never liked Fleur. I had my first interaction with her when she poisoned the water in the Grove and nearly killed Callista, one of the fairies on the Advisory Council. I found Fleur in the act that night, but her magic was tricky, and she eased away my anger to provide her escape.

I got into a lot of trouble over her with Crowe and the Sage. Being here in the same Coven as Fleur meant I had to wave a white flag to any hostility, but I still never came to like the witch. There was too much bad karma around her—too many dirty deeds.

Yet her passing leaves me empty, as if I *had* cared for her. Maybe it's the suddenness of her death or the fact that I hadn't even known she was sick. Hell, maybe it's just the idea that the Sickness can take *anyone,* both witches I know and witches do not, that's gotten in my head. Once again, I'm one of the last witches beside the grave, just staring down at the dirt and picturing the body wrapped in a white sheet layers below.

THE SAGE

It doesn't feel real. Unlike the first funeral, where every witch in the Coven supported one another, everyone is divided here. There's anger, tears, and even a fight breaks out. It's chaos—the kind that comes with panic. The kind that comes with fear.

Willow didn't come to the funeral. As strange as that seems, I understand it now, with the anger surging through the crowd. I know her; she'll come later and mourn in peace. For now, she's mourning in private, doing what she can to keep this from becoming a full-blown spectacle.

Maverick is here, and his eyes shine silver as he puts his magic to work. The rowdiest of the witches fall to their knees and collapse to the ground, temporarily paralyzed. The rest fall silent, watching their fellow Covenmates on the ground and sending Maverick disgusted, accusing stares.

"Everyone to the cafeteria, now!" he orders.

"'Bout time you tell us what's going on!" a witch toward the back of the crowd spits.

Maverick is in no mood for it. It's all over his face. His silver eyes turn toward the voice, and a second later, a choked sound rises. No one else speaks after that. The group turns away to make their way back to the Community Villa, and eventually, just Clio, Maverick, and I are left.

"That was rough," I say.

Maverick nods and drags his hand down his face. He's exhausted too, I can tell. I wonder how much magic he has left in his reserves and whether a meeting right now when tensions are so high is really such a good idea. We follow him through the purple plants anyway. By the time we make it to the cafeteria, it's full—fuller than I can ever remember seeing a meeting before the Sickness.

A few witches Maverick just put under his spell give him dirty looks, but the rest of them don't notice our arrival. Willow stands at the podium, her long, scraggly brown hair pulled into a messy attempt at a bun on the top of her head. There are dark circles under her eyes, and she stares down onto her Coven.

I don't envy her right now for having to do this. I prod into the minds of the nearby witches, and they're all hostile. If I was on the outskirts of information for something like this, I would be too.

I scan the sea of gathered faces waiting for Willow to speak. When I first joined the Elemental Coven, the group of Reanimates was small—a group within a group, because even the other Elementals tended to avoid them. They were scared and uncertain, depending on one another like a lifeline.

Now? The Reanimates make up almost half the Coven, and it's a jarring thought. I think about what this place would be if Willow lost her resurgence or had never had it in the first place—all the Reanimates would've been lost forever.

Then my eyes meet Alpine's, and I flinch, looking away as quickly as I can, though I know he already caught me staring. I don't have anything against him—Hell, I barely even know him—but ever since I saw his dead body lying next to Flora's in Alchemy, I can't face him. To think of him makes me think of her. It'll probably always be that way.

"Thank you all for being here tonight," Willow says, drawing all the attention in the room, Alpine's included.

The murmurs die instantly, and dozens of eyes bore into Willow from every angle. If I were her, my skin would be *crawling*.

"These have been some trying days," she says, tries to smile, fails, and continues. "But I fear they might not be over anytime soon."

"What's happening!"

"Are you losing your powers?"

"What happened to Alfred and Fleur?"

"Is everyone who's sick going to die?"

The questions grow more frantic, louder, and more desperate, and I reach up to cover my ears, wanting to block it all out. Clio reaches out from his seat beside me and grasps my hand, squeezing slightly. Willow silences all the questions at once by lifting her hand.

"As you all know, we have lost two very promising witches. The disease that killed them is unlike anything we have ever seen before." She pauses, enormous black eyes sweeping the crowd.

Don't say it.

"It's of a magical origin."

She said it. I squeeze my eyes shut.

Chairs knock over as witches hop to their feet, shouting and screaming insults and concerns. They're angry that Willow didn't protect them, that Willow allowed something so innocuous to infiltrate the Coven, while the rest are just scared for their lives. Fistfights break out, and that escalates into magic flying everywhere. Clio blasts fire toward a witch who strays too close.

Maverick jumps up too and lifts his hands above his head. "Enough!" he hollers, metallic eyes lighting up as his powers kick in.

Just as quickly as the brawl began, it stops. Witches in various forms of unconsciousness litter the floor; just a few who've been quiet so far were spared.

"Everyone will be required to receive daily attention from a Healer, and those who pass today's inspection will be moved immediately out of the Community Villa and all surrounding homes. After today, no one who isn't a Healer or infected will be allowed in the Community Villa. Am I clear?"

Maverick answers on their behalf. "Anyone who has issues with this new rule may speak to me in private."

Willow dismisses herself and has Grief walk her out before Maverick releases his magic. When the witches come to, a lot of them are hugging themselves, hugging each other, and a few tears are hidden and wiped away. The Coven clearly isn't anywhere near as angry as it is scared.

Permanent death.

What could be more terrifying than that?

Chapter Twelve

Secrets

*C*LIO, MAVERICK, AND I are the last ones in the cafeteria long after everyone else has moved to start packing their belongings. We don't speak for a while, thinking of the riots and the angry witches. A few of them weren't afraid to spit insults at us on their way out the door. Maverick only raised a threatening hand.

"This is serious," I tell him.

He bobs his head, face grim. "Yes, unfortunately, and it's only getting more serious by the day."

"Do you know where Willow went?" I ask. She might've been able to fool the others with her veneer of strength during the meeting, but it will never work on me; I see her pain and fear right through it.

Clio frowns and reaches out to tuck a lock of hair behind my ear. "I know you're worried, but I think she needs some time alone, Li."

I glance up at him but don't really see him. In my head, I see her face above the podium, the devastation in her eyes as her Coven turned on her. This day has probably been the worst of her life, and that's saying something, considering the fact that she actually *died*.

"I agree," Maverick says and takes his leave before I can

argue.

What a hypocrite. I know exactly where he's going—the same place he told me not to go. To Willow. I can't blame him, though. He has a different kind of special place in her life. I glance at Clio and try to put myself in her shoes. If I had the day Willow had, I would certainly want Clio to come after me.

"I don't like this. Feeling helpless," I say and untuck the lock of hair from behind my ear.

Clio turns to look at me once Maverick's footsteps fade away. "No one does. But if you need a distraction, there are still two other people you need to have a heart-to-heart with."

Fern and Ivy.

He's right, but part of me misses my sister. She's in pain, and I want to be there for her, even if I have no idea of how to help. Maybe just being close to one another will make a difference. Who knows?

"We can go see how your mother's settling in," he suggests.

I narrow my eyes at him. I was never more inclined to pick Ivy first out of those choices. "No. She deserves to sit and worry for a little bit. If she cares enough about Willow. Let's go find Fern."

Clio laughs but steps behind me to grab my chair.

"What's so funny?" I ask, turning to look at him over my shoulder.

"You. You're so *stubborn*. Sometimes, it's like nothing's changed. When I close my eyes, it's so easy to imagine we're back in Ignis and the war, being here, was all a dream. But then I look around again, and it's not. We're so different, and yet we haven't changed at all."

I take a minute to digest what he said. "I said something similar to Helena after I came here."

Clio's eyes move skyward as if he's lost in his thoughts. "I can't imagine she took it well."

I shrug, my mind shifting focus as we leave the

Community Villa. This is a weird moment of my life. I don't want to look at the past, because the memories of what I've already conquered are so heavy. But so is the thought of what the future may bring. I want to focus on the present, to stay in the moment, but somehow, even that seems like a terrible idea.

"So, do you know where Fern went?" I ask in a choked voice, desperate for any kind of distraction from myself.

"I have an idea," he says. "When we were in that other Coven, Fern... told me a lot about herself that I never knew."

"Like what?" I ask, furrowing my eyebrows and trying to keep the hurt out of my voice. I have always considered Fern to be one of my closest friends, especially after she took particular care of me as a child. The thought that someone else might know her better than I do actually hurts.

"She has a child," Clio says. "I never knew that was possible for fairies."

I let out a strained breath. "You're talking about Malcolm. Yeah, I've met him."

"Then why do you seem so lost?" I glance over my shoulder at him, and he laughs. "Oh, don't look like that. I'm just saying you already know where to look for her."

I do.

I wonder why I didn't think of that connection on my own. So I direct Clio through the maze of towering purple plants until we make it to the little mound of dirt somewhere toward the heart of the Coven. The area doesn't look like anything special, and the first time Willow brought me here, I was confused out of my wits. Now, the sight brings a welcoming peace.

"Fern? Malcolm?" I call. "Are you here?"

Fern pops up instantly, her radiant face brightening at the sight of me. I'm not used to people being *happy* to see me, so when they are, it fills some part of me that I keep forgetting is mostly empty.

"Lilith! It's so good to see you," she says and gives me

two tiny hugs, as if she feels one won't be enough to properly convey her feelings.

"I'm so happy to see you. And I never got the chance to thank you for keeping Clio safe."

"Any friend of yours is a friend of mine. Always." The sincerity in her smile melts my heart. In Ignis, Clio and Fern hated one another. Seeing the way they look at each other now makes it hard to believe that was ever true.

"I missed you so much, Fern," I tell her. The point has already been made, but I want to say it anyway. Just to make sure she knows as well as anyone within earshot.

"I missed you too, Lilith."

Malcolm pokes his head out. "Hi, Lilith," he says and turns enough to catch sight of Clio. Instantly, his head dips back into the safety of the shadows in his burrow.

"It's okay, Mal" Fern cooes to him. "They're friends. Both of them."

Malcolm's head slowly reemerges from the darkness. His nervous eyes open, full of tears, and he flutters out enough to hug Clio's leg. "Thank you for bringing my Momma back."

Clio's eyes grow wide with uncertainty, and he looks at me, lost for words. Unlike me, he's never been good with fairies. As a boy, he had a tendency to be crass and rough—things fairies don't particularly care for. "I-I didn't…"

Malcolm flutters away before Clio can finish, and Fern only smiles at Clio. "It's okay to let your guard down sometimes," she says.

"I've been telling him that for years." I say the words slowly with a half-smile at Clio.

He scratches behind his ear and stares at the ground.
"Fern!" A raspy yet familiar voice rises from the depths of the burrow. The recognition of it makes my stomach drop, and with wide eyes, I look between the opening of Fern's home and Fern herself.

She blanches and says, "One minute, Thorn."

84

THE SAGE

I open and close my mouth, feeling like I'm gasping for air and struggling for words. Maybe this is what a fish feels like when it's pulled from the water. Slowly—far slower than I have the patience for—my thoughts finally form a tangible hiss from my own lips. "*Thorn? Thorn* is in there?"

Fern bites her lip and looks from me to Clio. "Yes, but please don't tell Willow. She can't know... Not yet."

Clio takes a step back, his emotions working off of mine. "Who's in there, Fern?"

"The fairies from the Advisory Council," I reply, then meet Fern's gaze again and lower my voice. "Why are they here? Did you... did you *bring* them here?" The thought that Fern could be behind anything potentially malicious makes me sick.

"They were hurt," she says softly, threading her fingers together. "They didn't have anywhere else to go, but they couldn't stay *there*. People are... judgmental. It's easier to condemn than forgive."

"But they're *enemies,*" I say. "They can't be seen here. Willow won't understand. She'll think you've betrayed her."

Fern frowns, her wings beating more frantically. "That's the thing. They're not with the Council... They're not really with anyone. After Callista was poisoned, they've tried to pull out of the war and just focus on surviving in any way possible. Fairies... we aren't made for conflict."

"Fern, you *have* to tell Willow what's going on. If she finds—"

Fern lifts her hand to stop me. "I know there could be consequences, and if they come, I'll deal with them. I'll tell Willow eventually, but for now, Thorn and Callista need my help. And this is the only place they could go and not be found. The only real place they could go to heal."

I stare into her big eyes and feel myself melting into nothingness. Deep down, we all just want this war to be over. I can't begrudge them for wanting to get away from it all, but at the same time, this is dangerous. Besides the Sage, the Advisory

Council of Fairies are the most powerful beings in the Land of Five. Despite that, their previous ties to the Council could prove disastrous to us if Thorn and Callista's loyalties are more slated than Fern believes.

I want to continue the argument, thinking of how Fern was at one time a part of the Advisory Council before leaving it, but I can't do that. I owe her this.

Clio's lips are parted slightly, disbelief washing over his features. He looks as if he's about to protest, but I cut him down with one word. "Okay."

Fern smiles, but Clio looks sick as he whirls on me. "*Okay?*"

I nod. "She saved your life, Clio. We both know she didn't have to do that. She could've just let you die in that battle and then gone about her business, but she didn't. She risked herself to help you. To heal you. So I can do this to return that favor. Sure, it won't be easy, but what she did for you most likely wasn't, either. If you have any gratitude at all for her, you'll agree with me."

He reaches up to touch the ugliest scar across his neck—one we both know would've been a deathblow without Fern's magic. Silently, he looks away toward the purple plants so we can't see whatever other fresh emotions have risen there. Fern smiles, knowing as well as I do that she's won this argument.

Chapter Thirteen
We're Not Alone

UPON DEPARTURE, FERN gives me another little hug and sends Clio a hopeful glance. We have an entire conversation without a single word. Clio isn't happy with me, made obvious by his silence on the walk home, but he won't argue with me. He only asks one question. "Are you sure about this?"

"Yes," I say, though that's not the truth.

I'm not sure about anything at this point except my love for the people who matter the most to me.

Maybe Clio senses that, or he just has too much faith in me and loves me too much. Either way, we don't speak about it again. We go to our exams, both of us passing the screening for the Sickness, and retire to my room in Willow's mansion for the night.

I'M STILL AWAKE well after Clio and Kado fell asleep. I run my hand down Kado's silky side, enjoying the softness of his fur. He grumbles a bit, and his tongue lolls from his mouth, but he doesn't wake up. I watch him in envy. I can't think straight, and I wish I couldn't think at all. Between the virus, Fern and Ivy's reappearance, and the discovery of Thorn and Callista on the

Elementals' Grounds, I'm not sure what to process first.

I flip over again and groan at the tightness of the bandage on my leg. I tug at the top of the bandage, willing it to loosen a bit. This time, I earn a full, aggravated whine from Kado. His fluffy white head pops up, and he narrows his eyes at me before running his wet tongue across my cheek. Then his head sinks back onto the pillow.

I can't stop thinking about Thorn and Callista. Having seen them today brings up all the memories of the battle on the Council grounds and the hundreds of special witches who lived in the bunker beneath Headquarters. During my time on the Council, I never knew it existed.

My simplistic mind had assumed the Council was made up of five members—one for each Coven in the Land of Five— and the sixth member was the Sage. When Crowe took me back there as a prisoner, I learned the truth. The bunkers held the *real* Council—underground levels filled by witches with extraordinary powers, all hidden from the Land of Five.

After the battle all but destroyed Council Headquarters, I have to wonder what the Council will do. Moving all those witches would be impossible to hide. Somehow, I doubt they're even concerned about the Land of Five discovering them anymore.

Then I think of Crowe and the fact that Aquais warriors were in that fight. Could the Council have taken up residence at Crowe's mansion? The thought makes me sick, and I hate myself for it. Crowe always said his family maintained a fierce loyalty to the Council, and really, I hadn't put more thought into than that. Now that the image is in my head, it won't leave. Rena, Crowe's mother, was killed in the Battle of the Grove, but Willow made sure she was one of the first Reanimates brought back to us.

That influenced her loyalty—as Willow's magic has a tendency to do—but the rest of Aquais still stands strong in support of the Council. Because Rena had, once. I don't know if they're aware of Rena's fate, if they think she's still dead, or if they assume she was taken prisoner. But I'm sure the Sage has used her absence to keep everyone under her influence. Crowe's brother Kieran is the last of his family in that great mansion now. It's got to be lonely, being trapped among the memories of everyone he lost. He can't be blamed; he's no doubt in an agony of his own, doing what he thinks will continue his family legacy.

You can check, my intuition rings in the back of my mind.

I hate that voice. It's dangerous because nine out of ten times, it's right.

The astral trip is as easy as closing my eyes and going to sleep, but I worry about what I might see; *that* won't be as easy. I'm torn between the easy choice and the hard. One last time, I try to go to sleep, to just forget the world for a while. My eyes flutter open, and I look at Clio, the peace on his face as he slumbers. Wriggling closer, I press my face against his chest and breathe in his scent.

It warms me all the way down to my belly, but it doesn't help my troubles. With him come even more memories of the battle that tore us apart, all the agony of not knowing. I hate the Council. I really do.

With the fresh anger flaring through my heart, I give up on sleep. It'll be impossible now. Flipping over gently so as not to bother Kado or Clio, I lie flat on my back, staring up at the ceiling. One more time, I question myself. Is this really the best course of action? The answer comes quickly. It doesn't matter if it's the best thing I can do, because it's the *only* thing I can do. My eyes fight to open, but I force them closed. Crossing my hands over my chest, I lie as still as I can possibly manage. Finally, what feels like *hours* later, my breathing slow dramatically, evens out, and guides me into a meditative state.

When I'm sure it's time, I open my eyes and find myself outside my body. I take a moment to marvel at the sensation, looking at my glittery, shiny, not-quite-solid hands and then at my physical body nestled in the bed between my two favorite creatures in the Land of New Life.

I take a step around the bed, so grateful to at least have the use of my legs here. Traveling in this form is easy, painless, and I feel tears in the corners of my eyes as I make my way to the Grove. The logical, cruel part of me whispers that I'll never have this luxury when I'm awake. I just move faster.

When I make it to the Grove, the damage is bad. Even in astral form, I can smell the ruin the fires made of this place. In the low light, the grass glitters constantly, covered in millions of shards from the giant pane of glass that used to complete one wall of the building. The wind blows, and everything just looks cold. I can't feel the breeze, but I wrap my arms around myself anyway and keep moving.

Being here makes me uneasy, like I expect to be caught at any minute. That's highly doubtful. Headquarters is all but a pile of broken stones and bricks. It certainly doesn't *look* like anyone still lives here, but I've been fooled before. I press on, ignoring the chill running down my spine. Clio, Crowe, and I left the battle fairly early that day, so we never saw it escalate to this. The witches who stayed, though, had given it their all—on both sides. The garden is desolate, filled with so many lost souls that I swear I hear them *screaming* in the wind.

When I get to where the front door used to be, I pause. My mind slams back through my memories to the very first time I was here.

When I was one of them.

It feels like ages ago, like I'm looking into someone else's mind instead. I move on autopilot, carefully making my way through the rubble. Beyond the door to Headquarters, there used to be an expansive sitting area with thronelike chairs and décor representing each Coven covering the walls. It's all gone now, reduced to either ash or rubble, and I'm almost glad. I stumble through the wreckage. In a way, it's almost easier to pretend the entire thing never happened. I wouldn't have to face it again. Looking at the floor, I count my steps to where the entrance to the Sage's room used to be. The long, elegant stone hallway still stands—though the rooms on either side do not—and the sight hits me harder than it should.

It's like the building itself is trying to tell me something. *'We're not gone,'* it says. *'We're clinging to life. We've been hurt, but we're not gone.'* I close my eyes and try to block it out. In astral form, I could have walked through the walls, but I go around to stand in the open air. Once, this place belonged to the most powerful witch in the Land of Five. When the building still stood, the Sage's room was cozy, with books and a boiling cauldron, always smelling of the sweetest herbs. That's all gone, even her desk and chair, but the trapdoor leading to the bunkers survived the battle—the only thing that appears unaffected by the fire and tragedy.

'We're not gone.'

Swallowing, I put one foot through the trapdoor, then the other, and move through the floor to walk down the stairs. As I gaze into the blackness below, the thought that this might not be the best choice makes me pause. *'We're not gone.'* It's enough to get me moving again.

I reach the first floor without meeting any resistance at all, and that worries me even more. When I first learned of my ability to astral project, I tried to spy on the Council as a favor to Willow. There were so many charms and enchantments that I couldn't even get past the topiary garden. Trying caused me physical pain. It feels odd now to be this far within the Grove and not meet that magic again. Perhaps there really is no one here… or perhaps they've been expecting me, wanting to show me more.

As much as I hate to admit it, the Sage knows me in ways even Clio does not. She's sifted through my mind, tested my wits, and knows just how much I am capable of. When I joined the Council, she told me my abilities would be tested—to improve them, she said. Now, I wonder if the tests were just for her own secret store of knowledge, just so she could know what to expect of me in the future.

Based on what I know of the elderly witch, it sounds accurate. Now, standing in the ruins of Headquarters, I imagine her so clearly. If anyone could've anticipated me being here, it's her. I don't want to be right.

But if I don't keep going, I'll never know. My curiosity seems in direct opposition to my sense of self-preservation, freezing me here with indecision.

I breathe deeply and remind myself that whatever's waiting for me—if there's anything there—can't hurt me in this form. It's not completely reassuring, but it gets me through the first floor. It's so dark, and I absently wave my hands in front of me, as if I'll physical feel my way through. Now, I'm imagining the bunker's layout just as Crowe described it on our trip. This floor, the first floor, is Lynx's workshop. Just ahead are the distribution rooms where the Council prepared the food and resources it sent to each Coven. The third floor contains the Coven altar and bedrooms—the living space for the witches of the Grove.

I move slowly through each, but there's no proof of anyone still being here now. Floor after floor turns up empty, and when I stumble to the fourth and last floor—the Surveillance wing constantly lit by the electric lights from Mentis—I remember the files and the prison cells. I'm hugging myself again as I approach those tiny, cramped cells, turning away only when the memories grow too painful.

That's when I see the other witch here, and she's staring right at me.

Chapter Fourteen
Run

I WAS NEVER told much about Tabitha beyond the fact that she's in control of the Council's brainwashing. According to Willow, nobody knows she exists, because she can erase herself from a witch's mind at will. Willow met her shortly before her execution, and something about the timing of it—plus Willow's death and resurgence—made her the only witch alive to remember Tabitha at all. Even now, she's aware of the woman, though Willow admits her memory of Tabitha isn't the best.

For example, she's never described Tabitha to me in detail, so I don't know what she looks like. For some reason, that doesn't matter. I know this witch is Tabitha the way I know Helena and Clio.

I've seen her before. I shiver with the uncertainty of it. It's very possible I *have* seen her before but have no memory of the encounter.

That's a scary thought.

"It's you." Her raspy voice eerily reminds me of Iris. She takes a step forward, her ancient eyes bulging in her face. "I *see* you."

I gasp and take a step backward just before I slam back into my own body. I sit up, choking for air. Kado bolts to his feet with wide eyes, and Clio wakes up, grabbing me in confused surprise.

"Li! What is it? What's wrong?" His grip on me softens. One hand pats my back, and he watches my struggle with concern, just trying to help ease my ragged breathing.

Tears stream down my cheeks, and I bury my face in his shoulder, wanting to get myself under control before I even attempt to answer him. There's so much he doesn't know about me, and it's strange that this boy—the witch I feel the closest connection to in the entire Land of Five—doesn't know me as well as he thinks he does.

"I've acquired a lot of powers since you've been gone," I say at last and pull away from him enough to peer up into his eyes.

Clio nods, patiently waiting for me to continue. "Are they all Mentis powers?"

I shake my head, thinking of my fleeting telekinesis. "No. They've been coming from all Covens. Astral projection is the latest."

Clio blinks, narrows his eyes, opens them, and then frowns. "Wait, isn't that from Alchemy?"

"Yeah," I say and breathe in slowly. "When I sleep, I can travel to other places and see what's going on in real time."

"Uh-huh," Clio says, looking a lot more uneasy about the conversation by the second. "So where did you go?"

"Well, I started to think about the Council and Aquais. When we left the battle, it was early, and I wondered what happened after we left. I wanted to see… what was left of them. To see if I could figure out how they were surviving. I saw so many witches in the bunker when I was there, and I wondered if the Sage would make them stay in the Grove even if Headquarters was destroyed, just to keep their existence a secret."

"So you went?"

I bite my lip. "Yes. Headquarters is gone, but the

bunker's still there. The same as ever. I made it to the last level without seeing anyone, and I thought it was empty, but then I saw a witch."

Clio raises his eyebrows. "Was it the Sage?"

"No, but... it was someone worse."

"Worse? How could anyone be worse than the Sage?"

I breathe out, trying to carefully gather my words before I spew them. "When I first got to the Elemental Coven, I thought the same thing. Then Willow told me the truth about herself and what had happened to her. I had a hard time understanding why everyone forgot about her, especially since her execution wasn't that long ago. She told me the Council has a witch responsible for implanting and erasing information from the minds of everyone in the Land of Five."

Clio's eyes seem to double in size, and he sticks his tongue in his cheek, like he thinks I'm joking with him. "They do?"

"Yes. Her name's Tabitha. That's all I know about her."

"If she can erase information from witches' minds, how did Willow remember about her?"

"I think it has something to do with her resurgence. And the fact that knowing about Tabitha makes it harder for her to infiltrate our minds."

"I guess that makes sense," Clio says, running his finger along his jaw. "So... just now..."

"In the bunkers?" I ask.

He nods.

"She saw me."

Clio sits up so quickly that Kado yelps and jumps up too, ears flat in his best attack pose. I reach out to stroke his fur, easing him back into a sitting position.

"How do you know she really saw you?"

"She said, 'I see you.' Seems pretty self-explanatory." I toss the blanket off my lap.

"She was waiting for you."

"I thought so too," I admit. "It was strange that there weren't any charms or enchantments. Then she was there."

"Li, I hate to say this, but…"

I raise an eyebrow, hating the waver in his tone. "But what?"

Clio swallows and rubs his mouth. "Okay. This goes against everything I am, but we should leave. I thought we were safe here, but with everything going on, this place is just as dangerous as the Land of Five, if not *more* dangerous. We should go to that Coven where you were born and just ride out the end of this battle."

Run.

The word plays in my mind, but it sounds odd, foreign. I tilt my head, staring at him, and wonder if he really just said that. His eyes glitter in the dark as he stares back, waiting for my answer. I know I didn't imagine it, though that would've made this moment a Hell of a lot easier to process.

"Run?" I whisper.

Clio nods.

"Run?" I say it louder this time. "The Elemental Coven's on the verge of collapse, and that's your solution?"

His face is perfectly blank, but all the intention behind his words glitters in his eyes. He stands by what he said and doesn't feel the need to argue his point further. Seeing him now, like this, breaks something in me. I can't believe this is Clio, the witch I remembered being fearless—strong. Our Coven's *Adept*.

I could cry, though if it's from surprise, or sadness, or just an overwhelming surge of emotions, I don't know. I let out a long, raspy laugh and gesture to my legs. Even *walking* would be a struggle for me right now. "I can't *run* anywhere," I point out. "And if after everything, you still want to run and hide, I don't know what to say. You've never been a coward. Me and you? I thought we shared that passion to fight. That fire. The Council took everything from us." I glance pathetically at my wounded legs again. "And I do mean *everything*. So no, Clio. I will not run. Better or worse, I'm staying here with Willow, where I'm needed, and I'll ride this out to the end."

"You could die," he says. Despite his calm expression, I hear the first flares of anger.

I shrug. "And? All the best fighters already have. If I die here, Willow will revive me. It'll be like I just went to sleep. If I die out there, I'll be gone forever. You too. Why risk it?"

"You say *I'm* a damn coward. How can you be so foolish? If that witch really saw you, who's to say she can't find you? This sickness came from somewhere, and I'm willing to bet that the Council's responsible."

"Then why do you want to run right back into their clutches?"

"They won't expect it," he says.

"They expect more than you think," I retort. "How do you know seeing Tabitha wasn't just a diversion to flush us out? To get us to go back to the Land of Five so they can wipe us out forever?"

"Why would they need to go through all that effort if they can reach you out here? Any link to you at all isn't good." My face twitches with my urge to cut him off, but I let him finish. "This place isn't as safe as you think."

"That's the thing," I say. "Nowhere will be truly safe until this war's over." And as sad as it is, it's true. I think of the dead bodies that covered Alchemy and the ruins of Mentis. A tiny portion of Ignis survived its devasting wildfires, but I think that's only because Tarj managed to protect what he could.

Clio scoffs. "You can't be serious, Li."

I fold my arms across my chest, staring at him with all the fire and strength a broken girl can possibly manage. "As serious as the Sickness."

Clio stares at me, so much sorrow in his eyes but his face contorted in rage. "I know you think you're strong, and sometimes you are, but you're also stubborn as Hell and notorious for making bad decisions. Don't do anything you're going to regret later, Li. Let's just go. Then you'll see we're better off."

"No," I say, staring at him without blinking. I want him to see inside my mind, to see inside my *soul*, and know that I don't plan on changing my answer—in this life or the next.

"You're crazy." Clio stands from the bed, turns away, then looks back at me. His frown deepens, as if he expected my position to change just because he got up.

"You've always known that," I say, lifting my chin to keep his gaze.

With a grunt, he flings a dismissive hand at me and storms out of the room, whipping open the door with enough force that it bangs against the wall behind him.

Kado snarls after him and barks once. I imagine it's his way of telling Clio to stay out.

Chapter Fifteen
Sleeping Dogs

IN ALL THE years I've known him, I've only seen Clio angry on a number of occasions, and certainly never at me. We've had our petty squabbles, sure, but such a heated fight? Never. Kado curls back up against me, his fuzzy head resting on my chest. He senses my distress and does the best he can to cheer me up. I appreciate the effort, but after a minute of the closeness, I find myself missing Clio.

I reach out to feel the fading warmth on his side of the bed and just stare up at the ceiling, drowning myself in the poison of my mind. I stay in bed long after that, finding I have no willpower to do anything, even if it's just to turn over and go to sleep. I feel so alone... I haven't felt this way in a while, and I don't appreciate it.

It feels almost like I'm trapped in the hospital wing again, except this time, I don't have Clio eagerly awaiting my return. I stroke Kado's fur, running his ear through my fingers. "Was I wrong?" I ask him.

Kado lifts his head and whines before dropping it again.

"Yeah, I didn't think so either."

That doesn't make the crushing loneliness disappear. With a sigh, I press my palms against my eyes. For just a second,

I imagine this is what Ivy feels—all alone in her room, thinking about how much her two daughters have scorned her. I almost feel sorry for her, but then I regain myself and push it away. Whatever she feels, she had it coming from the very moment she put herself above Willow and me.

Kado shuffles positions a few times, nudging me with his nose every now and then to check if I'm asleep. Eventually, he hops onto the floor with his long legs and circles the bed, eyeing me in concern. Then he barks once, waits for me to look at him, and nudges my wheelchair.

"I'd love to, Kado," I say, "but I can't right now." Ultimately, I'm not sure how true that really is.

I'm not sure how long I stay in my self-created prison of anger and pity, but Kado grows tired of the room completely. He tries to claim my attention one last time, but when I don't move from the bed, he wedges his nose into the corner of the door, opens it, and slips out into the hallway.

"Goodbye!" I call sarcastically, watching the fuzzy stump of his tail disappear.

Even my dog left me. I let out a weird sound somewhere between a laugh and a cry. When someone knocks on my door, I sit up again, expecting Clio. Laura pops her head in instead.

"Morning, Lilith. I hope I didn't wake you. I saw Kado out in the hall, so I figured I'd drop by," she says politely.

I shake my head and look at the ground. Laura's a sweet girl; she doesn't deserve any of the venom bottling up inside me. "No, you didn't wake me," I say. I want to ask her what she's doing here, but I know it'll come out sounding rude. So I just wait for her to speak again.

"You're overdue for a checkup," she says. "So if you don't mind, Ambrossi wants me to take you to the hospital wing to cleanse your aura."

"I don't have a choice, do I?" I ask, thinking of Willow's face in the meeting room as she declared mandatory checkups.

Laura shrugs with a bashful smile. "No. 'Fraid not."

"Didn't think so." I look at the chair before glancing back at the tiny witch. "Are you gonna be able to move me?"

She nods, looking unoffended, and pushes the chair toward my bed. In one fluid motion, she slips her arm under mine, grabs me around the middle, and slides me from the bed to the chair. The landing is a bit rough, but it's better than what I expected from such a small girl.

"You okay? Anything hurt?" she asks, though her smile seems playful.

"No, you did good," I admit.

We don't talk at all as she wheels me to the hospital wing. Instead of easing me onto the table for the exam, she leaves me in the chair. I have the feeling moving me once already exhausted her more than she's willing to say, but I decide to be nice and not bring it up. Laura sifts through my aura, easing away what she can of the black spots while dispersing the others. While I don't fully understand her method of healing, I appreciate it. My mood's lightened quite a bit at the end of the session, and just before Laura can dismiss me, Katrina runs into the room to rummage through one of the cabinets for a small silver tool.

When she turns away to leave, she catches my eye, smiles, and says, "Long time no talk, Lilith."

I just wait for her expression to change from happiness to something else when she realizes how severe my situation is—just the way half the Coven has looked at me already. Or maybe she'll sense that something is off about me and that conversation is the last thing I want.

She lasts longer than most of the others before asking, "How are you doing?"

"Fine," I say, then glance at the tool in her hand. "How's Rena?"

"She's adjusting," Katrina says and lets out a sigh.

"That's good, right?"

"In a way." She runs her thumb down the side of the

device. "I think it's hard on Crowe... seeing his mother like that. And it hurts her to know he's like that."

I picture Crowe and Rena in the clearing again—the agony in his voice and the pure defeat in hers. I know the feeling. The first time I saw Helena alive again after her death, I fainted.

"It just takes time," I assure her.

"I know," she says. "That's what I told him."

"But he doesn't listen, does he?"

Katrina purses her rosebud lips, making them look twice their regular size. "No. How'd you guess?"

"Well, when Clio took me out in my chair, we kind of overheard Crowe and Rena. He was trying to help her dance, but she wouldn't do it, and he sounded so..."

A pained smile touches her mouth, then fades. "If you think that's bad..." I'm grateful that she doesn't bring up a worse, more painful memory. But then she decides to change the topic. "What's going on with you and Clio?"

I tilt my head, caught off guard by the question. "I didn't know you and Clio talk," I say simply. Especially about things as emotionally charged as our fight.

"Well, it was kind of hard not to. He was in the hospital wing this morning. Made a whole scene. We almost had to have Maverick put him out for a while."

"About what?" I ask, my eyes feeling huge.

"He said he wanted to learn how to heal."

That's new to me. "Did he say why?"

Katrina shakes her head. "Not that I heard. He just came in and demanded that someone teach him. Ambrossi and Laura tried to get him to leave, after Willow's orders, but he wouldn't go. He kept screaming about how pointless it was to sit on his ass. Eventually, Helena agreed to train him, and that was that."

I stare at her; really, I'm staring *into* her—into the memory she describes. I can't imagine what would drive Clio to want to heal. After our fight, it makes no sense. He wants to leave. Why integrate himself even deeper into the Coven?

"Anyway, we'll catch up later," she says. "I gotta run." Then she's gone.

Laura and I glance at each other. "Is all that true?" I ask.

A slight blush rises in her cheeks before she quickly looks away. "I wish I could say no."

"Did he tell you why he did it?"

Laura shakes her head. "If he told anyone, it's most likely Helena."

This would not come as a surprise to me.

"Want me to help you get to your room?" Laura asks.

"Nah, I've got it." I have a feeling she won't tell me any more about the incident with Clio, and to prove my point, I wheel myself out of there.

In the hallway, I'm not sure what to do with myself. There are so many loose ends at this point in my life, so much going on, that it's hard to tell where I should focus. I want to ask Clio what he was thinking, why he would do what he did, but I don't want to talk to him. Not before he apologizes first. So I push him out of my mind to think of Fern and Ivy instead, remembering that I haven't bothered to talk to my mother since that first encounter in my room.

I don't know why, but before I know it, I make the decision to face her, to see what she has to say for herself. Maybe it was the confrontation with Clio, or maybe it's something else entirely, but I'm on my way through the Community Villa. Then a chill runs down my spine—the same chill as when I went traipsing through the ruins of the Grove. It's odd to see all the empty rooms and the lack of life. I wonder if I'll see Clio, but given that I haven't seen anyone since Laura, I doubt it.

As I pass the cafeteria, I remember Willow's new rules and wonder if Laura just forgot about them all when she decided to bring me here. I know Healers work best in familiar environments, but it seems risky to search me for Sickness at

Ground Zero—even riskier for a non-Reanimate Healer to still be in here at all.

She's not the only one, though. There are Katrina and Clio too.

Now I wonder where Ivy could've possibly gone. I could always ask Fern, but I don't want to involve more people in this than I have to. It doesn't feel right to think about Ivy with her own room in Willow's mansion, so close to the daughter she left for dead. But under Willow's new rules, that has to be what happened, right?

I want to just wheel around through the mansion and find the room on my own, but the more I travel, the more of a Herculean task it is. I stop by my room for a break, scooping up the file, and get back to searching. I'm getting tired now and still have no idea where Ivy is, so I do what I didn't want to do. I ask around.

Eventually, I find what is now my mother's room. It's the farthest from Willow's, no surprise there, but it's also far from mine as well. I have the feeling Maverick was responsible for the room choice.

When I wheel up to her room, I breathe in, stare at the door, and reach out to knock. After this falsely polite gesture, I push the door open with my telekinesis before Ivy could have possibly opened it on her own. Then I push myself forward and stop in the doorway.

Ivy sits on the edge of her bed. Her eyes grow wide at my sudden intrusion, and other than standing quickly, she doesn't move. She stares at me, and I stare back. On the way here, I had a speech prepared, but now, looking into her terrified, uncertain eyes, my mind's been wiped completely clean.

"I-I didn't think you would come," she says, breaking the uncomfortably thick silence.

"Looks like you've settled in well," I say, glancing around her tiny space. If I'd acknowledged her statement, it wouldn't make her feel any better anyway.

"I have. Well, enough, anyway," she says. "Witches are kind here."

I press my lips together, unsure how to process that. When I first came to this Coven, I was met with hostility. In all fairness, though, I was Willow's favorite. Ivy is not.

"Has Willow talked to you?" she asks.

I shake my head. "Not about you, if that's what you mean."

She lowers her head, and I see the sadness in her eyes, though she tries her best to not show any emotion at all.

"Don't take it personally. She's going through a lot right now."

"The Sickness, right?" she asks.

I lift an eyebrow, wondering how much she knows about it.

"It's all anyone in the Coven is talking about," she clarifies.

"Yeah. Willow worries a lot about her witches," I say.

"She's a caring person." Ivy's just stating the obvious now, but I think she's also sounding out the words, testing them in the air, waiting for me to disagree.

"Yes," I agree, tilting my head and curious to hear what she'll say next about the daughter she barely knows.

"In Ignis, when I revealed myself to you, I was so scared of what you would think. Of how you would react. I thought it couldn't get much worse from the way you looked at me. I thought that would be the hardest part of all this, that I knew what hatred was. But Willow? She took it to another level. She looked at me like scum on the bottom of her shoe."

"Well what did you expect? She has memories of you, Mom. I don't. Don't forget that she *died* because of you. Whatever I've experienced, she's far surpassed, and that won't ever be easy for her to get over."

"I know. And I know I should be patient. Give her time and space. But this is hard. So much harder than I thought it would be."

"I have a hard time believing that," I say, honestly meaning it. "You really didn't think Willow would be skeptical when she saw you again? You thought she'd lock all her feelings away in a box and just be too overjoyed to know you're alive that she never opened it again?"

Ivy sighs. "Something like that. Whatever you may think, you girls are my heart. Lilith, all the days I spent with Helena, I thought about reuniting with you when the time was right. Willow… I didn't think I'd ever see her again. Last I heard, she was dead, and I never knew what she could do. No one did."

"You left."

"Huh?"

"Your speech is beautiful and heartwarming, of course, but your actions betray every single word. When the Council attacked us in Ignis… you abandoned me and Helena to whatever fate they had in store. I was captured and taken into Headquarters. The Sage threatened to execute me. I most likely *would've* been if it wasn't for someone else's change of heart. The only reason Helena avoided the entire thing was because she was already dead. If you cared about anyone but yourself, you wouldn't have left us like that. I can understand leaving me. You already did that once. But how could you risk Helena like that? She kept you safe for so many years, and you didn't even *try* to return the favor. I watched her sobbing over her beloved cat, but you didn't think about that, did you? You didn't think about me, either. If you loved me like a mother should, the way you claim you do, you would've fought for me. You would've tried to save me. You would've at least *tried*."

Ivy's eyes tear up, and I wait, expecting an excuse, but all she says is, "You're right."

"I know," I say.

"I've hurt you girls worse than our enemies have hurt you," she says.

"Don't do that," I say, disgusted by her self-pity. "At

least try to justify yourself. Try to explain your choices in a way I might understand."

"How do I do that?" she asks, looking up at me.

I sigh and dig a frustrated hand through my short black hair. If I wasn't bound to this chair, I would've walked across the room and shaken her by now. "When you didn't bother trying to help me or Helena, where did you go?" I ask. "After you saved yourself again?"

She plops back down on her bed, tucking her hands between her knees. "I know the image you have of me, so you might not believe me when I say this. I went to help Fern."

"You knew where she was?"

Ivy nods. "I knew since the Battle of Ignis. I knew where all of you were."

"How did you know she needed help?"

Ivy shrugs. "I've always had a special connection to fairies. It's... not something I understand."

I blink, staring at her because I *can* understand that. I've always had a special connection to fairies too. It's why I bonded with Fern as easily as I did.

"I just knew she needed help," Ivy continues. "At first, I thought *she* was hurt, but she... but she wasn't."

"It was the Advisory Council of Fairies, wasn't it?"

She nods. "I don't know them, but I wanted to help."

If her words are true, they're noble, but I have a hard time believing her. It seems so difficult to think my mother would've gone out of her way for *anyone* but herself. "So be honest," I say. "If she hadn't asked for your help, you still wouldn't have come back, would you?"

Ivy breathes out a loud, long sigh. "I would have. Eventually. But not until I could figure out how to make things up to you and to your sister."

I want to get angry. That's my go-to emotion for all situations like this, but part of me understands where she's coming from. I know what it's like to want to disappear, to start my life over and come back as a reinvented, better version of myself. I don't want her to know that, partly because it'll make her feel better—which she doesn't deserve—and partly because I don't want to admit there is *any* likeness between her and me.

"Your solution was to just stay away even longer?"

She shrugs and scratches the side of her neck. "I really didn't have too many other options."

"How about trying to be a better person than who you've been for the last two decades? The way to make it up to us is to do the opposite of what broke us. *Be* here. Be our mother. For Goddess' sake, stop trying to run away."

"I'm trying, Lilith," she says, then she looks down and catches sight of the file in my lap. "What is that?"

I glance at it, then back at her. "Honestly, I know more about you from this than I do from anywhere else. It's a file. From the Council. About you and me and Willow."

She closes her eyes, probably already knowing how bad that is, and I let her stew in her anxiety before launching into my questions.

"I think I know everything about you that I really care to know," I say, trying and failing to keep the disgust out of my voice. "But there's one thing this didn't tell me. Where... where's Dad?" I ask uncertainly. "I mean... is he really dead, or... is he hiding somewhere too? The file doesn't say anything about him. Like he never existed. I just don't understand how the Council doesn't have *anything*."

Ivy sighs, and her features sag like a wilting plant. I've never seen her happy, but I've never seen her this sad, either. I can't help but feel it pouring from her, and it almost hurts. I should feel bad for her. I should feel *something* for her, after all this time. I still don't.

"I wish he was," she says and reaches up to tap the corner of her eye. "But he was killed not long after you were born."

"That was when they caught Willow, wasn't it?" I wanted

to add that instead of trying to save her, Ivy just ran to cover her own ass. But I bite back the comment, which would only ruin my chances of her opening up to me.

"Yes," she says. "You were living with Larc then. He was Willow's first love. I'm sure she told you about him."

I don't know if Ivy realizes he's dead, but it's a sore subject between Willow and me. It probably always will be, since she blames me for his death. I didn't technically kill him, but she'd spent too much time in the battle stopping to help me. She should have spent that time on saving Larc. I'd like to think that Willow has forgiven me, but sometimes, I see a glint of pain in her eyes when she looks at me, and I know exactly why.

If I could just find a time-traveling witch, so many of my problems would be solved.

"Yeah, she has," I say and leave it at that. I wonder how far that answer will get us.

"When the Council learned of your location, learned of who you really are, they tortured Larc, stripped him of his powers, and passed you to foster parents. Witches who were more under their control."

"I knew all that," I admit, thinking of Larc's constant limp, so similar to my own. "What I don't know is *why*. Why would they do that to him for keeping an infant safe? It's not a crime."

"There is so much more to everything beneath the surface of what you can see. Your *history* made it a crime."

"You mean *your* history," I snap.

She winces but forces herself not to shut down. "Yes. They suspected him of helping us plot against the Council, but they had no proof to justify an execution. The only connection they had between him and us was you. Of course, he never changed his story. That he found you out by the oasis one day. With his own magic stripped, others' affected him… strangely. Mind-reading didn't quite work. The Council couldn't have their way, so they punished as cruelly as possible. They took Willow."

And Ivy let it happen. I force myself not to say it out loud.

How many times did this woman stand by and let other witches take the fall for her? Good people whose only crimes had been their own morality. No, I don't want to know. Willow probably has a better idea than I ever will. It certainly explains her absolute disgust for Ivy. I didn't think I could feel any worse about my own mother, but they say seeing is believing. I can't get the picture out of my head now—the Council ripping Willow from Larc's arms; me, a confused infant, screaming and crying as I watched and remembering none of it.

I wish Ivy had more powers than shapeshifting, so I could send this image straight to her. To make her feel the pain and the damage she inflicted on her own daughters. Maybe then, she'd understand why Willow can't stand the sight of her.

"You can keep this," I say and throw the file at her. "I don't want to look at it anymore." Not after how long I already tortured myself with it.

Ivy scoops it up slowly, tucking the loose papers back into place, and nods. When it's in her lap, she gives me a look that says she'll torture herself just the same when I leave her and the folder alone.

"I've made a lot of mistakes," she says, still eyeing the papers. "But that's the way you learn and grow, right?"

I just stare at her, not sure what I should feel. Out of all my emotions, I find disgust is the strongest. "Not from those kinds of mistakes."

Her eyes are wide, and tears well quickly in them. She's about to cry, I know that, and I also know that I don't want to be here when she does. I'm quickly growing surprisingly agile with the chair, and I use that to my advantage. I can't storm out, of course, but I make it out of her room and out into the hall without hearing her reply... or her sobs.

My heads swims, I realize I probably need to eat. Frowning, I try to picture the map of the labyrinth walls, imagining where I'll find the cafeteria, and make my way toward it. I hope I remember how to get there, because I just don't have it in me to search all day.

When I round the next corner, I bump right into Willow. Her eyes are wild, her naturally curly hair unkempt and tangled. She's brushing it and doesn't see me at all, nearly falling over the wheel of my chair.

"Willow," I say.

She stumbles away from my chair, stops, then turns around to face me. "Lily, good morning. Have you had your checkup today?"

I nod.

She frowns, as if she doesn't believe me. "How's your leg?"

"Improving as much as it can. Ambrossi thinks he'll be able to heal everything like Grail did, but I doubt it, considering."

She nods and casts me a tired look. "If Ambrossi says he can do it, I wouldn't put it past him." She looks up toward the end of the hall, then back at me. "I hate to cut this conversation short, but Maverick is expecting me."

In a fluid motion, she tries to duck past me, but I reach out to grab her sleeve, holding her in place. Her exhaustion is clear, but this distant version of her doesn't seem like the Willow I know. It makes me uneasy, as if she's drifting away from me.

"What is it, Li?" she asks. There is no irritation in her voice, but by how perfectly straight her spine is, there is plenty. She's antsy to get on her way, to find Maverick and discuss whatever needs to be said, but this is important too.

With a glance over my shoulder toward Ivy's room, I ask, "Have you talked to Mom yet?"

Willow pulls her lip back into a sneer, the exhaustion replaced with fury. "No. I haven't talked to *Mom*. I've been busy. As far as I'm concerned, she's at the very bottom of my priorities list."

"I understand, but if you get a moment, I think you—"

"Two more witches have died from the Sickness, Lily. Can you understand *that*? Two more souls lost forever, and we're no closer to a cure. There are dozens of witches now sick with the same thing, and you want me to… what? Waste time I don't have on a woman who's never cared about anyone but herself? No. I'm sorry, but I'm not going to do that. She can leave for all I care." She yanks her arm free, storms away, then stops. When she glances at me over her shoulder, some of the rage has lessened everywhere but in her eyes. "I'm glad to see you're out and about on your own."

The words are supposed to be kind, but they hit me like a bucket of ice water. It's not exactly a *good* thing that I'm out alone. I'm only here because Clio and I fought—a fight for which neither of us are willing to apologize. His absence slices through me again, and I shiver in the cold only I can feel. Maybe she realizes she made a mistake, or maybe she said it to throw me off. Either way, she takes off for her mission again, and I'm alone.

I don't move for a long time, just staring down at my hands in the middle of the lonely white hallway. I feel useless like this. All the strength I'd carried in my conversation with Ivy is gone now, and I don't understand where it went. Something about the look in Willow's eyes broke me. She's struggling in a fight neither of us can pursue. I can't even go into a normal battle. Not like this.

But there's still so much I can do.

I realize this as soon as my spiraling thoughts land on Fern and her allies.

Grief's voice floats into my mind. *'They're grown witches.'*

And? Then I shut him out. He always sneaks into my head at my lowest, and I hate myself for forgetting he can do that whenever he wants.

For a few long minutes, I wonder why, only twelve hours ago, Clio's plan to run away seemed like such a bad idea.

THE SAGE

Chapter Sixteen
Trouble

'VE ALWAYS HAD a difficult time expressing myself, no matter to whom. So it comes as an unwelcome surprise when I break down right there in the middle of the hallway.

I remember when Rayna's brother Quinn first came to the Elemental Coven; he had a similar breakdown in the hallway. I was there to comfort him—to provide a shoulder to cry on. Thankfully, there are no other witches here to see me like this. A few of Willow's tigers sniff at me, one them going so far as to put its head in my lap and offer a comforting purr. But other than that, I'm alone. The thought only brings more tears.

When the last tiger walks away, I try to stop. Some restrained and broken-sounding noise escapes me. The tiger swings its head around, but it doesn't come back. Now I'm fully alone. I wipe away my tears and stare up at the ceiling, trying to remember how to breathe properly. When I can see again, I find Crowe standing there at the end of the hall, hands at his sides and looking completely unsure, as if he can't decide whether to approach or turn around and run.

I smile like I didn't just break down entirely, but he's no fool. I can see the indecision on his face in his narrowed eyes and pursed lips as he approaches me. "Lilith, are you okay?" he finally asks.

"Saw that, did you?" I stare at the line where the wall and floor connect.

"Just a little," he admits.

I shake my head and grip the arm of my chair even tighter. "C-can you help me back to my room, please?" I'm in no mood for conversation, or the possibility of it, but I don't see a way to get what I want without using words. My muscles feel gooey, and I'm just too worn down to conjure my powers. I couldn't leave on my own even if I wanted to.

"Of course," he says, quickly circling the chair to grip its handles. Then he pushes me down the hall. For a few steps, the only sound is the swish of his robes. "Care to let me in on what's going on?" He rounds the bend in the hall. "Is it too dramatic to say everything?"

"I'd say not... considering your circumstances."

"You've heard about Clio too, then?"

He falls silent, and I know it's because he stumbled into a conversation he doesn't want to have

"I'll take that as a yes."

"I heard it through the grapevine," he admits. We both know who that is.

I fold my arms and decide it's best to not to say anything else as he finally approaches my door. With my elbow on the chair's armrest, I prop my chin in my hand and watch Crowe from the corner of my eye. His flitting glances toward my legs are hard to miss. If even *he's* worried about it, I don't know what to say.

He opens the door. "Need me to help you inside?"

"No, but it would be great if you did anyway," I say, staring into the prison of my room and suddenly not wanting the isolation anymore.

Crowe laughs. "Fair enough." He pushes me into my room. Kado yips in excitement, spinning circles around us as

Crowe pushes me to the bed and lifts me out of the chair, setting me as gently onto the fabric as he can manage.

"Thank you, Crowe," I say.

"You're welcome." He moves my chair to the side before he turns, eyeing the door.

"How are you holding up... here?" I ask. I have the feeling he'll leave anyway.

Instead, he turns slowly, raising an eyebrow. "Do you want my honest answer or the answer everyone expects of me?"

"The honest answer," I say. "That's the only one I ever give."

He sighs and reaches up to ruffle his red hair before sitting beside me. The look of advanced aging washes over his face again, his eyes dull and his face draws tight. I'm not going to like his answer. "I know I belong here," he begins.

"That's not what I asked," I say, tilting my head.

He sighs again and leans forward, resting his elbows on his knees. "It's like I'm half the person I used to be. When Mom died, I thought I lost her. And part of me died too."

"But she's doing well now, right?" She seemed well enough when Clio and I witnessed Crowe and his mother in the field. I stare at his profile, at the shape of his cheekbones and his lips, wondering how his face would change if I admitted to having seen them that day.

Crowe nods. "If you can even call it that. Willow revived her, but she's different now. I used to think of her as unbreakable, but she just..."

"Gives up?"

He turns to me with narrowed eyes. "Yeah. How'd you know?"

I take a deep breath before answering. "The other day, I saw you out in the field with your mom. You were trying to get her to dance, but—"

"She wouldn't." His smile doesn't look remotely genuine. "Like I said, Willow might've brought her back to me, but she's not the same. The part of me that died with her? That's still gone. I don't think it'll ever come back."

"It's an adjustment, what you're going through. What she's going through too. From what Willow's told me, it takes them all some time to remember who they are. After all, death is no small thing."

"I've told myself the same thing," Crowe says, "but it doesn't stop me from wondering if I should've stayed at Headquarters. Maybe I made a mistake in coming here."

"Why would you think that? After everything you heard from the Sage herself, you know better than that."

"Yeah, but this place isn't what I thought it would be. When you said Katrina was here, I thought it would feel like home. But... she's different too."

I tilt my head, silently urging him to continue.

"I've been here a week now, and I've barely spent any time with her. It feels as if every time I try to get closer to her, she's gone again. Like she's... avoiding me."

"She's a busy woman, Crowe. Willow depends on her a lot, not to mention the fact that she's been caring for your mom and the other sick witches. Last time I saw her, it looked like she'd barely slept."

"I know I should be understanding," he adds. "This just isn't what I imagined it would be. I miss Kieran and Aquais. And with the Sickness? I just keep thinking what if she gets it? What if I lose her forever?"

"You can't worry about that," I say.

"But I am, and I do. She's still there in the Community Villa every day, even though Willow told her not to go. Healers are so stubborn."

"It's frustrating. I get that. All we can do is live day by day. Take it hour by hour if you have to, and eventually, you'll get through it."

Crowe takes a sharp breath; at first, I think he's mocking me. Then I realize he's *crying*. Fat tears pour down his face, redness blooming under his eyes and across his cheeks, and he doesn't try to hide it. That's probably the worst part.

I cringe instantly. The only thing I hate more than crying is being next to someone else who's crying.

"I just… I don't know why I thought this would be so easy. I thought… joining the Elementals, I'd see Katrina again, and we'd be happy together. Like we used to be. But…"

"There's no such thing as a happy ending in war," I point out, sitting forward enough to set my hand on his knee. My mind flares out at the pain of every loss he's encountered since joining the Council, and I pull my hand away quickly—perhaps too sharply.

He looks at me, his face streaked with tears. "So what's the point?"

It's a fair question—one I've asked myself a number of times and for which I've never come up with a solid answer. I don't want him to know that, though—to feel the same level of hopelessness I've reached. A little uncertain, I reach out to pull him into a hug. He doesn't resist at all, then he's leaning against me, his tears soaking the fabric over my shoulder, chilling my skin. "The point is to live another day," I tell him. "Survive with the hope that one day, you'll get to live your life and have your happy ending. Everything will be okay in time."

He wraps his arms around my ribs and holds me so tightly that it's hard to breathe. I don't complain; I just fall into companionable silence as he cries it out, marveling at this new scenario. Here he is, this man who's really nothing more than a boy—my *mentor*—crying in my arms. Just as that thought passes, he looks up at me, like he's about to speak. Then he kisses me.

I freeze. I have no idea how to react to this, to *him*. Before I can decide, he pulls away from my arms, staring at me with red-rimmed eyes.

"I'm sorry," he says and hops to his feet, as if he's ashamed to even be near me. "I don't know why I did that."

"You're hurting." I try to sympathize, though really, I

have no idea why he did it, either.

"That's not an excuse," he says, wiping his face. "I guess I thought it would make things better. I'm such an idiot."

"You're not an idiot. You're just in pain."

"What's the difference?" he asks with a snort. "*Kids* do things they know they're not supposed to do. Not responsible adults. Pain or no pain, I have no excuse."

"Crowe..."

"I just... I want the anger to come back. I held onto that for long enough. During the Battle, it was so much easier to think, to take control of my life with that anger knocking everything else to the back of my mind. Sadness? I don't know what to do with that... It's crushing me."

I understand him better than I've ever understood anyone. Anger certainly does make it easier to stand strong, but it also makes it easier to hurt those around us and not care.

"Anger is more destructive than its worth," I tell him. "I learned that the hard way. Letting go of it was one of the hardest things I've ever had to do. And sometimes, I still struggle with it. But you know what? It was also the most rewarding thing. It let me see the world around me for all it's worth. Yeah, there will be times when it'll hurt you, but it'll comfort you too."

"That... that doesn't help me," he says. "I'm sorry."

I purse my lips. "Well, what if I told you that anger is just one phase of sorrow? The sadness you're feeling now was always there. It's just showing different faces. Maybe the anger helped you for a while, but always feeling it like *that* would hurt you in so many ways. Sure, being sad makes you vulnerable. It also make you more willing to compromise, forgive, and move on. You just need to learn to let go."

"I'll keep that in mind," Crowe says and walks across the room. He stops at the door and looks back at me, face still blotchy from crying. "Can I ask you for a favor?"

"Anything," I tell him.

"Don't tell Katrina about what just happened, please. I'll

tell her eventually. You have my word on that. But not right now. Not when I'm like *this*."

I draw a line across my lips, and Crowe gives a hint of a smile before it drops. Then he's gone, the door swinging shut behind him.

Chapter Seventeen
Blessed Be

I DIDN'T THINK it was possible to feel worse than I did after fighting with Clio. After Crowe left, I was proven wrong. Now I feel completely empty. A chill sweeps across my skin, giving me goosebumps despite the lack of any real breeze. Kado sees me shiver and jumps up on the bed to rest his head in my lap.

I stroke his ears and the puff of fur on his head, trying to distract myself. Did that whole thing with Crowe really just happen? I poke at my lips, still feeling the brief contact of his skin on mine. I know it was real, and I wish it wasn't.

"Am I a terrible person?" I ask Kado.

He looks up at such a sharp angle that the whites of his eyes show beneath the color. A tiny whine vibrates up his throat, and he butts his forehead against my stomach.

"At least *you* don't think so," I say, slightly relieved. He rests his jaw on my lap again.

As much as I don't want to think about Crowe, I can't help it. In its usual fashion, my mind bleeds those thoughts into so many others, and I try to block them all out just by closing my eyes. It doesn't work.

"I wish there was a spell to make me stop thinking," I

tell Kado.

His slitted eyes open, then he lifts his head and leaves a wet kiss across my cheek. Then he glances at the pillows again and whines. I've gotten pretty good at reading my zombie dog, and even now, when I'm not fully present, I know what he's trying to say.

Lay down. Relax.

So I do. I give up on trying to stay upright and slide down to rest my head on the pillows, staring at the room's opposite wall. Kado curls up beside me, right against my stomach, his warm, soft fur grazing my chin.

"I don't think I ever told Willow how much I really love you," I tell him.

He nuzzles deeper against me, but I feel the tiny *thump thump* of his wagging tail.

I wrap my arms around him, fully comfortable in this new position. Hard to believe I've been awake for only a few hours; I feel ready to fall asleep again, wrapped up with the only creature who's bothered to stay by my side. I think of Willow and Clio and wish either of them would walk through the door at any moment to at least attempt making amends.

But they don't. I have no idea why I torture myself by hoping they might.

Being stubborn isn't new to me, but neither is the prospect of dealing with witches just as stubborn as I am. What if they never miss me enough to *want* to make peace? When I think of never talking to Clio or Willow again, that freezing loneliness washes over me completely.

If I don't come out of my room, Helena will come check on me. At least, she will if no one else does first. I do know that much. The only problem is that she's not on the short list of people I really want to see. I stare at the tiny mark the doorknob made left in the wall when Clio flung open the door. That fight really was stupid, and I wonder if he's come to the same conclusion yet.

Kado lifts his head again, licks my cheek, and stretches each of his long legs. Then he jumps to the floor and stares at me, rubbing his nose against my fingertips. When he whimpers, I reach down to pet his muzzle. At the very least, I know he'll never leave me in my time of need. He whines again, and I try to give him another small, reassuring smile we both know is fake.

"I'm okay."

I reach out to scratch behind his ear and feel suddenly embarrassed. Crowe's fingers reached up to caress my hair almost exactly the same way when he kissed me.

Just like that, the desire to leave my room is gone. How can I go out there and face running into him—or Katrina?

Damn him. Did he *have* to do that? Did he really have to make things worse than they already are?

When I eventually tell Clio what happened, he's never going to stop being mad at me. I know that with almost blinding certainty. In my mind, that crack in the wall doubles and then triples in size, and I'm falling into the vortex—into another world where everything is right.

He'll probably just leave without me. Though I remind myself with such desperate ferocity that he'd never do that, I realize I just don't know him like I used to. I close my eyes for a long time, trying just to forget about all the doubts I still have.

Suddenly, a bath seems like the best idea in the world. I practically throw myself to the floor.

Kado jumps backward and yips before dropping low, his nose by my face. He sniffs frantically and barks again, looking toward the door as if trying to summon help.

After the pain of impact fades, I let out a deep breath and lift my hand. Kado stops to watch me. "It's okay, buddy," I tell him. "I'm okay."

He whines but stops trying to get someone else's attention. Then he trots slowly beside me as I drag my body into the bathroom to hoist myself over the white tub and turn on the water. Using my telekinesis helps me sit up against the basin filling with water. As quickly as I can, I use a combination of telekinesis and pure willpower to slip out of my clothes. Then I force myself over the lip of the tub and into the water.

I'm just lying here, feeling the warmth on my skin and imagining it's coming from someone—anyone—who hasn't given up on me.

***

A SERIES OF knocks jars me awake, and panic overwhelms me when I realize I'm not in my bed. I'm still in the bathtub, my neck and the back of my head radiating with pain from lying there so long. The water's cold now, and I try to sit up—to cover myself and climb out of the tub with some dignity—but I can't. The slick edge makes it so much harder to get back out than it was to get into the tub in the first place.

Kado sniffs my fingers and barks as I claw at the edge of the tub. Then he dashes out into the room to greet whoever's at the door. I try one more time to get myself out of the water but slink back down in defeat.

I take a breath, squeezing my eyes shut, and call, "Who's there?"

"Katrina." She's in my room now. "Are you in the bathroom?"

"Yeah…" I pause when Kado reappears in the doorway. He looks back toward Katrina, then at me again. "If it's not too much trouble, could you help me out of the tub?"

"Oh, of course." She appears in the doorway, looking tired and disheveled, her blue hair falling everywhere from the bun in which she tried to contain it.

This is the first time I've really looked at her since we returned from the Battle of the Grove. I wonder when she last slept, then feel a twinge of guilt. Every witch I see is exhausted. I'm probably the only witch in the entire Coven who hasn't been missing out on extra sleep.

Katrina kneels beside the tub and dips her fingers into the water. Then she jerks her hand back. "Lilith, it's freezing. How long have you been in here?"

I shrug. "I don't know."

"Must've been a while," she says. "Between the water and Kado."

"Kado?"

She nods, helping me to sit up then slipping her arm under my knees. "He came to find me."

"All the way in the Community Villa?" I ask, glancing with wide eyes at my dog.

"Yeah. That's why I was concerned." She pulls me out of the tub. A little hesitantly, she leaves me on the floor to grab me a towel. I wrap it around myself, grateful for the tiny bit of warmth it offers, and then Katrina wheels my chair over to the doorframe and helps me up onto it. Manuvering into my room, she helps me climb onto my bed and ruffles through my dresser to find me something to wear. When she comes back, she hands me a purple dress.

I take a minute to dress myself, then Katrina sits beside me on the bed, and I have to look away from her intense blue stare.

"What's going on with you?" she asks.

I blink. "Nothing. I'm fine."

"Nobody falls asleep in the bathtub when they're fine. Clio says he hasn't talked to you since you guys fought. No one else has seen much of you at all the past few days. Clearly, something's going on."

Her eyes bore into mine, searching for the traces of answers. My cheeks burn with guilt and the memory of Crowe's kiss. How can I possibly tell her what happened without losing her too?

"Clio's still in the hospital wing?" I ask.

"Last I saw, yeah." Her voice softens. "I could get him for you, if you want."

I shake my head. "No, I'm not ready to talk to him. I actually, um…" After my promise to Crowe, I wonder how I'm going to force this sentence out. But if I don't say anything, I'll lose Katrina's trust when Crowe finally does tell her. Katrina's eyes narrow as she stares me down, and a chill wiggles down my spine.

She knows. She has to. She's just waiting for me to open up to her, as a friend should.

"You haven't tried talking to him yet?"

I shake my head. "I talked to Willow earlier, and she told me the Sickness is getting worse." I won't mention her anger over Ivy, because it doesn't seem important. In a way, it really is.

Katrina nods. "Between you and me, she's been getting on the Healers. She only wants Reanimates in there now. Any Healers still alive like Ambrossi and Laura, Willow wants to pull. Me too, actually."

"I'm guessing none of you will go?"

Katrina shakes her head. "We take precautions. Wear protective gear, and all that. But at the end of the day, I'm not sure it'll make a difference for them or for us."

"That's Healers for you," I say, though now I'm worried for Ambrossi. From the time of my 'accident', he's always looked after me. I've thought of him as my brother for years, even though we don't share a drop of blood. The thought of losing him forever turns my stomach; I imagine I have an idea of the agony Crowe subjected himself to earlier.

"Willow tried to have Maverick take Clio out too," Katrina adds.

Willow told me she was on her way to a meeting with Maverick. Why didn't she tell me it was about Clio? "And?"

"Clio went right back when he woke up. I don't know if she knows, or if she's just given up."

I purse my lips. I might lose Ambrossi *and* Clio, if he's not careful. If the Sickness doesn't get him, he could end up in trouble for his attitude alone.

126

"Probably a combination of both," I admit.

She tucks a loose strand of blue hair behind her ear. "Have you talked to Crowe recently?"

My heart pounds, and I can't look at her, convinced she'll see the thought in my eyes. This is it.

"He's locked himself in his room since this morning and won't come out to talk to anyone. Not even me. It's just so unlike him."

My shoulders sag in relief. So maybe she *doesn't* know … yet. This just means I'll have to be the one to tell her. "Something happened," I begin, letting out a breath as soon as her intense blue eyes meet mine. "Between me and him."

"Oh?" Her nostrils flare, but the rest of her remains calm.

I realize I'm about to burn my last bridge to a friend right now. The longer the silence drags on, the more anxious she becomes. Now she's shooting me an almost hostile look, and I freeze up, unable to say the words I need to say.

'You have to do this,' a voice says in my head.

It's not my own.

My nose wrinkles, as if I've smelled something disgusting. *'Grief, stay out of my thoughts.'* Then I put up a metal wall of energy in my mind before he can respond. For a witch with the power of invisibility, he sure does have a habit of getting in my way.

"He kissed me," I say quickly—so quickly that it almost blurs together into one weird word. "It happened real fast and—"

Katrina holds up a hand, a small, bitter smile on her face. "Woah, girl. Breathe."

"But I—he—"

"Breathe. Relax. Then tell me what the Hell he did."

"Well… I got into a fight with Clio, but I've also been fighting with Willow about Ivy and Fern—" I stop myself there, deciding I shouldn't say more than that about the tiny woman.

"Anyway, I had a breakdown in the hall, and Crowe saw. He took me back to my room, and I told him what was going on. He told me how he's been feeling about you and Rena. He thinks it's wrong. Willow's resurgence. He said he doesn't feel close to you or Rena like he used to. He said he never gets to see you anymore, and I guess he thought the kiss would be comforting? I don't know, but he regretted it instantly. I could tell. And he even said as much."

Katrina nods. "That explains it."

I raise an eyebrow at how calmly she speaks. I was so prepared for rage or tears or something dramatic. Almost no reaction at all takes me by surprise. "Aren't you upset?"

She shrugs. "A little, but everyone is so stressed right now that we're all hurting. Fighting hate with more hate is never the answer. Crowe will figure himself out eventually."

"Good point." I chew on my bottom lip. She smiles at me, poking the corners of her lips to try to get me to smile too. My lips don't even feel capable of smiling anymore. "Just so we're clear, I'm sorry for what happened. He didn't want me to tell you because he said he wanted to do it himself when he didn't feel quite as ready to fall apart. If there's any way you can make it seem like I kept his promise, I would really appreciate it. I think he would too, honestly."

Katrina pulls me into a tight hug. "No worries, just as long as you promise to do something for me."

"Anything," I reply as she releases me.

She reaches up to brush my hair from my eyes. "I know it's probably the last thing you want to do, but you should talk to Clio. Fix whatever's making him so uneasy. It seems ridiculous for you to both miss each other as much as you do and not push past a silly disagreement."

"It wasn't just a disagreement, though," I admit. "It's the first real fight we've ever had."

"Ever?" she asks, lifting an eyebrow.

I nod. "When I first came here, Clio was the one who

128

kept me going. I didn't even know if he was still alive, but the thought of one day seeing him again was enough, you know? Now, he told me he wants to run away, just me and him. He's scared of the Sickness, and when I told him I wouldn't go, he got really mad. And I haven't seen him since."

"I didn't know that," Katrina says. "I'm sorry."

My lips pull tight as I feel the burning in the corners of my eyes. "I finally get him back, and he wants to leave again. It feels like all the work of searching for him, of worrying about him, of wondering if he was alive or dead was just all for nothing. I think I missed him far more than he missed me."

"You're overestimating what that fight really meant."

"How? He hasn't bothered to check on me in days."

"Yeah, that's pretty awful of him, but he didn't leave the Coven. Those fears he expressed to you? He still has them, but he didn't let them stop him. Instead, he went down to the hospital wing and demanded to learn healing skills to try conquering those fears. Is he happy about being here? No, but he's doing it. For you. That boy is crazy about you, and one fight isn't going to change that."

"He shouldn't do it," I say. "The healing. He's only ever been able to manipulate fire, and trying to mess around with herbs now... It's too dangerous. I almost got him killed once, back in Ignis. Isn't that enough?"

"He's a big boy. He makes his own choices, and no matter what happens between you and him, just remember that you're not responsible for what he does. Regardless of whether he properly learns how to use healing or not, there's always a chance he could get hurt or sick. There's a chance we could *all* get hurt, and facing our future, hating one another doesn't change that or make it better. Love has no limits. Like it or not, his feelings for you mean he's just as deeply involved in everything as you are. You can't keep trying to shield him."

I stare at the floor, hating how right she is. Now I'm jealous—truly jealous. I've always heard that Aquais witches have a better hold on their emotions than the rest of the Covens, but I never truly believed that until now. Seeing how composed she is, when she has every reason to scream at me, to grab me and want to fight, hits me deeply.

"You're right," I say at last.

Chapter Eighteen
War Changes Everything

KATRINA HUGS ME, pats Kado a few times, and walks to the door. She pauses in the doorway, her long fingers gripping the white paint as she looks back at me. "If you need anything, let me know," she says. "My door is always open."

I nod, and she leaves. Kado stares at me, waiting for me to make a move. I just gaze at the empty doorway, at the white wall of the hallway beyond, and think about Clio. I wish our relationship was even a fraction as strong as Katrina and Crowe's. I feel sick knowing Clio's still mad at me; he'll probably be even angrier if either Katrina or Crowe decide to tell him what happened before I have the chance.

More than anything, I wish that he would just come through the door, more concerned for my wellbeing than his feelings over our stupid fight. He would grab me and say how sorry he is and that the whole thing never should've happened. I savor the image for just a second before I push it away with a despondent sigh. Holding onto fantasy won't make it true. Besides, if I saw him right now, I don't know what I would say—or worse, I'd start by saying something stupid.

I'm notorious for it.

So, I decide to look for him during my next checkup. A

place with plenty of witnesses might work in my favor.

Kado tilts his head, studying me, and then I realize how truly empty the day before me is. I used to fill my afternoons with battle training, but that's impossible now—maybe impossible for the rest of my life. I haven't even seen Sable since my return from the Battle of the Grove, and I've seen even less of Maverick than I have of my own sister.

"How do you do it?" I ask Kado.

He yawns and barks.

I smile at his small, excited bounce. "I guess that's enough wallowing for now. Maybe Fern could use some company.

***

AT THE BEGINNING of my journey, I assumed the worst part would be getting myself in my chair. It's unfortunate how wrong I can be sometimes. As much as I love Fern, I have to question why she and Malcolm created a burrow so far from everything and everyone else. By the time I make it, I'm sweaty and tired and wish I'd just stayed in my room. The wheels of my chair dig down into the soft earth and take more energy than I can afford to get them loose. Once, I think about calling it quits and turning around to go home, but I don't have the energy to do even that.

If I make it to Fern's, she can cast a spell to wipe away all my exhaustion. If I stay here, I'll have to face it alone.

Soon, the tiny mound of dirt grows visible in the distance, renewing a bit of my strength. Fern is quick to greet me, and she even offers a small cup of water, which I graciously accept.

"Good to see you," she says, her voice always bright.

I nod. "You too, Fern."

"You came alone?" She glances over my shoulder. "Where's Clio?"

"I'd really rather not get into that," I say, surprising myself with how emotionless I sound.

Fern's bottom lip juts out into a pout, and she taps my forehead, easing my physical and emotional pain. "I understand."

"Thank you." She flutters down to land on the arm of my chair. "How are Thorn and Callista doing?" I ask.

"Better," she replies. "Callista is doing better than Thorn, but you know what they say. It's all mind over matter."

I nod and glance toward the Community Villa. I wish that saying could explain everything that went wrong in the recent week. When I narrow my eyes, it's almost as if I can *see* the fog of Sickness surrounding the building—an ugly gray against the beautiful purple glow of the air and plants.

"You're worried," she says and frowns.

I try to look away, but the tiny fairy flits toward me until she's staring me in the face. "What is it? Did something happen to Clio?"

"No, I'm just... thinking of the Sickness. Willow is so distraught over it, and we lose more witches every day. Clio... Clio decided to take up Healing to do his part... but what if he gets sick too?"

"He's tough, Lilith. Think of everything he's been through so far. You just have to have faith that he knows what he's doing."

"I've never questioned that." Well, maybe one time. "I just know it's impossible for anyone to control everything that happens to them. That's the hard part. If we could just make it so that nothing bad ever happened, no one would suffer."

"That's a fair point," Fern says. "But then nothing good would happen either, right? We'd have no idea what good was without being able to compare it to the bad." I stare at her so long that she starts squirming in midair. "What is it?"

"You... were part of the Advisory Council of Fairies at one point, right?" Fern nods. "I don't think you ever told me why you left. Clearly, you still care about Thorn and Callista. Why leave to begin with?"

"We had our differences, just like you did with the Council. Even though you despise them as a whole, you walked away feeling something different for each individual witch. You built a friendship with Crowe but ended up hating the others."

"Something drove you away from Advisory Council."

Fern shrugs. "Nothing personal. Callista and Thorn don't believe in motherhood for Fairies. They think it's below them. That beings like us should be treated like queens."

"How is it wrong to be a mother?"

"My sentiment exactly. We argued about it when I found out I was going to have Malcolm. It was enough to draw us apart, but I really do care about them. They're my sisters in wings."

"Are they still the most powerful fairies in the Land of Five, even after giving up their positions?"

Fern nods. "Yes, of course. So am I. You're still one of the most powerful witches, right?"

I shrug. "As far as I know."

She smiles. "What are you thinking?"

"When I first joined the Council, Callista just touched me and the pain in my bad leg disappeared for a little while. It didn't go away completely, but that instant of magic was more than Ambrossi had been able to do in years. This Sickness... I know it's magical, but do you think it's possible for them to find a cure?"

"Maybe, if they know who's responsible."

"Even if they don't, could they find a way?" Ferns wings flutter faster and faster as she wrings her hands and refuses to look at me. "Could *you* do something?" I ask.

Rustling rises at the entrance of Fern's burrow, like a creature digging through crispy leaves, and then a face I haven't seen in ages appears. It's Callista. She's paler than I remember under her blue pixie haircut, and her cheeks are sunken, but it's her.

She comes out of the hole, opening her shimmery pink wings to take her place beside Fern on my chair. Her huge green eyes stare up at me, full of kindness and love—things a lot of witches have given up on in this war. "It is possible for us to do something. For a complete cure, I'm not sure, but we can extend the length of the Sickness until you figure out how to stop it."

"Really?" I ask, warmth blossoming in my chest.

She nods, her weak chin tucking down toward her chest before she looks back up at me. "Yes, but I must ask you for one favor first."

I narrow my eyes to slits. Everyone wants something done for them. It seems as if no one has the kindness to go out of their way to help for free anymore, not even the beings I've always considered the kindest of all of them.

War changes everything.

"Anything, Callista," I tell her.

"Watch out for us. Have our back. Give me the promise that if our hiding place is compromised, we won't be banished from the Coven."

"Done," I say instantly. Though like with my promise to Crowe, I can't imagine being able to hold up my end of the deal if that time ever comes.

Chapter Nineteen
Contamination

*B*Y THE TIME I return home, I'm dirty and exhausted. The bath I took earlier feels like it never happened, and all I want to do is curl up in bed with Kado and go to sleep. Fern's magic carried me through only half the journey; the rest I managed by sheer force of will alone. Kado greets me as soon as I open the door, circling the chair and sniffing me from all angles to ensure my safety. I pet him, and he relaxes to watch me push my chair beside the bed before I haul myself up onto the blankets. I lean over to push the chair to the side, and he jumps up next to me. I hold him like a giant teddy bear—the way I held Clio when we shared the bed.

I stare at the empty spot where he used to lie and wonder if he'll come back tonight or find somewhere else to sleep. The thought of him sleeping on the floor of the hospital wing makes me sigh. It sounds very much like something he would do, and since he hasn't talked to me in days, I assume he's already done it a few times. After the day I've had, I don't have the energy to go all the way down to the Community Villa and convince him otherwise. So instead, I lie in bed, torturing myself with memories of today.

Kado flops over, encouraging me to rub his belly as he drifts off to sleep. That keeps me distracted for a little while, but when his breathing slows and he falls asleep, I'm back inside the cage of my own mind.

Willow has become a woman obsessed, Ivy is just as selfish as ever, Clio has lost whatever sanity he had left, Crowe and Katrina are impossible in opposite ways, and Thorn and Callista expect too much of me.

I just can't catch a break.

***

I WAKE UP to Helena's gentle murmurs. When I open my eyes,

I'm actually excited to see another witch, especially one I haven't pissed off recently. When my grogginess clears and I get a real glimpse of her, I realize how tired she looks. As a Reanimate, she doesn't *need* to sleep, but at the same time, it's obvious she hasn't. It puts another little sliver of doubt in my heart, though not much, simply because I don't think there's room to carry any more than I already have.

"You look terrible," I say without thinking.

"I know." She tosses a lock of orange hair over her shoulder and helps me dress.

"It's worse, isn't it? Willow said two witches died and a whole bunch are sick."

"They did," Helena says. "That's why we're doing your exam here today instead of the wing. It's not safe for anyone who's still alive to go there right now."

"The witches who are sick... are any of them—"

"What? People we know?"

I nod, chewing on my lip.

"No one I know, but that doesn't make it easier. Ambrossi's convinced that someone is doing this on purpose. It has to be another witch, judging by the way this kind of magic is acting."

"Yeah, but Lazarus also said there's never been a witch who could do that."

"As far as he can *remember*," Helena reminds me and shoots me a look that says I should've known better.

Horror dawns on me as the gears in my head start spinning, putting a few more pieces together. "That must be why they took out Alchemy," I say slowly. "They were planning this all along."

"That's my thought too," she says. "Okay, now I need you to close your eyes and take a few long, deep breaths." I obey, hearing the whisper of fabric as she moves around me, studying me from all angles. "Go ahead and open your eyes," she says.

My eyes open to watch her pace back and forth. She lifts her hand, pressing her finger to my brow right between my eyes. The cold brush of her skin makes me shiver, and she drops her hand. Then she steps back.

"Am I clean?" I ask.

"Yeah, you are. For now." Helena reaches into the folds of her robe to pull out a tiny serrated leaf. "Chew this."

I take it from her slowly, studying the bit of plant. "What is it?"

"It'll help keep your immune system up," she explains.

I pop it in my mouth, prepared for a bitter taste, but the leaf is sweet and goes down without much effort. "Thank you."

"You're welcome. How are your legs doing?" She pokes at the bandages.

"Better," I say. "I kept the bandages off yesterday."

"Really?" She pulls the edge of the bandage loose enough to see my leg. I nod. "Well, if you want, you can leave them off for a bit longer. It'll do them some good to air out."

I let both of them unravel and slump to the ground—ugly strips of beige against the dark floor. Kado yips and bows down, pouncing on one of them to give it a thorough sniff.

Helena studies the rugged cuts and bruises on my legs before she meets my gaze again. "Okay. You're set for now, but don't hesitate to find me if you need new bandages. Stay away from the hospital wing, though."

"Have the others left yet? Clio? Ambrossi? Laura?"

"How'd you know they were still there?" Helena asks.

"Katrina told me. She said they've all stayed against Willow's orders."

"They have. Everything Willow's tried, they've ignored. They're still working to do what they can against the Sickness. Or at the very least to keep those with the Sickness comfortable."

"And none of them are sick?"

"As far as I know, yesterday, they were all well. We'll see

what today's results turn up."

That certainly doesn't sound promising.

"Don't look so worried," Helena says, squinting in concern. "If they've been okay this long, they'll probably still be okay."

Just then, my door bursts open, and Maverick stands there, his metallic-colored eyes shining bright. Helena jumps, and Kado barks, making the most vicious sounds I've ever heard.

Maverick ignores all of it. "Emergency meeting. Now!"

"What's happening?" Helena and I ask at the same time.

"Ambrossi's sick."

Chapter Twenty
Balance

THE WORLD IS funny in the way that everything balances out. For every friend, there's an enemy. For every good, there's bad. For every witch who's still healthy, there's one who falls sick. My head spins as Helena pushes my chair. We follow Maverick into Willow's throne room and look around with wide eyes. Since the Community Villa is closed, this is her new meeting room. I stare at the tigers milling around inside the pit, then look back to Willow sitting slowly in her regal seat. The room is already packed with witches, though there are noticeably fewer gathered now than at the last meeting.

"For those of you who have not heard, our best Healer, Ambrossi, has caught the Sickness," Willow begins, her voice full, sad, and wavering.

Panicked, angry shouts fill the room.

"What are we going to do without a Head Healer?"

"Who's going to take his place?"

"I thought you said no one else would get sick!"

"And they won't," Willow says coolly. "No Healers who are not Reanimates are permitted to be in the hospital wing. This has been the rule for a few days now, but I've been lenient. There are no exceptions anymore."

"You'll have to tell Clio yourself," Helena says. "He's the

last one not sick."

"Katrina and Laura?" I ask, horrified.

She shakes her head. "No, they've just had enough sense to keep their distance."

"I'll talk to him," Willow says, though the way she says *talk* makes me sure she'll do more than that if it comes down to it.

"So what do we do in the meantime?"

"Any progress on a cure?"

"What if Reanimates are carriers?"

Willow has nothing to say to that, and neither do I. I never considered the possibility that Reanimates could aid in infection, but now that it's been said, it's what we're *all* thinking. Even Willow, and the heartbroken look behind her eyes makes it perfectly clear that she's blaming herself too.

"What are you going to do?" someone demands.

Willow says nothing. I don't mean to, but my mind reaches out to prod at her mind. She's defeated, completely unsure of how to proceed, and without any ideas for moving forward. I feel so guilty. I have the answers she needs, but it would require a real heart-to-heart. Last time I tried to do that, I only made her feel worse—angry.

I can't worry about that now.

"We have a plan," I say about the low hum of questions and doubts.

Dead silence fills the room as all eyes turn toward me. Even the tigers pause in whatever they're doing. Willow's mouth pops open into a small 'O' as she stares at me, hopeful, confused, and determined.

"What is it, then?" someone asks.

"We'll tell everyone as soon as the details are ironed out," Maverick adds from his place beside Willow's throne.

I look at him gratefully, but he doesn't return it.

"You don't really have a plan," the same witch accuses.

"You'll do well not to talk back to your superiors,"

Maverick says, keeping his gaze trained on one spot in the throne room. Now that he's in the spotlight, Willow whispers something in his ear. Maverick closes the meeting for her. Willow stands on uncertain feet and walks around the edge of the pit toward me.

"You have a plan?" she asks breathlessly as Maverick leads the witches out of the room. Even her whisper is filled with hope.

I stare at her, at the darkness under her eyes and the way her words slur with desperation. She's drunk on exhaustion and fear.

"I do," I say and grasp her arm.

When I release her, she takes charge of my chair, pushing me away from Maverick and Helena. I wait until we're out in the silent hall before speaking again. Sensing my sister's distress, one of the tigers follows us, its nose twitching as it takes its place beside her.

The first thing that enters my mind is the situation with Thorn and Callista. I want to tell Willow about them too, but that would be foolish right now. She's already upset, and discovering that I've been keeping a secret from her will only upset her more. Especially since they don't have a cure yet.

I'll tell her when the time comes. And hopefully by then, they'll have a cure on order. One thing at a time.

"There's somewhere we can go to truly get away from the Sickness."

Willow's eyes glaze over, and she grabs my shoulders. "Where?"

I bite my lip, knowing how completely her attitude will change when I tell her.

"*Where*, Lilith?"

"The place I was born."

The hope in her eyes dims. "You mean in the file, right? Where Ivy used to live?"

I nod. "It's still in good standing. Fern took Clio there to heal, and the Council doesn't know about them. It's safe."

"The Council knows about them plenty," Willow says stiffly. I frown, but she bites her lip and continues. "Say we were to go there. What's the catch? Why not suggest this sooner?"

I take a breath; at least I prepared for *that* question. "The catch is that you have to talk to Mom."

Willow's eyes narrow. "We don't need her."

"Have you ever been there yourself?" I ask, raising an eyebrow.

"No, but... well, if Fern was there, she can take us back."

"No!" I shriek, terrified that she'll seek Fern out on her own. The last thing I want is for Willow to discover firsthand exactly what I'm keeping from her.

"What do you mean, no?" She steps away from me.

I freeze, panicking, searching for a way out of this situation I've created. "Think about it," I say. "She just left that place, and she's finally back with her child. She hasn't seen in years, Willow. She deserves this time to rest."

Willow purses her lips but does not argue. I take that as a good sign. "You're absolutely sure there's no way to get there without Ivy?" she asks, glancing sideways at me.

I shake my head. "She's our best bet."

Willow swipes her hair from her eyes, and the anger drains from her face too. All that's left is a sad, broken girl driven by desperation and the tiniest bit of hope. "Okay. Let's go."

She peeks back into the meeting room, letting Maverick know she'll be back in a little while, and I hear him offer to come along. She turns him down, and now we're moving. My heart beats harder than it should as we make our way down the hall and closer to Ivy. Even the tiger picks up on my mood.

This has to go well. Ivy needs to feel like Willow is being honest. Otherwise, she'll most likely refuse to lead us there. Or worse, she might leave in the middle of the night and leave the rest of us stranded with the Sickness.

As much as I hate to believe my own words, they are the truth. Ivy really is our best hope of getting out of here.

WHEN WE REACH Ivy's room, Willow looks at me expectantly. Yes, this is a fairly dire situation, but I know she won't be the one to knock. The small amount of dignity she still holds ensures that. But I lost all my dignity a long time ago, so I knock for her.

At first, there's no response. I have the sickening thought that Ivy's already left, saved herself once again, and we're wasting time. Pushing the thought away, I knock again, louder and harder, praying to the Goddesses that my honest conversation with this woman has done something to change her.

Willow eyes me sideways, sarcastic grimace tightening her features.

At last, the door opens. Ivy's red-rimmed eyes grow wide as she looks between both of us. "Girls. This is a surprise."

I dip my head, but Willow merely folds her arms and looks away down the hall, as if she expects Maverick to save her from this situation.

"Come in." Ivy steps aside so we can enter.

I wheel myself much farther into the room than Willow, aided by my own telekinesis. Ivy stands beside her tiny bed while Willow remains just inside the doorway, arms still folded.

"What can I do for you two?" Our mother manages to summon up a small, patient smile.

Willow takes a deep breath. "We need a favor—"

"Mom, I wasn't born in the Land of Five, was I?" I ask. Willow narrows her eyes at me. Her curiosity brings a small smile to my own lips.

Ivy looks back and forth between us before sighing. "No, you weren't. When I got pregnant with you, Willow, your father, and I lived in Mentis."

"Why did you leave to have me?"

"This war has been ongoing for decades. Some witches have always opposed the Council. Your father and I were two of them. We never meant to have a family, but it happened."

Willow scoffs, and I have a feeling she's on the verge of storming out. But she doesn't.

"When you were born, Willow," Ivy continues, "we loved you so much. We did everything we could to keep you safe. But the Council had an eye on you from the day you were born. There were charts, graphs, everything keeping careful track of what powers you had, what you *could* have, and we knew what they were doing, searching for anything that didn't belong."

"And did they find it?" Willow asks, jutting out her chin.

I look to my sister, sharing in her curiosity. Of all the things I've asked her about our past, I never bothered to ask what types of powers she had before the Council sentenced her to death.

"No, they didn't," Ivy says. "As far as they knew, you were telekinetic."

"Just like me," I blurt without thinking.

Ivy nods. "Willow passed their inspections, but the Council was always suspicious of us. I knew that eventually, it would all come out. When I got pregnant again, I feared they would do the same with you, Lilith. And that you might not be as lucky. I feared what the Council would do if they got their hands on you, so I... we..."

"You pretended I wasn't your child," I say, giving weight to the words she will not say.

"That's how Larc ended up raising you for a time," Willow adds, her voice sharp and raw with pain. "He was a few years older than me, but he was barely an adult. I don't know how you could've done that to him."

"We never made anyone deal with something they didn't willingly take on," Ivy says.

Except for Willow and me.

Willow returns the look, and I see my thoughts reflected in her eyes. Larc will always be a touchy subject for her, but I can't say I blame her. If Clio died, that's just one more wound that would never heal.

"And no one questioned why he was suddenly caring for an infant?" I ask. "If he was barely older than a teenager, someone had to be suspicious."

"His parents died in the war, and he kept to himself. No one knew."

"But someone did. Someone had to have known if he was turned in."

"To be honest, I don't know what happened, how the Council found out you were connected to me, or how they found you with Larc. All I know is how it ended."

"So your point is that you spent more of your life pretending you weren't a mother than actually being one," Willow says, drawing out each word as she studies her nails with forced apathy.

Ivy closes her eyes, as if this conversation brings her great pain. It hurts Willow and me a lot more, I'm sure. "Yes."

"You were never my mother, even when you could've been," I say.

The woman looks offended, and Willow frowns, seemingly torn between righteousness and disbelief. I'm surprised Ivy doesn't argue with what I've said. "That's right."

I smile to hide the pain, laughing at the irony of it all.

"You need a favor?" Ivy asks.

I glance at Willow, hoping she can pull all her diplomatic skills together to manage this. "I think the only way to stop the Sickness from spreading is to go where the person responsible for it can't follow us. The only chance we have is that other Coven. Otherwise…"

We're doomed. It's possible that Ivy's included in that, even if she decides to run. We still don't know how the Sickness spreads, and if it *is* some type of Aens magic utilizing the air, we'll all probably fall prey to it anyway. Ivy seems to be considering the same thing.

"If I sent a team of witches who have been cleared, can you get them in?" Willow asks. Then she pauses, her eyes closed. Without looking up again, she adds, "Please, Mom?"

Ivy swallowed, her eyes wide in disbelief. I'm sure I look very much the same. It's a strong play on Willow's part, and when a smile spreads across Ivy's lips, I know it was the *right* play.

Chapter Twenty-One
Double-Edged Sword

WILLOW TELLS ME to prepare before she goes to work gathering all the witches who've passed another exam by Laura. I'm left with Ivy to ponder what the future has to offer. She helps me through the halls and back to my room, where she releases my chair and hesitates.

"We're going to be okay," she says. Then she smiles and steps back out into the hall.

Her statement buzzes through my head as I open my door and call out for Kado. He leaps off the bed, padding to my side, and jumps up to put his paws in my lap. I pet him for a minute, enjoying the company before I start gathering what few belongings I have into a tiny blue bag. When I finished, I tie the bag around the arm of the chair and move back out to the hall. Kado follows by my side as we move through Willow's mansion. I really don't like the fact that I'll have to leave him behind. As a Reanimate, he has too great a chance of being a carrier.

I take a shuddering breath when we exit the mansion, glaring down the hill through the purple plants toward the Community Villa in the distance. I'll have to leave Helena behind too. *And* Willow. The thought never really occurred to me until right now. I haven't seen much of her since we returned from the Battle of the Grove, but it doesn't feel right to leave without her.

"I need to tell her goodbye," I say to Kado.

He yaps once, and I imagine he's adding his agreement.

With a quick glance around, I check to see if anyone notices me, but I'm alone. So I encourage Kado to move ahead, and we make our way downhill. The dog doesn't leave my side, pressing his nose against my chair's wheel every time it gets stuck. Thankfully, that only happens twice.

It's quiet at the bottom of the hill. I study the Romanesque building with the decorative towers, then take the silence as an invitation to move faster. Usually by now, I can hear the other witches moving around inside, or at least their voices. Or *something*. But this ... this is what our entire Coven would sound like if the Sickness wins. A shiver rolls down my spine.

I take a breath, tingling with the excitement of doing something I know I shouldn't be doing, and wheel myself inside with Kado a step ahead of me.

His bark echoes down the hall. A few seconds later, the sound of hurried footsteps precedes Helena appearing around the corner. "Lilith! What are you *doing* here?"

I frown and open my arms so she'll at least hug me first. She does, I pull her so close against me, I hear her breath catch in her throat.

"What's going on?" she asks. When she pulls away, her gaze drops to my bag tied to the armrest.

"Willow's moving everyone who isn't sick to a new Coven. Reanimates are... are staying here."

Helena's eyebrows draw together; she looks as unsure about everything as I feel. "When was this decided?"

"Today. Kind of a spur-of-the-moment thing when news got out about Ambrossi." Now I frown. "How is he?"

"As well as you can imagine."

"So not good."

Helena nods and purses her lips. "Go back a minute. Why do Reanimates have to stay?"

"Willow's worried you guys might be a sort of carrier host for the Sickness to spread. For the... magic of it."

Helena narrows her eyes; I have always recognized this as her instant method of pulling her emotions back under her control. "Based on what we've seen with Ambrossi, it's definitely possible. He dealt with the Sickness day in and day out, and it didn't seem to affect him. He only got sick when Willow dragged him and a few others out of the hospital wing."

Most of the time when I end up being right, it doesn't actually feel good. This time, being right is a tragedy I never wanted.

"Can I see him?" I ask. "It just... it doesn't feel right to leave without saying goodbye. Since he might... he..."

"Of course." Helena's eyes grow wide as she glimpses into my mind. I know she can see just how close to the edge I really am. She circles my chair to grab the handles, then pushes me down the hall. Once again, Kado leads the way.

Before we make it to Ambrossi's room, she stops. Her icy fingers send a shock through me when she grasps my hand. "You'll have to wear protective gear," she says, then plucks a mask from a bag beside the door.

I look at her for what feels like an eternity. "That's not necessary, Helena. If I haven't caught it yet, there's a good chance I won't."

"He said the same thing, you know."

"Well, what's life without a little risk?"

She doesn't look convinced, but she also doesn't argue when I wheel myself into the room. There are two beds in here, divided by a single white curtain. It's drawn. so the other bed is impossible to see except for the silver railing on the end. I ignore it and move right to Ambrossi's side. He's pale—paler than he's ever been—and his red hair is matted into so many knots, it looks painful. At our approach, he tries to lift his head.

"Lilith. You... you shouldn't be here," he rasps, immediately breaking into a coughing fit.

"Maybe not, but I always do things I'm not supposed to do. And I couldn't go without seeing you, Ambrossi. You're my... my Healer. Always."

I reach toward him, but he pulls as far away as he can on his tiny bed. "I know you think you're invincible, and maybe you are. But on the off-chance that you aren't, Lilith, I do not want to be the reason you get sick. All I've ever wanted is for you to heal and be happy."

"You can't save everyone." The words are sour in my mouth, and the sting of his rejection brings tears to the corners of my eyes.

Until this moment, I always imagined that Ambrossi would be okay, that his body would be so used to healing others that he'd be immune to this, that he'd be the one witch the Sickness could not destroy. Looking at him now, I see how human he really is. He's actually dying, and unless Thorn and Callista can work some new type of magic to push back the symptoms, he'll be dead forever.

"No crying," Ambrossi says before I realize the first tear has already broken free. "I've had a good run, and I'm not afraid to die. I'm not even sad. I've done my part, and you've grown up well. You've become such a warrior."

I drop my head and start to cry, weeping loud, ugly sobs that radiate through the room. Ambrossi's fingers reach out to caress my cheek, his skin as cold as Helena's, and I wonder how much time he's got left.

"This seems hard now, but it's *this* pain that'll help you keep fighting. Unfortunately, it's a double-edged sword. Promise me you won't let this pain destroy you."

I've been through more pain in my twenty years of life than most other witches will ever experience. It's inevitable, like I'm some kind of magnet for chaos. After all the years of being kicked when I'm down, I understand why stray dogs have a tendency to bite. This, though, is a whole new kind of hurt.

Looking into Ambrossi's eyes, I want to tell him that I won't let it destroy me. I want to just agree with everything he says. I want to do whatever's in my power to make him as happy as I possibly can.

"And that's your problem," Helena murmurs.

Ambrossi and I glance at her, but he understands that she's read my mind and nods. I can't say another word. This is hard enough as it is, so I hug him and turn to Helena, desperate to escape.

Then I hear someone say my name from the other bed.

Helena shoots me an apologetic glance, and the sorrow deepens. Now I can't move at all, because I already know what's about to happen. And it'll hurt me more than I've ever been hurt before.

Chapter Twenty-Two
Their Love is Pure

"WHO IS THAT?" I ask Helena, but I'm already on the move to see for myself.

"Lilith, you might not want to do that."

I pull the curtain aside. It's Clio. "No, no, no," I moan, moving as close to the bed as my chair will allow.

It's easy to forget that we fought the last time I saw him. All I can think about is how much I hate myself for driving him here, for never checking on him. This is why he never came back to find me. They've all been lying to me.

"How did this happen?" I ask him. Then I turn to Helena. "How did this *happen*? Why didn't you *tell* me?"

"He's stubborn," Helena says.

Clio smiles, but his lips are so dry, I imagine the tiny movement cracking his skin. "I caught it... yesterday," he says and coughs. "It really does kick in fast."

"This can't happen," I say, pinching my underarm.

His smile looks painful. "But it is."

"Clio, you were right... We should've left. We should've—"

Hushing me, he reaches out to cup my cheek. "It's not so bad, really. I know you have a mission. A job to do. Let's face it, I would've held you back. You… you're destined to do amazing things, Li. You don't need me. You never did. And this way, I can see my parents again."

"It shouldn't be like this, Clio," I tell him.

He shrugs. "We don't get to decide, remember? That's the thing about destiny."

"That's bullshit." I can't—I *won't* accept that I've been fated since the beginning to lose everyone I care about. "We're going to find a cure. You'll see. Both of you." I say the last part loud enough for Ambrossi to hear.

"Li," Helena says, the pity so clear in her voice that it takes everything in me to not lash out at her.

"I came here to say goodbye," I tell her. "But not like this. Why didn't you tell me?"

"We all worried… how you would take it," she admits and bites her lip.

"These witches are *dying*. My *feelings* are the last thing anyone should care about. We have options. And I won't accept saying goodbye to either of you until we've exhausted all of them."

"What options?" Helena asks. "I've searched everywhere for a cure, but—"

"Fairies," I say.

"Huh?"

"We have *fairies*," I say, looking at Clio.

He nods; I know he remembers the secret we both vowed to keep.

"They know so much more than we ever will," I continue.

"And how do you know they'll help us?" Clio asks.

Because we agreed to help them. "Because they're kind creatures, and we look after one another."

Helena narrows her eyes. "What are you not telling us? I know you're not talking about Fern and Malcolm."

"No, I'm not."

Ambrossi tries to sit up so quickly that his muscles quiver. Coughing, he lies back down. "Thorn and Callista? You found them?"

I wince at the sound of their names. Once they're out, there's no taking it back. I wonder how he knew. Maybe Ambrossi has more to his magic than I ever bothered to think about before.

"How'd you guess?" I ask, tilting my head.

"I don't know much about fairies, but I know that they're strong. Stronger than witches. That kind of magic... it can't be hidden. It might be harder for some to sense it. To me, their magic is a shining beacon. Those creatures are some of the strongest beings to ever inherit the Land of Five. Their love is the purest form in existence. When they come to care about someone, anyone, that bond is there for life."

Chapter Twenty-Three
One Day

*L*EAVING CLIO'S SIDE is the hardest thing I've had to do in a long time. Helena spends a good half hour trying to persuade me to go on my own, but I won't budge. I can't. I've thrown myself off my chair, lying on the edge of the bed beside him. His cold hand rests in mine, but I focus on the feeling of his skin pressed against mine. Helena's voice fades into a drone in the back of my mind, easier to ignore the more I focus on Clio. All I can think about is that this might be the last time I see him—or Ambrossi. It makes me want to stay here until I catch the Sickness and die right beside them.

I can feel it—the damage so deep, so thorough, that I can never be broken in the same way again. It's a blessing, in a way, I suppose. No pain will ever compare to this. Without Clio, my life will be like chewing the same mouthful of food over and over forever—flavorless and bland. Empty. I already feel it seeping into these moments with him. I'd spit it out if I could, but there's no easy solution for this ... if there even is one.

I lift his hand to brush my lips against his cold skin, fighting back tears. It feels as if he's already half dead, and when I look up to meet his bloodshot eyes, I see that same sadness and fear.

THE SAGE

Helena taps my shoulder and wraps her arms around my waist to help me sit up. "Come on, Li. You need to go."

"No." I tighten my grip on Clio and lie here, without moving. If Helena wants me out, she'll have to carry my dead weight.

"Li, please don't do this," Clio says in his raspy voice.

"I don't want to leave you," I tell him, burying my face in his chest and regretting it almost instantly. He doesn't smell the way I remember. Instead, he reeks of vomit, of infection, of *Sickness*, and the smell reminds me more of death than I would ever admit out loud.

Helena tries again to physically move me off the bed, but I scream and cry, holding tighter to Clio. He's too weak to push me away. I'm so unhinged at this point that my telekinesis unsheathes itself; things are flying off the shelves and skittering across the floor without intention. Herbs rain through the air, tangling in Helena's thick red hair. She shakes it out, frowns at me, then looks at the door. The moment her scowl softens, I know what she's planning. Then she dashes out of the room.

I'm sure now I only have a few minutes left, so I look at Clio—really force myself to see him, Sickness and all. "I don't want to leave, but I know I have to," I tell him. "No matter what, please promise me you'll hold on. That you'll keep fighting. Because I can't leave you too. I can't."

A tear runs down my cheek, and Clio lifts an icy finger to brush it away. "You know me, Li. I'll fight to the end."

I smile at him, but it's bitter. Though we're both still thinking about our completely foolish fight, neither of us mentions it now. It doesn't matter, and we don't have long before Helena returns with Willow in tow. My sister looks more panicked than I've seen in a while—even more than at the meeting where her entire Coven had been about to turn on her.

"Lilith! What are you doing? You have to get out of here," she says, marching toward me.

"Be gentle," Ambrossi's voice croaks.

Willow doesn't stop to acknowledge him. She grabs the handles of my chair and pushes it up against the edge of Clio's bed. I don't say anything, just bury myself in Clio's chest again, breathing in his scent and trying not to let it make me sick. Her gaze lands on him, and her mouth pops open in surprise.

"Lily, I'm sorry. Just as I'm sorry to see this has happened to you, Clio. I am. But we have to go. Everyone's ready to leave, and they can't go without you."

"Why?" I hiss. "What's so special about me that I can't be one of the witches they leave behind?"

"What would be the point? You're a strong warrior, you're loyal, and you're my sister. I'm not going to let you stay."

"I'm not a warrior," I say, gesturing to my battered legs and the painful wounds bared for all to see. "Or have you forgotten?"

"Just because you can't fight anymore doesn't mean the Coven has no use for you. You're brilliant. You can do anything you want to do. You're not going to be left behind."

Tears pour from my eyes now.

"I know this is hard, but you'll find all the strength you need on the other side."

"You don't know anything." I sit up so fast that her eyes lock on mine before she can decide against it. All my pain and confusion burns through her gaze and directly into her mind. She gasps and takes a step back, her lip trembling.

"I know this hurts, but once you're over there—"

"The Council's going to pay for this," I tell her. "The *Sage* will pay."

"One day, yes."

But not today.

"That's not going to happen if you die here," she tells me.

I can't be mad at her—not about this. I turn back to Clio and press my lips to his forehead. "Please hold on," I whisper in his ear. "I'm going to find a cure. Just please hold on."

THE SAGE

He looks back at me, eyes glazed with the Sickness. "I love you," he says then turns over to vomit onto the floor.

I can't help it anymore. The stench of dying witches, my despair, all this rage. A few sobs escape me, then the rest of my world turning completely upside down sends me into blackness.

Chapter Twenty-Four
Twists

WHEN I OPEN my eyes and see the world moving around me, I assume I'm in the middle of another astral episode. But I quickly realize that it's only Maverick carrying me. It makes sense that Willow summoned him. She never would've been able to get me to leave otherwise, and maybe she knew that. I peek up at him, trying to gauge what he's thinking. Usually, he's expressionless, but he's frowning solemnly now, his lips pressed tightly together. I know he's going to miss Willow just as much as I'll miss Clio.

At the very least, we'll always have that in common. I open my eyes fully and turn my head enough to survey the witches around us. There aren't as many as I thought there would be, and the realization curdles in my stomach. Crowe walks beside us, a tiny, folded-up version of my chair in his hand. Someone's wrapped up my legs again, but the bandages are just a bit too tight.

I lift my head off of Maverick's shoulder, trying to see who else is traveling with us. "I thought you'd be out until we crossed the portal," he says.

"We haven't left the Coven yet?" Now I see the budding purple plants just ahead.

He shakes his head and scratches the corner of his mouth. My episode cost them more time than I thought it would, and he's not happy about it. I use the silent moment to study the group of witches again. Maverick has every right to be as solemn as he looks; our number of witches healthy enough for this trip is incredibly small. I pick out familiar faces—Sabre, Crowe, Katrina, Quinn, and Laura.

"Where's Grief?" I ask.

Maverick's eyes answer that before his one-word sentence. "Dead."

I set my chin back on his shoulder and close my eyes. Who says there's no such thing as a stupid question?

Zane, the great hulking muscle of a man standing guard at the portal, greets each of us as we cross. When Maverick and I take our turn, all he says is, "Good luck."

It feels both meaningful and pointless at the same time.

"Ready?" Maverick asks me.

I don't answer before he pushes through the portal. When we emerge on the other side, we're somewhere near the border of Aens. I recognize the open moors and the houses far in the distance. The breeze blows through my hair. After everyone comes through, the portal seals again in an instant, as if it never existed.

"Onward we go," Maverick says. In this group we've been forced to create without the Reanimates, I realize, he's now our leader.

"Wait!"

I narrow my eyes as Ivy pushes through our group to approach Maverick and me. Both of us stare at her in equal parts curiosity and annoyance.

"Yes?" he asks, meeting her stare directly.

"Let me hold her."

He looks down at me, as if asking for permission; I have no idea how to answer or even how to feel about the request. Ivy doesn't seem the type to give affection just for the Hell of it;

she's calculating something. If she wants to *hold* me, there's a reason, and of course I want to know what it is.

"Okay," I tell him.

He stares at me intensely and conjures a question in his own mind. *'Are you sure?'*

I nod. With great consternation, he passes me to my mother.

Her arms are so much thinner than Maverick's; the rough edges of her bones push awkwardly against my spine and into the muscles of my legs. I grit my teeth. Even the bandages aren't enough padding to ease the discomfort.

"Sorry," she says. It takes her a minute of adjusting me to find a hold that's comfortable for both of us—or comfortable enough, anyway.

"Why?" I ask, mad at myself for the incomplete sentence.

"We're almost there," she says proudly, as if that's a real answer, and picks her way to the front of the group again.

Maverick follows closely in Ivy's wake, keeping just a step behind. Not enough to overshadow her but enough that he can see me if I need him again. I blink at him in appreciation. Actions really do speak louder than words. I rest my chin on Ivy's shoulder, not sure how to feel.

My mother's arms should be a comfortable place; I should feel safe and protected. I don't. Maverick and Crowe are more comfort to me than Ivy; she's as unpredictable as her footsteps, which jostle me into aggravation.

If there were anything to see around us, I would have focused on the scenery to distract myself. Though we began at the edge of Aens, we still haven't entered, staying on the border for a little while before drifting in the *opposite* direction of the Land of Five. There's nothing was trees, bushes, and grass around us—not even any other Covens. The thick forest here reminds me of Alchemy, though this is a wilder, more untamed version.

THE SAGE

"Are we almost there?" I ask, keeping the confusion from my voice as I reach out to brush my fingers across the moss of a passing tree.

"This is it," Ivy says.

I blink and look around, thinking I've missed something. With all the foliage around us, I can't see anything. These witches may have an underground Coven like the witches in the Bunker, but there's no sign that anyone has ever been here. I wrinkle my nose and glance at Ivy. "There's nothing here."

She lets out a loud, low whistle. It sounds beautiful at first but quickly grows into a dissonant shriek. The other witches with us look as caught off guard and disturbed as I feel; some go so far as to put their hands over their ears. When Ivy's whistle ends, the witches appear.

Shadows jump from the air, slip around trees, and seem to sprout from the *ground*. In a flash, they surround us, figures cloaked in black robes. Our group huddles tighter together.; there are more of them than us, and that's never a good way to start a fight. Their apparent leader is a tall figure in a black cloak adorned with purple swirls around the edges. The hood covers her eyes, but a few wisps of long black hair still escape.

"Ivy?" The woman pulls back her hood to reveal the burn scars covering the left side of her face. Her left eye is clouded over in a white haze, but the other eye staring at Ivy is ice-blue, the color of the sky. Like Ivy's eyes and my own.

"Hello, Sissy. I've brought Lilith back to you, and she's in desperate need of your help."

Chapter Twenty-Five
The Wilderness

"*iSSY?*" I try to lean closer for a better look at this woman. "You're my aunt?"

A hint of a smile touch her lips as she nods, gazing at Ivy. "She is not the only one in need of assistance." Her sharp, eerie eyes sweep over our little group until they come to settle on me. "Why have

you come?"

Ivy and this woman are like an older, more complicated version of Helena and me. They've been through a lot together, and the times they've seen have rarely been good. The woman's face doesn't lack in kindness, but a man steps supportively up beside her—like Maverick to Willow whenever she found herself under duress. The man wears a cloak like the rest of them, and when he pushes back his hood, I'm transfixed.

He's breathtakingly beautiful, with a sculpted face, wispy blond hair, and haunting blue eyes. He's older than me by a good decade, but something about his face transfixes me. When his eyes meet mine, I look away, feeling more than a little guilty for these thoughts. I summon up an image of Clio wasting away from the Sickness back in the Land of New Life, and it's enough ground me into myself again.

He extends his arms toward Ivy. I realize what she's about to do just before she hands me over to him.

"Mom!" I try to catch her eye, but the man holding me has turned around just enough that I can't see her from his grip.

"Howdy, Little Miss," the man says.

I look away, refusing to make eye contact. Crowe and Maverick inch closer, as if this entire situation leaves them with the same awful feeling in the pits of their stomachs as I have in mine. Even then, they still keep a distance, wary of the other cloaked figures who haven't moved, spoken, or revealed their faces.

"My name is Darrius," he tells me.

"That's nice."

Darrius raises an eyebrow, but I've caught sight of Ivy again.

"These witches seek shelter from the Council," my mother tells the woman with the burns on her face.

The other witch nods. "You know the Wilderness has always functioned as a sanctuary in an unforgiving world. But... there are so many of you. It makes me uneasy."

"I hope you know I would never do a thing to hurt you. We are desperate. This is all that's left of an entire Coven. The rest are sick or dying, and if you turn us away, I'm afraid we'll all suffer the same."

Her words make me wince. Willow would have used far more tact and grace, which she obviously didn't get from Ivy. What leader would willingly harbor other witches who may or may not be carrying the Sickness with them?

The woman's lips are pressed together in a concerned frown. She's going to turn us away, and the thought turns my stomach. But then she sighs and looks at Darrius and me. "Take her to the Den and make sure she's comfortable." To Ivy, she adds, "I'll find accommodations suitable for all your witches."

Darrius takes us farther into the forest. I grip his arm, listening to the murmurs of the group fading away. The cloaked witches disperse only after Darrius pushes through them. Crowe stares after us but doesn't follow. I'm going to be alone with this strange witch, in a strange place, and the realization makes me sick.

I try to tell myself that Ivy wouldn't intentionally leave me in a dangerous situation, but that thought almost makes me laugh. That's *exactly* what she'd do; it's what she's *always* done. So I distract myself by studying where we are. The thick bushes along the paths are much like I Alchemy, but the vines and heat remind me of Mentis.

As we move farther from my Coven and I can no longer hear them, I look at Darrius and realize there's nothing else here. "Where the Hell are your buildings?"

He laughs. "Just a very sweet thing, aren't you?"

I raise an eyebrow. He has no idea. "Look, I don't know you, and you don't know me, so I'll just say I've been through Hell and back. I'm under no obligation to be sweet to you or anyone else."

"I can respect that," he says, nodding slowly.

My eyes starts twitches. "I asked you a question."

"Ever heard seeing is believing?" As soon as he says it, he stops beside a tree. "This situation falls in that category."

I frown at the tree and then at him again. "It's a *tree*."

"Ah, patience, child."

"Child? What are you, five, *six* years older than me?"

"Age is just a number. Our character is what defines us." Darrius shuffles me in his arms, pressing our chests uncomfortably close together.

"Hey! What are you doing?" I struggle against him as he lifts both hands and claps once. "Personal space is still a thing, you know."

He ignores me, clapping again in a series of bursts that echo in the silence around us.

Nothing else happens. I tilt my head. "Let me guess. Patience?"

He nods, smiling so wide the corners of his eyes crinkle. "Now you're getting it." A white rope ladder tumbles out of nowhere, nearly smacking me in the head. "See?"

I push the rope against the tree, feeling the tough strands beneath my fingers. Darrius presses me against him again and grips the ladder, preparing to climb.

"Onward and upward we go!"

"Let me get this straight," I say. "Your Coven lives in the *trees?*"

"One with nature." He smiles like he's never been prouder of himself. "Hold tight." I obey, wrapping my arms around him a second before he hoists us up the ladder.

The speed with which he climbs brings a cry of surprise out of me. It's also incredibly impressive. I clutch onto him, more out of instinct than anything else, convinced he'll drop me at a second's notice. Green branches sway around us as he climbs, hand over quick hand. Just when I think I'm about to hurl, we're at the top. I can't help but glance down, and my stomach lurches again.

"Hold on," he says, letting go of the rope to pull himself up onto the wooden planks of a solid floor.

I clamp a hand over my mouth, more nauseated than I care to admit. When he stands, I realize we've climbed right up into a house like any other—only built into the treetop.

"You weren't kidding," I say as he crosses the room.

"No, I wasn't." Darrius bends down to set me on a chair padded with pillows.

I take the opportunity to stretch, trying not to look too grateful. My body aches from the journey, being shuffled around like cargo, but I try not to let any of that show, either.

He smiles and cups his mouth with both hands. "Hazel! Come out and meet my friend."

"You don't even know me," I say, folding my arms. "And I don't appreciate people who pretend they do."

"Really, now? Then tell me your story so we can change

that. What puts a girl like you in your position?"

I sneer at him, thinking of the first time I met Crowe—how full of himself I thought he was. Now, seeing this witch, I realize just how wrong I'd been. Apparently, it can always get worse.

"My *story* is *none* of your business," I say slowly, enunciating every vowel.

"It kind of is, though, right? Since I'm part of it now." His foot taps against the floor as he tilts his head. "After all, you're going to be living in my Coven. My world is now *part* of your story. How great is that?"

"Hazel!" I shout. I have no idea who she is, but I don't want to be alone with this guy anymore.

Darrius smiles and swipes his hair away from his face. "She's coming. She's coming."

"Who is she?" I just wish he'd say something helpful or stop talking.

"I'm a Healer." The sugary-sweet voice rises from the hallway as a tiny girl makes an appearance. She looks my age, but she's so small that it would be easy to mistake her for much younger—even a child. She walks with a little bounce to her step, her pixie-cut brown hair fluttering a little around her face. She reaches toward me with an outstretched hand, holding my gaze as she approaches. I appreciate the fact that she doesn't once look at my legs. That kind of restraint doesn't come easily. "Who would you be?"

I feel Darrius' stare burning into the side of my head, but I don't look at him. I already like Hazel far more than I'll ever like her friend, and I take her hand when she reaches me, surprised by how much longer my fingers are than hers. "My name's Lilith."

She nods. "A good name. If I can guess, you've been through a bit." Her gaze finally drops to the bandages on my legs, which are now rumpled and sweaty from the journey. Until this moment, I hadn't even realized how much they *smell*. "How did that happen?"

"Two separate accidents."

"Tough girl," Darrius says, sounding truly impressed.

I roll my eyes, wishing he would be on his way and let me talk with the Healer alone. From what I've already seen, Darrius has nothing to offer me. "I was a child for the first," I add. "The second was more recent. To make it a long story short, both were magical damage, so I can't walk."

Hazel studies the sagging bandages again. "Might not be able to walk, but I'm willing to bet there's still more healing to do before calling it quits."

"Yeah, maybe. To be honest, I'm not sure how they're doing. I've let them air out a few times, but I haven't looked at them much."

"Well, I *would* say you're in luck, but that's not quite fair of me to say. I *will* tell you that it's good Darrius brought you to me. I can at the very least help your legs *look* the way they used to."

"There are herbs for that?"

Hazel tilts her head. "Not so sure about herbs. I specialize in water healing."

"Huh. I've never met a witch who could do that." I wonder just exactly what goes into her healing.

"Well, who knows? Some physical therapy might do you wonders."

"That sounds great, actually." I admit, especially after all the days I've spent lying around instead of getting the exercise my body needed—the exercise it had been so used to receiving before everything went to Hell. "When do we get started?"

"As soon as possible," she says. "Today, though, I'll just change your wrappings, if that's okay. When you start to feel more comfortable, I'll get you in for some water therapy. You're probably pretty eager to get back to your Covenmates and get settled in."

Not as much as when I was alone with Darrius.

Something about Hazel brings out my much more peaceful side; I already feel close to her, as if we knew each other in another life. She smiles and sends Darrius to get a fresh cup of tea. He scurries out of the room, and I realize why she really did it—and why she declined starting therapy today; she sensed how uncomfortable he make me.

I respect the Hell out of her for that.

Hazel offers a sly smile before excusing herself to gather supplies. I sit alone in this room, looking around and feeling oddly comfortable. I have to give Hazel all the credit for that. Now I feel like maybe I belong here.

Darrius returns first, and my peaceful calm wavers. He smiles at me and sets a mug on the table before taking a seat on the couch across the room. I watch the tendrils of steam rise from the tea, vowing to ignore him until Hazel returns.

"It's a shame about your legs," he says, "but keep your chin up, girl. One day, your pains will make you a warrior."

My heart breaks all over again at the memory of Ambrossi's last words and the very same promise he made me. At the time, I wasn't sure I could live up to it. Now, I make myself a new promise. I'm ready to be strong again and nothing else.

I reach for the mug and say, "I already am."

Chapter Twenty-Six
Convergence

WHEN HAZEL COMES back, arms full of supplies, Darrius and I are glaring at each other. For the most part, she pretends not to notice. She drops the materials on the table and approaches me. Her work is quick and efficient. When the bandages are off, I look at my legs—at the thick patches of scabs beginning to heal. The edges have lost their reddish tint, and I can almost believe that one day, they'll heal completely.

Almost.

Hazel grinds up some flowers and herbs, the poultice a red color I've never seen before, and rubs it into the wounds. I grit my teeth, expecting a sting, but there's no pain.

She looks up at me when she's done. "It's a little stinky," she admits, "but it'll help with the pain. At least enough to get you through the night."

I dip my head gratefully. "Thank you."

"You're very welcome." She looks back at the mound of stuff on the table. "Would you like them bandaged?"

I shake my head. "I'll let them air tonight."

Hazel smiles, and the corners of her eyes wrinkle. "Good decision."

She stands to gather her supplies again when a bell tolls

somewhere in the distance, loud and long. It chimes once, the sound fading before it repeats a second and third time. I straighten in the chair and look to Darrius and Hazel for answers.

Darrius laughs. "Relax."

"It's the dinner bell," Hazel explains. "A little early today, but Molly most likely wants to say some things before we eat."

"Molly?"

"The witch you met coming in." Darrius rolls his eyes.

I press my lips together and cast him a scathing glance.

"Your aunt, I believe," Hazel explains in a much sweeter tone.

"Where do we eat here?" I ask.

"The cafeteria is its own building," she says.

The minute amount of bliss I'd managed disappears at the thought of Darrius carrying me again.

"You're not gonna hurt me, right?" Darrius asks.

"I'm not going to make promises I can't keep." But I don't fight as he scoops me up.

"Play nice," Hazel says, eyeing him.

"All right, all right."

Hazel gives me an encouraging smile as she steps toward the rope ladder and leads the way down. Now that the sun has set completely, descending from the house in the trees is like dropping into the belly of a beast—one likely to swallow us up so we never see the light of day again.

When we reach the ground, I can't see anything. The trees are nothing more than shadowy outlines, and I wonder how they know exactly which one is the tree they're looking for. Finally, Hazel stops, and I hear a few leaves and dirt scatter as she leaps to grasp a ladder.

I look up at Darrius', dreading this climb too.

"Remember, don't hurt me," he says.

I glare fiercely at him, despite knowing he can't see it.

Maybe he can at least *feel* it. The treehouses seemed like an amazing concept at first, but I'm already beginning to turn against them. With my body in this condition, I'll always need someone else to help me up; if that person is going to be Darrius every time, I'd rather sleep on the ground.

Darrius swings me around him, adjusting me for a piggyback ride, and climbs. Halfway up, I hear the drifting sounds of chatter, laughter, and cheers. My heart pounds at the sound. This sounds so much like the days before the Sickness in the Elemental Coven.

At the top, Hazel helps Darrius pull me up onto the ledge. It's warm and bright inside this house, the wooden planks of the wall and floor giving it a cozy feeling. There are a dozen long tables at least, all surrounded with pillows instead of chairs.

"It's more comfortable," Hazel promises and leads Darrius toward the nearest table.

I catch Katrina's gaze as he sets me down, but other than that, I don't have any contact with my Covenmates, almost as if I'm no longer one of them. I see Sabre, Crowe, Laura, and a few others. A witch from my Coven, a girl whose name I never bothered to learn, sits beside a girl from this Coven with long black hair pulled back in a blue ribbon. The sight makes me smile. I take it as a good sign that our Covens are getting along so well this soon.

"Comfy?" Hazel asks.

I nod.

"Let me know if I can bring you any more pillows."

I grab her arm and hold her in place. "Please don't go."

She smiles, nods, and takes her place on the empty pillow to my right. Darrius sits on my left. Hazel gives my knee a comforting pat just as someone whistles and the room falls silent. The only witch standing is the witch with the burns who greeted us—my aunt.

With a wide smile, she gazes around the room, glancing at each witch from both Covens. She looks much friendlier now than at the border.

"Fellow witches of the Wilderness," she says at last. "You must be wondering who all these new witches are."

There are a few calls of agreement. The girl with the black hair and blue ribbon smiles at the Elemental witch beside her, as if she already has the answer.

"They are sisters and brothers of ours," Molly says. "These are witches down on their luck. Witches in need of help. Of shelter. They are enemies of the Council."

That brought a round of cheers and shouts of encouragement. Hazel settles her hand on my shoulder and gently squeezes.

"Don't be afraid to welcome them in," Molly continues. "Some of you have already been assigned roommates, but to those who have not, feel free to welcome these witches into our Coven and your homes."

Across the cafeteria, Wilderness witches reach out and hug the nearest Elemental. Hazel hugs me, and we're all surprised by the warmth of these people. The compassion is exactly what we need—exactly what has been missing from ourselves and our own Coven.

For once, it feels good to belong.

Chapter Twenty-Seven
Without a Word

WHEN THE MEETING is over, Hazel leaves to plan our first therapy session, and Darrius goes with her. I'm relieved to be back with witches I know. Maverick takes charge of carrying me after we receive our individual assignments within this new Coven. Hazel's poultice helped dull the pain in my leg a bit but not as much as I hoped it would. As Maverick carries me down the rope ladder and through the darkness of the undergrowth, the pain flares up again. I can't wait to go to bed and just put an end to this day.

A lot of the witches did as Molly suggested and paired up with Wilderness witches as housemates. Crowe, Katrina, Maverick, and I, however, decide it's best to get a house together. Molly suggests a few witches from her Coven who could live with us for guidance, but Maverick politely declines.

I still haven't seen Ivy since she dumped me into Darrius' arms. I assumed she would've wanted to at least check on me, but she seems to have disappeared. I'm sure she's staying in the same house as Molly—her sister—but it hurts. They're my family, and yet neither of them even extended the offer for me to stay with them.

Our new house with this Coven has the same cozy feeling of the cafeteria, with wooden planks and boards making the walls and floor. There are black-leather chairs and a few shelves with herbs. The kitchen has a decent stock of food, and overall, I'm content with the simplicity.

"Chin up," Katrina tells me as Maverick sets me down on the couch in the living room.

I smile but have no intention of obeying her. I miss Hazel, and oddly enough, I wish she would've let me stay with her. But as the Wilderness' Healer, she most likely lives alone; most Healers prefer it that way.

Crowe finishes his entire scrutinizing lap around the house. "It's not bad."

"Not at all," Maverick agrees.

As the witch with the most kitchen experience, Katrina is automatically in charge of cooking dinner. Crowe gives me a worried look when she leaves the room, and I pretend not to notice. I pretend that everything's fine, like I wasn't separated from them earlier and like I'm not secretly hurting inside.

It makes things just a bit more tolerable imagine that I'm fine—that *we're* fine. The tension leaves my shoulders after Katrina and Crowe go to the kitchen, and then it's just Maverick and me, staring at one another.

"What do you think of these people so far?" he asks.

I shrug. "I just met them."

"You were alone with them for at least an hour," he replies. "Did they treat you okay?"

"Their Healer's kind." I keep my feelings about Darrius to myself.

"That's good." There's a hint of a smile on his lips.

I raise an eyebrow. "I feel like you've got something else to say."

Maverick laughs, rubbing his finger along his chin. "I've been studying you."

"Studying me? And here I thought we were becoming friends."

"Hear me out," he says. "Now, I might be wrong, but

176

the more I talk to you, the more I feel like you have one more power you haven't discovered yet. An Aquais power."

I frown, dumbfounded. "What?"

Maverick nods. "It might not *seem* like much, but you... you rely on your intuition a lot, don't you? You can read people within seconds, and that's without your mindreading. You just *know* whether or not they're good people. You know whether you can trust them or whether you should keep things to yourself."

I blink at him. That really *doesn't* sound like much of a power. "Common sense isn't a power, Maverick."

"No, but divination is. It can be a powerful tool. And I think you had it long before you joined the Council. It explains your fascination with Iris. And your reasons for saving Tarj."

I lift a hand to stop him. It makes sense, sort of. Except for the Sage. The first time I met her, I really believed she was a good person. That quickly turned out to be a lie, and the only reason I discovered that was because the Sage told me herself. Not my intuition.

After a heavy silence, Maverick stands. "Just something to think about. I'm gonna go lie down for a bit. Did you want some help, or..."

I smile at how nervous—how *uncertain*—he sounds. "No, Maverick. I'll be okay. Thank you."

He nods and heads down the hall on the opposite side of the room. I stare into the empty fireplace, feeling a sudden all-consuming homesickness for Ignis. This place feels a little too comfortable, but I can't figure out why. We're beyond the Land of Five, in the territory the Council always said would kill us.

They were completely wrong. It probably never would've harmed us to cross the border. All along, keeping us inside the Land of Five was just another ugly trick. I burst into laughter until I cry, and Katrina and Crowe bolt out of the kitchen to check on me. I've devolved into a horrible, weeping mess when they reach me, but I convince them I'm okay. Katrina eventually returns to the kitchen, but Crowe stays stubbornly by my side.

He bites his lip, and I know he wants to comfort me but can't think of anything to say. Instead, he glances briefly toward the kitchen. "Hey, I never got the chance to thank you for not... you know." He drops his gaze.

"You tell her yet?"

Crowe nods. "She took it better than I thought she would."

"Good." At least something has had a positive outcome.

"You know I meant no harm by it. I'll apologize to Clio too if you need me to." Then he frowns. "Where *is* Clio?"

The tightness in my chest returns but without the laughter this time. Tears pour down my face, breaking through the dams and levees I set up to keep them contained. Crowe doesn't hesitate to hug me this time, and when Katrina emerges from the kitchen, her only reaction is to drop to her knees beside us and hug me too.

Chapter Twenty-Eight
Water Therapy

WHEN IT'S TIME to turn in for the night, the awkwardness in our new house flares up again. I don't know what the Wilderness witches were thinking when they designed this place. There are two bedrooms, meaning only two beds. *These* witches might be used to hugging and loving each other, but Elemental witches aren't cut from the same cloth. It makes sense for Crowe and Katrina to share a bed, but Maverick and I fight over the other, both of us insisting the other person take it. It doesn't surprise me that we're both too stubborn to admit we deserve something as simple as a bed.

I imagine, like me, Maverick probably won't get much sleep tonight, anyway. Anxiety runs rampant in new places like this, and it doesn't help that we're both in the middle of desperately missing someone back home. Until now, I never realized how truly similar he and I actually are. The realization stares me in the face, daring me to overlook it.

In the end, Maverick wins the bed fight by dumping me on the bed, where I have no way to chase him down and argue. Then he sets up camp in the living room. I spread out on the bed, staring up at the ceiling, and wish I had Kado for company. The bed seems entirely too large without him in it. I try without success to sleep, but I keep tossing and turning, knowing I'm going nowhere for all the effort. I reach down to stroke the healing wounds on my skin, wishing I had some of Hazel's poultice. Maybe if they'd stop hurting for a little while, I could sleep.

But I can't.

So I let my mind win.

This, of course, is never a good idea. I think about the incident with Tabitha in the Council bunkers and wonder what would happen if I scoped out Aquais. If Tabitha traced me back to the Land of New Life, she wouldn't expect me to return from somewhere else.

Would she be there too, in the bowels of Crowe's mansion, or would the Council even know I was in Aquais? Once the questions start, it's nearly impossible to dislodge them.

"Here goes nothing," I mutter and close my eyes, easing my breathing.

In what feels like seconds, I'm in my misty astral form, staring down at my still body. I squint, hating how fragile I really look, then sigh and make my way out of the cabin. Climbing down the ladder is so easy like this; I'll miss it when I'm awake. But for now, I distract myself by marveling at the beauty of this place. Even in the darkness, it's so different from anywhere else I've ever been. I find a brief moment of partial respect for my mother and understand why she came here.

I still don't understand why she left.

"Focus," I tell myself, but that doesn't help.

I don't know where I am. I know I can find my way from the Wilderness to the portal into the Land of New Life, but I have no idea how to get from right here to Aquais. So I take the long way, stepping through the portal and into the Land of New Life. It's not a good decision; I know it's not, because all I can think about is spying on Clio while I'm here.

And I might not like what I find.

True or not, I still have to know if he's still alive.

I rush to the hospital wing and all the way to the door at the end of the hall. I try not to let jump to conclusions or panic over the unknown, but I can't help it. Finally, I slip into Ambrossi and Clio's room. Clio is alive and well, but the blanket in the other bed has already been pulled up over Ambrossi's face.

I'd be lying to myself if I said he was sleeping. The sight breaks me enough to tear me right out of my astral projection. I open my wet eyes, embarrassed to see Maverick, Crowe, and Katrina crowded around my bed.

"Where did you go?" Maverick asks, his voice calm and patient. "And what did you see?"

I bury my face in my hands, my tears slipping through my fingers. I don't know how I can still be embarrassed to cry in front of them, but I am. "I went back to the Land of New Life," I begin. "I saw Ambrossi."

Katrina gently lays a hand on my knee, silently telling me I don't have to continue. I accept the offer. I don't think I can keep going now, anyway.

***

THE FOUR OF us say a little prayer for Ambrossi with a tiny ceremony in his honor. Katrina lights a candle, and we let it burn out on its own before any of us speak. We use the silent time to think about him, what he meant to us, and what our lives will be like now that he's gone. At least now, there are tears in everyone's eyes.

After the candle burns out, Katrina turns to look at me. "I'll take you to Hazel's."

"She's ready for me?" I ask, surprised she came and went without me being any the wiser.

Katrina nods. "She said something about water therapy. That sounds interesting."

"You're welcome to stay for the session," I tell her,

almost hoping she will. Although I'm comfortable with Hazel, I want to be with someone who feels Ambrossi's loss just as deeply as I do.

"I'll do that." She scoops me up into her arms.

We shout goodbye to Crowe and Maverick, and, with some difficulty, she gets us down the ladder. On the forest floor, she turns in a full circle and looks at me. "Which one is Hazel's?"

I don't know how I know, since I've only been there once, but I point it out quickly without any doubt. Katrina walks us toward the tree and calls for the rope to be lowered.

The long stretch of silence during Ambrossi's vigil made sense. Silence between Katrina and me now doesn't. "Things are all right between you and Crowe?" I ask as she helps me onto the ladder.

I grip the rope, grateful for the chance to at least try climbing it myself.

"Of course everything's fine. I don't know how you can think about *us* with everything else that's happened. I mean, if that's true... if Ambrossi's really gone..."

"Yeah." Just another needle in the pincushion.

"Something wrong?"

"No, just tired." I can't remember the last time I got a good night's sleep, and I'm still wishing for a witch with the magic to make me sleep. Maybe if I annoy Maverick enough, he'll grant me a favor with his knockout magic.

Katrina just nods, and judging by the bags under her eyes, I know she understands my exhaustion like no one else. Slowly, I pull myself up, hand over hand. Without my legs, it's hard to do on my own but not impossible, especially after all my time spent wheeling myself around in that chair. My arms burn from the strain, but I make it to the top and pull myself up onto the ledge with a grunt. The door is already open again, and I have a feeling Hazel keeps it that way so her Covenmates feel welcome in her Den.

As a Healer, that kind of thing is important.

When we slip inside, Katrina sets me on the same chair, and Hazel makes her appearance. She smiles at me, genuinely happy to see me, then turns her gaze onto Katrina. Though her smile dims at the edges, she doesn't look any less friendly.

"I don't believe I've met you yet." Hazel extends a hand.

"No, you haven't. I'm Katrina. I hope it's all right to watch you work a bit. When Lilith said you do water healing, it caught my interest."

"Ah. A Healer, I take it?" Hazel retracts her hand without missing a beat.

"A bit." Katrina sits down. "I've helped out a little, and I know the basics."

Hazel nods. "That's good. Hopefully, you'll learn something new." Then she looks at me. "How are you feeling? Are you ready?"

I bite my lip and look up at her uncertainly. "Will it hurt?"

Hazel shrugs, her big eyes drifting across the room. "It might. A little. But I'll try to make this as painless as possible for you."

I stare at her for a long time. Yes, I have trust issues. That's not something I'm ashamed to admit. But when she says this, I believe her. I have no reason not to.

"Follow me to the back. I have the water already set up," she says.

Katrina nods and meets my gaze before lifting me into her arms. Then she waits for Hazel's instructions, holding me loosely in her arms as the smaller witch moves through her house. Katrina follows her down the hallway at a patient, unassuming pace.

At last, the hallway brings us into a large green room. I stare with wide eyes, taking in the details. One wall is covered in plants; ivy and roses stand out, though there are a variety of other greens I can't easily name. The walls and floor are covered in small square tiles, and the large tub is set *in* the floor—a deep, yawning pit reminding me of the tiger pit in Willow's throne room. The water in it is so clear that the tub looks empty. Without the water lilies floating on the surface, I wouldn't have known otherwise. The room smells sweet, and I somehow manage to relax.

"This is the Water Room," Hazel says.

I look into the tub again. A few steps lead down to a seat inside. I look to Hazel for instructions as Katrina sets me down on the hard floor. "How's this work?"

"Lilith, this might make you uncomfortable, but I've found that the water helps blood flow and aids in healing when you enter au natural." Hazel hands me a towel.

A blush flares in my cheeks, and I grasp the towel. I glance at Katrina for guidance, but her wide eyes remind me that this is my decision. So why not?

When I've stripped off all my clothes, Katrina picks them up, folds them neatly, and sets them aside. I wrap the towel around myself, grateful for the bit of privacy it gives me as I move myself down the stairs. My feet touch the water first, and the warmth tickles my skin, luring me forward. When I slip under the surface, I feel like I'm floating in a warm, comfortable haze. I could fall asleep in here; if not for the other witches in the room, I probably would have.

Once I'm sitting on the bench and the water rises past my shoulders, Hazel says, "Good. That's good. How's the water?"

"It's nice." I let my arms float and my fingers relax.

"It's not too hot?"

I shake my head.

She nods and sits at the edge of the pool. "We'll start out slow." Her fingers dip into the water, and she closes her eyes, muttering a small spell. A trail of bright blue slips from her fingers into the water. When it touches my skin, it's like a tiny jolt of lightning. It recharges me, pulling away the fatigue and pain in my muscles.

"May I see your leg?" she asks.

"Which one?" I meant it as a joke, but it seems to go right over her head.

Her wide eyes narrow in sadness. "Whichever one you would like."

I lift my recently injured leg, since my original injury is impossible to cure; Ambrossi already proved that much. Hazel grasps my toes so gently that I barely feel her touch. Then she brushes her fingers over every rugged bruise and cut. Very gently, she pushes my leg toward me before pulling it back again to stretch it. The motion relaxes my muscles even more.

"How does that feel?"

"That's amazing," I say, wishing I could stay in this moment forever.

She smiles.

"Are you using magic for this?" Katrina asks, sitting beside Hazel to observe her work.

The Healer shakes her head. "It's all about the pressure points on the body."

Katrina nods, eyes wide with fascination as Hazel switches to my bad leg. Looking down, she studies the scars, old and new, and frowns just a little. The process with this leg is the same, but it clearly bothers her; Hazel knows as well as I do that there's no curing this one. The pain, however, has dulled so much that by the end of the session, it's hard to believe I was ever in pain at all.

Finally, she releases my foot into the water again. The warmth surges through me, and I feel like I'm floating on a cloud. I close my eyes, enjoying the moment, reveling in what it's like to not be in pain.

"How do you feel?" Hazel's soft voice drifts into my head.

"Amazing," I breathe. I'm so relaxed that I don't think I can ever move again.

Something prods my shoulders, and I struggle to open my eyes. Katrina crouches beside the pool to offer me her hand. I groan, already on the verge of sleep. Feeling this good is dangerous. Groggy, I lift my hand, breaking the hold of the water and grasp her fingers. She eases me out of the pool and hands me the towel. I pat myself dry, she grabs my clothes, and we work together to get me dressed again.

"I'm gonna put fresh bandages on your legs," Hazel says. "After the therapy, they help to keep your blood circulating."

I nod, and she disappears in search of supplies.

"That was some unique healing," Katrina muses.

"Do you think you'd be able to do it?" I ask. Someday, I plan to go home, back to the Elemental Coven, and if there's a witch there who can help ease my troubles like Hazel just did, I would be forever in their debt.

"Maybe," she says. "If I had some more training." Her eyes sparkle; she's *excited* by the idea of learning Hazel's techniques. Win-win. "Ready?"

I nod and let her pick me up to take me back out to the comfortable living area. She sets me on the closest seat before plopping down next to me. I stifle a yawn, glancing around for Hazel.

Then I hear someone climbing the rope to her house. Katrina and I both turn to see the witch who greeted us at the entrance to the Wilderness. My aunt. She smiles at me then Katrina as she moves into the room to take a seat with us.

My peace and gratitude disappears. I don't know what to say to this woman, if anything at all. If she's here, that means *she's* got something to say. Even if it's just to Hazel.

"Greetings," Molly says.

"Hello." Katrina offers a pleasant smile.

I don't move, waiting for cues as to what I should do, because I'm still grasping at straws.

Hazel appears then, supplies in hand, and gasps. "Miss Molly, my apologies. I didn't hear you come in."

"That's all right, Hazel. I don't mean to intrude. Just wanted to take a moment to talk with our new witches. See how they're settling in."

Hazel nods and approaches me, kneeling on the floor to spread out her supplies in a semicircle around her. I'm impressed with her attention to detail and find myself watching her pick through her supplies instead of looking at my aunt.

"Lilith, you've grown so well," Molly says, leaning back in her seat.

My eyes dart toward her. "You knew me when I was little?"

"Did I ever!" She nods with tears in the corners of her eyes. "You were the cutest baby. Ivy was so proud of you."

I stare at her tears, not understanding this reaction. "Oh, really?" It almost sounds like Ivy sent Molly in here just to talk her up, and I'm confused on multiple levels.

I look down at Hazel smearing a poultice on my leg, rubbing the green liquid in circles over my skin. Beside me, Katrina watches too.

"I know you find it hard to believe," Molly says, "but she was."

"*Was.*" I laugh. "What happened?"

"Life, I suppose. To make things simple, I *know* about you. Ivy told me everything, and I want you to know we're going to do what we can to keep you safe. Always. You're part of this Coven." Then she looks up at Katrina and adds, "You too, of course. But you, Lilith. You're important."

I look up at her. "In what context? We're *all* important. I don't want to be special. I've told Willow the same thing. I don't want to be protected unless the other witches in my Coven receive the same. They deserve it too."

Molly smiles; it's kind, full and warm, and entirely aggravating.

"What?" I snap.

"Ivy wasn't lying about your fire," she says, not at all

offended by my tone.

"Ivy lies about everything. That's the thing. Before today, I didn't know I had an aunt. She never mentioned you." Molly flinches. I don't mean to hurt her, but there's no way to say something like that without any sting at all. "Why didn't she?"

"You were rather young the last time you were here." Now the smile is completely gone. "I don't know why she never talked to you about me... I'm surprised. You lived here for such a long time."

"To be fair, I didn't know I had a mother for a while, either. I was adopted by a couple in Ignis. I really only met Ivy recently."

"Yes, she told me that too."

Did she tell Molly about abandoning me to be captured?

"If you're my aunt, why didn't I stay here with you when Ivy went into hiding? Why did she leave me with Larc?"

Molly sits quietly, tapping her fingers together in deep thought. "All families have their tragedies, and I'm sorry to say there's still quite a bit about your past that you seem unaware of."

I raise an eyebrow. "Like what?"

"Your, um... *sister* lived here for a bit too at one time." She clears her throat.

Katrina looks at me, so I ask the question we're both thinking. "Why are you talking about her like that?"

"Willow's not your sister. She's your cousin."

My jaw drops, and I gape at her. That was *not* the answer I expected. "No, she's my sister. She remembers."

"Willow doesn't know the entire story, either," Molly says. "She may be older than you, but she was still just a child when you were born."

"Oh, my Goddess." I press a hand to my forehead. Every time I think I know the truth, the rug gets pulled out from under me again. I'm starting to lose interest in the whole idea of truth. If I'm never going to learn it, my efforts might be better placed elsewhere. "I found a file in the Council's storage rooms. *That* says Willow and I are Ivy's daughters."

"And that's what they believe. *Willow* is Ivy's daughter." Molly pauses and licks her lips. "And you're mine."

"What?" I sit up so fast, I almost fall off out of the chair. Katrina catches me with a steadying hand. "*What?*" I nearly shout it this time.

Molly bows her head, eyes slightly narrowed in preparation for and dread of this reaction. "You're my daughter."

"So why am I just finding this out now? Why does *everyone* think Ivy's my mom?"

"She took care of you when I couldn't," Molly admits. "Your birth was... hard. I almost didn't make it, and the Healers had a difficult time getting me well again. I wasn't right for a long time. Mentally. And Ivy... did what she could to help. The Council saw her with you, and one thing led to another."

"I can... almost understand that," I concede, reading the honesty in her eyes. "But why did I have to leave this place? My home?"

"I didn't trust my Coven," Molly says, and I see a piece of myself in her then. "I was young and new to this Coven, and I didn't trust a soul with my precious daughter. Only my sister. After everything that drove me to come here, Ivy was the only person I could trust."

"Not my father?" I ask, raising an eyebrow.

"No, not even your father."

Katrina tilts her head, and I look at her as I ask my next question. "Who *is* my father?" I ask. "Or is that another question I'll never get the answer to?"

Molly doesn't say anything.

I breathe heavily through my nose. "Willow told me our dad died in the battle. When Ivy disappeared."

"*Willow's* father disappeared that day, but yours... we were never close. We spent one night together, and I never told

189

him about you."

"So where is he now?"

"I don't know," Molly admits. "We went our separate ways and never saw each other again. There's a good chance he's dead."

"Well, that's depressing." Honestly, it really doesn't bother me either way. I wasn't exactly close with Howard, my adopted father, and when he passed, it was much easier to live with the idea of not having a father than not having a mother.

"Maybe, but that's the full truth of your origins," Molly says with an empathetic shrug. "I promise."

"Is it? There aren't any more secrets being kept from me? Because this joke is getting old."

"Well, that's the story as I know it," Molly says.

"Then tell me what this place is," I demand. "Why are you here?"

"This Coven was here long before the Land of Five ever existed," she says calmly.

"What?" I tilt my head and frown at her.

Molly nods.

"I mean why are *you* here, specifically? I'm assuming you and Ivy were both born in Mentis."

"And we were. I came here as a fugitive from the Council when I was a few years younger than you are now."

I gesture toward my own face and study the charred, withered flesh on Molly's. "They did that to you, didn't they?"

She nods. "The Adept in my class was a... jealous witch. During our Arcane Ceremony, the Council looked to me instead of her, and she didn't take it well. She set my home on fire. Ivy got out just fine, but I... didn't. I was hurt for a long time, and the Council reconsidered their decision. That witch got what she wanted and took my place instead."

I cringe. Though this happened years before I was born, the pain in her voice is as strong as if this happened yesterday. I can understand her pain probably better than any other witch.

Even with magic, burns are hard to get over.

"And from then on, she tortured me every chance she had, going so far as to convince other members on the Council that I was a spy. I ran away... to protect Ivy and my parents. The fire could've killed any of them, after all, and I knew this witch didn't care who she hurt as long as she hurt *me*."

I frown at the ground. I hate to admit that I've met many witches like the one Molly mentioned—that there are more of them than good witches. "Unfortunately, that's how ninety-nine percent of the Council witches are. Wait. If the Council knows you're here, why haven't they come after you?"

Molly laughs. "Who says they can? Centuries ago, when Myalis led the Equipped away to create the Land of Five, we stayed here. Mostly, this Coven is made of the UnEquipped. Those with magic decide whether or not they want to use their powers, and if they do, we find them work suitable for their talents.

"Then witches from other Covens started to come to us, and we gave them a home here. We might not have understood the pressures that made them leave their Covens, because we only answer to ourselves. But we are a powerful group. We have thrived on the idea that no matter the situation, we provide shelter to witches who are hurt and in need."

It seems like an anomaly that this group can exist without the aid of the Council for all these centuries and still be virtually unchanged. Goes to show just how toxic the Council is. Even most of the land under their care is destroyed.

"If you're really mostly UnEquipped, how did you take care of yourselves for so long?"

"Everyone will fight when the things they love are at stake. regardless of whether they have powers."

Chapter Twenty-Nine
Mistakes

KATRINA AND I leave Hazel's house before Molly does. I can't take much more of whatever the witch has to say. We shuffle down the rope, and at the bottom, Katrina lifts me into her arms, staring through the forest.

"Where are we going?" I ask.

She shrugs. "I don't know. I figure you probably don't want to go back to our place yet."

"I really don't," I admit. In front of Crowe and Maverick, I'll have to act normal, like everything's the same when what I've just learned changes all of it.

"What are you going to do?" Katrina asks.

I don't know. How could I? "Is there anything I *can* do?"

"No, but... you must feel so lost."

I squint at her with just a bit of sarcastic appreciation. "That's been true for a while now. This changes nothing."

"Are you going to tell Willow?"

"I have to." And I wonder how she'll take it. "I mean, I'll have to let *everyone* know eventually, but not until she knows first."

Katrina nods. A bell tinkles through the darkness. She tilts her head to stare up into the mess of invisible branches far above our heads. "Hungry?"

Not really, but it's as good of an escape as any. "Yes." I let her carry me to the cafeteria, trying to forget everything Molly told me.

All the surviving members of the Elemental Coven have gathered in the cafeteria. Some of them stand in closer groups than the others. Quinn steps up beside Katrina and me as we get our food, and I look at him gratefully. I haven't had much time to connect with him lately, so even the small talk as we eat is fairly soothing. Ivy doesn't make an appearance during our meal. Neither does Molly. Maverick finds his way toward us halfway through the meal. I focus on eating, but I keep thinking about Molly and Ivy's disappearance. Has Molly told her sister yet that I know everything?

"You haven't seen your mom since you've been here, huh?" Maverick whispers in my ear so even Quinn doesn't hear.

I tense at the question, feeling tears stinging my eyes. My life has never been easy, but this morning showed me that it could be *easier*. I shake my head, not trusting myself to speak. I don't know if I should be worried, but with so much already in my head, I decide to push it aside. I can only take care of myself.

I set my fork down with a clang as soon as Darrius enters the room. I haven't seen many of the Wilderness witches—the UnEquipped in particular like to mind their own business—but the witches I *have* met I've seen quite a bit.

I scoff in audible disgust.

Quinn looks up at the entrance and laughs. "Not a fan?"

I shake my head and glance at Maverick. "When you're done, can you take me back to the cabin?"

"I can take you," Katrina says.

I cast her a sideways glance. I have nothing against Katrina. In fact, after this afternoon, she knows me better than anyone in the world. And for that same reason, I need my space.

Maverick must sense something's off, because he instantly sets down his fork. "Of course." When he stands, I reach toward him and let him pick me up like I'm two years old.

Katrina frowns at me. I've hurt her feelings, but with everything else going on, it's easy to file away. She'll be okay tomorrow.

"It's been a long day," I say, my mind drifting again to places I would rather not visit.

Maverick doesn't ask questions as we move through the cafeteria. When we pass Darrius, I accidentally catch his eye, and he grins.

"Leaving so soon?" he purrs. I try to ignore him—I'm in no mood for his shit—but he mutters, "Such a shame."

That gets under my skin, and I pat Maverick on the shoulder to stop him.

"He's not worth it, Lilith," Maverick mutters but he stops anyway.

I stare over his shoulder at Darrius. "What, pray tell, is such a shame that you have to whisper it *behind my back?*"

"You. Your whole attitude. When Ivy talked about you, I imaged you as... well, something completely different. And now?" He laughs and sticks his hands in his pockets.

"Now what? You're *underwhelmed?* Is that it? You're so caught off guard that you have to harass me every chance you get? Are you trying to change your image of me, or can you just not handle the fact that you don't have everyone's attention anymore? Not enough of your own drama?"

Darrius merely smiles.

"Let's just go," Maverick says and starts walking again.

"What? What is it? Why do you keep harassing me?" I snap at Darrius.

He lifts his hands in apathetic surrender. "I'm sorry. I meant no offense. It's just you look so... *soft* for being the Sage's apprentice."

Those words make Maverick stop again, and he turns, both of us glaring at Darrius.

I narrow my eyes at him. "And you think you know me

194

just by listening to the rumors? Or maybe you think *Ivy* told you everything you need to know about me. My... mother, who's been in my life for less than a year. I'd love to hear how many great stories she has of her and me together, because she is the *least* accurate source for that information. You don't know a damn thing about my life. Sure, you could've taken the time to ask me, but I get it. That's kind of hard to do with your head so far up your own ass—"

"Lilith, enough." Maverick takes a breath through his nose and turns again to leave the cafeteria. Multiple people stare at us now, and I can feel Maverick's discomfort. "Let's go."

"What? I'm giving him a dose of reality, and for those who've never had it, it's downright bitter."

Darrius sneers but doesn't say anything else as Maverick helps me down the rope. Normally, I'd be upset with Maverick for interrupting me, but I'm glad he did. I don't know when to stop, and I would've kept going if Maverick didn't call it quits. That doesn't change the fact that I'm so tired of people dumping their assumptions on me. Opinions are one thing; that's part of life. But I'm done with people constantly shoving those opinions down my throat.

"I'm not sorry for standing up for myself," I say once we're halfway down the rope.

"I didn't say you should be," Maverick replies, his voice wiped of emotion. "I can see why you don't like him."

"I wouldn't have had to say any of that if he'd just minded his own business."

"I understand." Maverick just nods, not irritated or offended but merely tired. I'm find with that, because I'm not in much of a talky mood either now. He gets us quickly back to the tiny, familiar enclosure of our cabin and takes me to my bed.

Either he's ready to be rid of me, or he senses just how finished I am with today. Whatever the case, I'm looking forward to sleep.

"Are you sure you're okay?" he asks, setting me on the

silver blanket.

I'm *really* not, but what difference would it make to say that out loud? Admitting how close I am to losing my mind won't bring Ambrossi back to life, it won't make Clio better, and it won't cure Willow of her beliefs that she's failed.

And it definitely won't erase Molly's words from my memory.

"I'll make it."

He nods, a flash of respect in his eyes. Again, I'm left with that feeling that he understands me more than he'll ever say. "Call if you need anything." Then he shuts the door.

I stare after him and lace my fingers. It's a hell of a punishment to feel restless and also be unable to walk.

But I can still go places.

If only that were enough to take me away from here forever.

Giving in, I close my eyes and relax against the bed. My fingers play with the soft edges of the blanket as I steady my breathing and slowly slip deeper into unconsciousness. My last astral journey brought me more than I could handle, so I vow not to go back to the Land of New Life again. Not until I absolutely have to. That leaves me with one place to explore—Aquais. Since Headquarters collapsed, I've had my questions and suspicions about Crowe's home Coven.

Now would definitely be the time.

I see my own feet moving across the ground, still amazed by my astral ability. Then I'm drifting toward Aquais, taking the same route Crowe used to take me around the Land of Five. When I cross the border, I don't feel the marshy waters saturating the ground. I glide through them with ease and remain comfortably dry. It's almost like I still have Kieran's stone—the magic one that keeps Aquais witches from getting wet.

I look up, at the giant hill in the middle of the Coven. There's Crowe's mansion—a grand structure housing both his family and the Aquais Adept. And who knows who else?

Crowe's a special witch, not just for his abilities but because he comes from the most important family in Aquais—the founders of the Coven. Seeing his home again brings all that information up to the surface.

Inside the mansion, I'm inundated with memories. Rena and Kieran and how warmly they welcomed me into their home. But the place is cold now. There's no greeting, no one excited to see me. The foyer is dark, and as I travel farther into the house, there are barely any lights *anywhere*.

It's weird, but I keep going, ignoring the discomfort in my gut. It *is* nighttime; they might all be asleep. Maybe. I shiver, and in the back of my mind, I'm thinking about my meeting with Tabitha. She knows I was snooping. Of course she did. They added so much information to that file, and if they haven't forgotten about me since I left, it'd be foolish of me to do the same.

The Sage probably told her to keep an eye out for me, though I'm still surprised that she guessed I'd come to them on *this* Realm. What else does the elderly witch really know about me?

I drift through the cafeteria, looking at the table and fighting back more memories. I'm sick with them. I travel on and on, but I don't find any other witches at all. I didn't know what I expected, but this certainly isn't it. It reminds me too much of Alchemy, the day we found all the witches dead.

At the very least, I should be able to find Kieran. Rain or shine, this *is* his home. I can't imagine him abandoning it now. I make it to the master bedroom and look inside, but it's empty. I check the room across the hall and find Kieran tucked into the blankets.

His face is scruffy and unshaven, and the warmth of his character in my memories is gone. He looks at least a decade older. These past few months haven't been easy for anyone, it seems. I stare at him, wishing so badly that I could reach out and ease his pain, let him know that his family is alive and well—in a manner of speaking—but I can't.

This is something he'll have to handle on his own, and I pray he has enough strength to keep himself afloat. With great effort, I leave the room and find Grail, the Aquais Adept, a few doors down. I have no sympathy for this witch who took away my ability to walk. It's probably a good thing that I can't move objects in this form, or I'd be even more tempted to suffocate him with his own pillow.

I leave his room, eager to see who else I'll find. One of the other bunker witches, Sabrina, is asleep in the next room. Lynx occupies the room after that. It's just as I thought; the Council is working on something in Aquais. I keep searching for the other Council members and eventually find Rayna but not Hyacinth.

That's definitely odd.

I drift back into the hallway and stop when I see Tabitha again.

"Hello, girlie!" she bellows.

I scream myself awake in my own body, staring at the darkness outside my window. My gut churns; I may have just made a big mistake I won't be able to fix this time.

Chapter Thirty
Divination

*T*HAT FEELING THAT stays with me for the rest of the next day. Surprisingly, no one heard me scream last night, and when I wake for the second time hours later, sunshine streams through the veil over the window. I blink and cover my eyes, grateful that at least I won't have to lie about what I saw.

Katrina takes me to Hazel again for my water therapy session, and then we all eat lunch in a group—Katrina, Hazel, Crowe, Maverick, and me. Barely touching my food, I say as little as possible just to get through the meal. No one seems to notice my withdrawal, and I start to wonder if they actually *prefer* me this way. That, of course, makes me shrink farther into myself.

When we return to the cabin, I try to drag myself into my room, but Maverick stops me. He pulls me back into one of the chairs in the living room and sits down with me, watching my intently. "Something's wrong," he says.

"Yeah." I stare into his eyes, waiting for him to look away first.

He widens his eyes, urging me to speak. If this continues, he'll win our staring contest.

"I... took another trip," I begin.

"To see Willow?" he asks, cocking an eyebrow.

I shake my head, hating how disappointed he looks. "To Aquais."

He frowns and tilts his head, as if I've said something profound. "Why there?"

"I've had my suspicions for a while," I admit. "After Headquarters was destroyed, I figured the Council would find a new base of operations. And I was right. It seems they're setting themselves up in Crowe's mansion, which makes sense. He always said his family was their number-one supporter."

Maverick nods. "I can see that, actually."

"I was partly right," I say slowly. "There were witches there from the bunker, along with Rayna and Lynx, but I didn't see Hyacinth or the Sage."

Maverick shrugs. "That's not too strange. Maybe Hyacinth went to Aens to stay with her mother and the Sage is hiding somewhere else."

"Yeah, maybe. Where would she go" It both does and doesn't make sense that she would seclude herself. Isn't she worried of being attacked?

But I guess when she's the most powerful witch in the land, she doesn't have to waste her time worrying. My nose twitches in irritation.

"What else did you see?" Maverick sounds a little impatient now.

"More like... someone saw *me*."

Maverick hunches over beside me on the couch, his eyes wide with desperation as he leans so close, his fingers press into the couch. "Who?"

"Tabitha."

"T-Tabitha." He puffs out a huge, surprised breath. "Tabitha. Okay, well, um..."

"It's bad," I say.

He straightens, ruffling back his hair. "It might not be."

"And that might be an honest statement." I scoff. "This is terrible, actually. More than terrible, since this is the second time she's seen me."

"Shit."

I couldn't have summed it up better myself. "Yeah, that's what I said."

"Have you told anyone else about this? Molly or Ivy?"

The mention of their names makes me pause. I try to speak, but it's like my tongue is choking me, preventing anything from coming out.

"We should tell them. Molly, at least. She deserves to know, just in case. So she can protect her people," Maverick says.

The thought makes me sick, but I nod. He's right. I had the same thought. I couldn't bear it if I brought harm to Molly and the Wilderness after the kindness they've all extended to us.

Even if it is for biased reasons.

When Maverick doesn't leave, I realize he wants to do this *now*. Since I've already agreed, I can't back out. So I pretend that nothing's wrong, that I'm in this mission one-hundred-percent just like him. "Help me find her?"

"I will in a minute," he says.

Now I'm confused.

"I want to try something," he explains.

I raise an eyebrow. "Try what?"

"Your divination."

"I don't have divin—"

He shushes me. "We'll see one way or another." Maverick stands and quickly leaves the room before disappearing down the hall.

I throw my hands up in exasperation and let them fall back to the couch. I miss being able to chase people down when they walked out on me mid-conversation. "Okay, fine. What are you thinking?" I call, hoping he can still hear me.

Maverick doesn't answer. But he does come back with a

bowl of water, grabs a handful of ashes and soot from the fireplace, and tosses them in. Once he mixes it with his finger, he hands the bowl to me.

"What the hell do I do with this?" I groan, convinced he's going to ask me to *drink* the concoction.

"Patience," he says and moves across the room to grab a book from one of the shelves.

"You know, I'm getting real tired of people telling me that."

"Then maybe pick up the skill, and we won't have to say it anymore," he jokes.

"You're hilarious." I roll my eyes.

"I know." Maverick lifts the book. "Now, I'm going to hide this, then you tell me where it is."

"And I need the water for that why, exactly? I can just read your mind."

Maverick sighs and rolls his eyes right back. "Since you want to be a spoilsport…"

I see the metal wall go up in the front of his mind. "Not playing around, then," I say. "Okay. Fair enough. Hide the book."

He smiles and prepares to do just that. I look down at the murky water in my lap and stare so long, so hard that I feel like I'm parting the individual molecules with my thoughts alone. I don't hear Maverick return until he says, "Okay, tell me where I hid it."

I stare into the water a few moments longer and blink to break the connection. Setting the bowl on the floor, I reach up for him to lift me from the couch. Then he settled me on his hip, and I guide him down the hall and into my room.

"Put me down," I tell him. He does and studies me closely. I drag myself across the floor, trying not to focus on how dusty it really is, and toward the bed. Then I prop myself up with one hand and reach between the mattress and the bedframe with the other. It's just too easy to find the book.

THE SAGE

When I look back at him, he smiles. "Still going to say you don't have it?"

Chapter Thirty-One
Strengths and Weaknesses

*A*S MAVERICK TAKES me to Molly's, my head swims with what I've just learned. Divination is powerful, and it now means I have a power from every Coven. How could Maverick know when I had no idea? Do I really have such little faith in myself? I look down at my hands and then my useless legs. It's hard to believe that a being as pathetic as I am really possesses all these powers.

That's irony for you.

I'm so lost in my own head that I don't even realize we're reached the next tree until Maverick starts climbing. This tree is smaller than the others with the easiest climb we've managed yet. When we reach the top and Maverick picks me up again, we stare at her home. Not only is Molly's tree the smallest, but so is her house.

Unlike Hazel's den, Molly's door is closed. Awkwardly, Maverick arranges me so that he can reach out and knock. After just a few seconds, she opens the door. Her thin lips spread into a smile.

"Lilith and Maverick. This is a surprise! What can I do for you?"

"We'd like to talk to you for a moment," Maverick says.

What an understatement.

"Of course, of course." Molly steps aside to allow him in.

The house has accommodations for only one witch. She looks comfortable, though, as she encourages us inside. Maverick sets me down on a couch and sits beside me.

Molly takes a tiny wooden chair from the kitchen and settles it across from us, sinking into the seat. "So what's on your mind?"

Maverick looks at me, but I'm at a loss as to how we should begin. It seems crass and rude to blurt out that I might've brought harm to this woman's entire Coven, especially provided the secret we share.

"I'm not sure you're aware of everything Lilith can do," Maverick starts for me. "But one of her abilities is astral projection."

Molly's eyebrows lift quickly. "Ah. That's impressive." That twinkle in her eye goes beyond pride and simple adoration.

I hate it. "Yeah, but I—"

"What did you see?" Her voice is far calmer than my own.

"Tabitha saw *me*. Tabitha is—"

"I know all about her," Molly says. "The Council spy."

"I'm sorry. I really didn't mean to."

Molly smiles. "What are you sorry for? You've done nothing wrong."

"But the Council—"

"Has always known we are here. Fighting them is not anything new, nor is it something we are unprepared for. Though we are outside the Land of Five, I'm afraid that doesn't quite spare us from their reach."

"So… you aren't mad?" I ask, sounding small and innocent like a scolded five-year-old.

"No. We'll do what we must to survive. That's what we've always done."

For a moment, it feels as if *we* refers to her and me on a more personal level rather than the entire Coven. Either way, she's right.

"If the Council are coming, we'll be prepared. Just like we always are," she assures me. "Don't worry."

"That's a relief." Really, she has no idea *how* much her words have placated me. The idea of damning these people, Hazel and Molly, makes me sick. I never would've guessed they could be ready to go to war at the drop of a hat, but I don't doubt Molly's words. That stare of hers is chilling, making it so easy to believe that she's seen things that would break most people. Willow has the same look in her eyes. Even though it's hard for me to *want* to trust anyone, I trust her.

Maybe it's dumb, but I have to let myself trust *someone*.

"If I may say so, you are an impressive young witch, Lilith. Ivy didn't tell me you were capable of such a power."

I open my mouth with only venom on my tongue, but Maverick stops me from unleashing it. "If you think *that's* amazing, she has powers from all the Covens."

Molly leaps to her feet like someone just shoved her out of the chair.

I tense, watching her uncertainly and preparing for her to walk away.

She shakes her head, her black hair barely moving, before she sits back down again. "I-I'm sorry. I… have never heard of such a thing. A couple powers here and there, sure. But *all* of them? Together?"

"That's why the Council's after her," Maverick says.

I shrug. "What can I say? I'm an anomaly."

"And you should wear it proudly. It's a title not just anyone earns." The puckered scars on the left side of her face twist as she smiles.

Maverick laughs. I might have taken that comment as an insult at one time, but today, I don't. I like what she said, and she's right, in a way. Instead of being ashamed of myself—ashamed of my abilities—I should embrace being so powerful that witches have been out for my blood since before I was born.

***

I'M UNEASY FOR the rest of the evening. As much as I wish I could sleep, I can't. I keep thinking about the conversation with Molly, like my body knows something my brain does not.

Divination does not lie.

Maverick and I tell Katrina and Crowe about my run-in with Tabitha, and I know I'm not the only one finding it difficult to sleep. I don't like to pry into the minds of the witches close to me, but in the stillness of the cabin, it's impossible not to. I hear Katrina and Crowe every few minutes. Maverick's voice fills my ears less frequently, but it's there, nonetheless.

It's like we all know we're standing on the verge of something and we've made a subconscious link, prepared to leap into battle at the first sign of danger. I hear movement in the room behind mine and again down the hall. Everyone in here is awake, preparing in their own ways for what's to come. After everything Maverick learned about me and the Wilderness, Maverick's perhaps the most prepared. Poor Crowe is the least. He's kept to himself since we got here, and as far as gaining new information goes, he's paying for it.

I push my Covenmates from my mind and try to tap into my telekinesis, desperate to test out *something*. At one time, this was my strongest power, but as the others emerged, it waned to just a fleeting ability.

Still, curiosity is a demon. I reach with my telekinesis, using my original power to first lift a book. This I lift up and down a few times, testing the threshold of my powers like lifting weights. They seem as strong as the last time I used them, but somehow, I doubt that's the truth. I sit up, setting the book back down onto the wardrobe, then look down at my legs. The floor seems miles beneath me, and I barely remember what it feels like to walk. I try to imagine it, but even the awkward gait I used ninety-percent of my life doesn't come to mind. What little walking I'd experienced feels like a memory—a dream in someone else's head. I study the distance again, playing with fire just to see how bad it really burns.

"What the Hell…" I sharpen my mind and step slowly off the bed. Razor-sharp pain shoots up both legs, and I grit my teeth, trying to keep myself upright. The magic isn't enough.

I collapse to the floor with a heavy thud and a shout of pain. Footsteps race down the hall. Maverick bursts into my room, closely followed by Crowe and Katrina.

"What happened?" Katrina asks, wrapping her arm around my waist as soon as she reaches me.

"Nothing." I stare at the floor. My cheeks feel hot, and I don't know why I'm *embarrassed* to say what I did—to admit that not even my primary power can help me past the damage to my legs.

Judging by the next minute of silence, I can tell they've all guessed it anyway.

"Let's get you off the floor." She and Maverick ease me back onto the bed.

I say nothing. Oscillating between depression and shame, I have no brain capacity left for speech.

"Lilith, it's going to be okay," Crowe says uncertainly from the doorway.

I blink and scowl at him. "Says the guy who can literally be anything."

He drops his gaze and hunches his shoulders, and I feel instantly guilty for going for his throat.

"Can I just be alone, please?" It comes out so quietly, I'm worried I'll have to repeat myself just so they hear me.

"Yeah." I actually appreciate that knowing look in Maverick's eyes now.

THE SAGE

He and Crowe leave quickly, but Katrina hesitates. She stands beside the bed, staring at me with her powerful blue eyes. "You're a strong witch, Lilith. You're going to get through this. Somehow, some way, you're going to make it through. Just remember what Molly's gone through. You two share the same blood."

"I appreciate it. Really." I close my eyes. Her words might be sweet, but they don't warm me the way she probably hopes they will. I just want her to go away.

When I open my eyes again, she's standing beside the door. "Let me know if you need anything, okay?" She starts to close the door but stops with wide eyes.

"What is it?" I follow her gaze out the window and see it too—the kind of light that only comes from a fire.

The Council have arrived.

Chapter Thirty-Two
Battle of the Wilderness

"**L**ILITH, STAY HERE," Katrina orders, already in battle mode. She looks around the room and at the door, searching for a way to lock it. When she finds none, she gives me another stare over her shoulder and hurries out.

"Wait! Bring me with you!" It's no use.

She doesn't come back; she doesn't want me to go. I scream anyway, hoping I'll catch Crowe or Maverick's attention. After a minute of trying, I realize the cabin's completely silent. Empty. They've all gone to join the fight, leaving me here like the burden I am. I've never felt so useless in my entire life. Then I remind myself that at one time, I didn't have *any* powers. Even when Willow had her doubts about me, she brought me with her to battle to see how I would do.

I've always been at the center of every conflict. And that's not about to change now.

I stare at the ground and throw myself to the floor anyway. My wrists, elbows, and knees flare with pain, and I wait for the agony to subside before I pull myself across the floor, tears welling in my eyes. I don't know if they're from the pain or my humiliation.

It takes forever to drag myself out of the room, but I try not to focus on that, on how slowly I'm making progress. I try to content myself with the fact that I *am* making progress.

When I finally pass through the hall and across the living room, I stare at the rope ladder disappearing into the abyss below. Down there are the sounds I've grown accustomed to—curses of pain, spells, and death blows. Except this battle is so much worse. There are UnEquipped in this fight, more of them than in any other Coven in the Land of Five. Every UnEquipped I've ever known runs at the first sign of conflict, hoping to stay hidden until the battle is over.

These ones are much more capable. They fight back—with rocks, swords, and their hands—in any way that can to protect themselves. Staring into the darkness feels just like staring into that bowl of water. The images filling my mind make me freeze, mostly because I quickly focus in on the witches I know. I see Quinn, his arm still wrapped in bandages, trying to conjure his telekinesis before he's sent flying across the forest floor. Then I see his opponent—*Rayna*, his own sister.

I can hardly believe what I'm seeing as she moves toward him with a giant rock lifted over her head. She's going to kill her own brother.

"Quinn!" I cry.

I want to help Quinn, to save him, but there's no way I can make it down in time. Ignoring the burning tears, I try to block out the image before I see the end, positive that Rayna will win this fight just because she has the upper hand.

Then it changes.

Quinn's eyes glow, and Rayna laughs, assuming it's his faulty magic. I see a discarded sword lying on the ground, just out of Rayna's sight. When she's a step away from her brother, the sword plunges forward through her neck and out the other side. Neither of them move. Then Quinn begins to cry, a broken man, watching his sister slump to the ground beside him, covered in her own blood.

Next, I see Crowe in full snake form, biting into Councilmember Sabrina's arm. She swats him away but collapses a moment later. I already know she'll never get up again. Crowe's giant snake form disappears into the shadows.

"Lilith!" a voice yells beside me, and I jump, pulling my vision back to my own surroundings.

Willow crouches on the threshold beside me, her black eyes wide in the darkness.

"Willow? What are you doing here?" I gape at her.

"Ivy brought me. We need to get out of here."

"But what about—"

"We can't worry about them," she says, clearly frustrated. "We need to get you somewhere safe."

"Why *me*? Witches are *dying* down there."

"And Goddess willing, I'll be able to bring them back when the time is right. Now let's go."

"But the Sickness—"

She pretends not to hear me, glancing down at the ladder just as Maverick makes an appearance.

"This is no time to be stubborn, Lilith," he says.

He's right, but he jumps up onto the threshold and scoops me into his arms before I can admit it. Grabbing the rope, he makes his descent, Willow shuffling down a moment behind. Then we're in it—the same carnage I watched from the treetops. Maverick and Willow run through the trees, ducking and dodging away from the sparring masses. Maverick's ability makes it easier, literally leaving witches on their knees as we pass.

In the shadows, the witches who have already fallen are rough shapes against the dark undergrowth. I try not to see faces on any of them as we rush through, and for the most part, it's easy. I can tell myself they're nothing more than part of the background, the scenery, and in that way, it's almost like they were never alive at all. Then Willow stops, causing Maverick to turn back frantically. She drops beside a body, and beyond its size, it's hard to make out any details. Maverick brings us closer, and a passing glint of torchlight reveals shaggy aquamarine hair and matching eyes.

It's Lynx, the Council's healer—the only witch who's ever been able to cure magical damage. And he's dead.

Willow bends over, trying to slip her arms beneath his massive form.

"Willow! What are you doing?" Maverick demands.

"We can't leave him here!" She grunts and shifts around, trying to move him. She's too small, and no matter her position, she can't pick him up.

I'm stunned by this display, not sure whether we should help her or drag her away. "But he's one of them."

"It doesn't matter." She grunts again and sits back. "He was just doing what he had to do. We *need* him. I won't let him die like this."

Maverick growls, but he knows better than to argue with Willow, especially when she's like this. She won't leave until she gets her way, and the longer we stay here, the more danger we face.

"I got him," he tells Willow.

When she turns to face him, he passes me over into her arms. She grunts in surprise and watches Maverick heave Lynx's enormous body off the ground. Blood pours from the wound in the Healer's neck, but Maverick doesn't seem to notice. It soaks through his clothes, and he keeps moving, shooting us a look that keeps both Willow and me silent all the way to the portal.

Chapter Thirty-Three
The Last Hope

ANE OFFERS A grim welcome on the other side of the portal, his eyes grazing over the boy in Maverick's arms. I thought I'd be relieved to see the purple plants and the strange, empty sky in the Land of New Life again, but I don't feel anything close to that. My heart's still thumping wildly as I keep reliving the battle we just escaped—all the witches we've left behind.

We go straight to Willow's mansion, though I'm not sure who's leading whom since none of us speak. The silence is so complete, I wonder if I've lost my hearing. I reach up, clap a hand over my ear, and move it just to make sure.

Maverick opens the door for us then leads us to the very first bedroom. With a hefty sigh, he rests Lynx on the blankets.

We all stare at the Healer, at the glazed look of his empty eyes and the blood smeared all over his neck and torso. "I'll go get Lazarus." Maverick takes off for the Community Villa.

Willow sets me down in an armchair in the corner of the room and purses her lips. She looks like she'd be crying if she was still physically capable of doing so. The sadness with which she eyes Lynx tugs at my heartstrings. It's hard to believe they're strangers.

THE SAGE

"What's wrong?" I ask.

She bites her lip, swiping a lock of brown hair over her ear. "I'm terrified I'm going to fail again."

"You won't." I reach out to lay a hand on her crossed arms. The gesture is meant to make her feel better, but it's awkward, made worse by how flimsy my words sound. Under the circumstances, it was the best I could come up with, but I have no faith in them. I don't even know if her magic will work now.

After the Sickness, I've come to doubt everything I thought I knew. One thing is for sure—if it *doesn't* work, if Lynx is gone forever, I don't know what we can do to fix this. Maybe there's nothing we *can* do.

Willow holds my gaze, then turns away. Her tiny form strides across the room before she gently strokes Lynx's cheek with the back of her hand, like a mother caring for her sickly child.

"Won't know until I try." She says it so quietly, I almost don't hear her. Then she takes a deep breath, her chest rattling, and a purple light shoots out of her, tying her to the prone form beneath her. The light wraps around Lynx and then Willow, glowing brightest through her eyes. Halfway through the spell, Maverick dashes into the room, wide-eyed and out of breath, with Lazarus in tow.

Lazarus' eyes are blue pools of sorrow, and he crouches down beside the bed opposite Willow, staring at Lynx's face. He doesn't blink or flinch away from the blinding light of Willow's magic, and I have to give him credit for it. I can hardly *look* at my sister ... cousin ... whatever she is, but Lazarus is so concerned about Lynx, his prodigy, the light of all his apprentices, that it doesn't matter. Like Willow, I assume that if Lazarus could cry, he would.

Maverick, still standing close by the door, catches my gaze. We're both thinking the same thing; there's a lot weighing on this moment, and everyone in the room knows it. Maverick

215

didn't want to hurt Willow's feelings, but I suspect he's been worried since we found Lynx—worried that maybe she was losing her magic.

At last, the light fades, and Willow drops to the floor. Maverick rushes forward to catch her, cradling her to his chest as he always does after a spell. He glances at me again, desperate for answers, and I look at the bed. There's no movement, and we're all dreading the same thing.

It didn't work. My heart sinks into my stomach with a painful flip. I look away from Lynx and Maverick to stare at the floor, praying to the Goddess with everything in me.

"D-did it work?" Willow's small, trembling voice lifts into the silence as she stirs from her fainting spell.

Maverick and I lock eyes again, unsure who should be the one to break the news. He opens his mouth. "Uh…"

The best sound in the world cuts him off—a massive gasp from Lynx.

Chapter Thirty-Four
Fall Apart

EVERYONE LEAPS TO their feet at the sound. I lean sideways, propping myself up with as far as I can with one arm. It's a crummy view, but it's enough to see what I need to see. Lynx coughs, and Willow goes to him, whispering comforting words in his ears. She smoothes his hair from his face just as his eyes open, the once aquamarine orbs now black pits with just a hint of blue in a thin ring. He looks around, seemingly unaware of everyone else until his gaze lands on Lazarus.

Lynx opens his mouth, but no words come out, only a strangled series of croaks and gasps. Maverick gently touches Willow's back—a gentle attempt to pull her away—but she struggles for her space, staring down at her newest creation. She swipes at his hair again, and I look at the ring on her finger. When I first came to the Elemental Coven, Maverick told me what that ring really does; it connects her to all the Reanimates. Watching this scene now, I wonder just how deep that bond goes. Does she *feel* what Lynx feels? Can he really communicate with her through a piece of jewelry?

Maverick drops his hand and steps back, realizing he's interfering more than helping as he looks at me again. Then he steps toward me and mutters, "Let's give them a minute."

Irritation flashes through me. I don't want to leave, not even for a second. I want to be here for Willow if something goes wrong. I don't know what *could* go wrong at this point, but life always has a way of surprising me, and I don't trust this—the sudden feeling that everything's going to be okay.

"I don't *want* to go," I say, trying to look around him at the group of Reanimates.

"This moment… isn't about you," he says and picks me up anyway.

"Hey!" I struggle against him, turning back to look at Willow.

"Let them get Lynx situated."

I huff and fold my arms, but he's made his point. So I let him carry me outside and wait until the door closes before I ask, "Where are we going?"

"You have some business to attend to, if I remember correctly."

"What?" Nothing could be as important right now as what's going on in the room we just left.

Maverick raises his eyebrows as we make our way out of Willow's mansion, and now my mind turns to Clio and Ambrossi. Willow saved Lynx, and maybe that means Lynx can save Clio. It's too late for Ambrossi. Astral projection gave me a glimpse of what happened, but seeing it in reality will be harder, more painful.

We're silent as he traverses through the maze of purple plants. The first time I saw them, their beauty amazed me. They do nothing for me now. Deep in the pits of my grief, they do nothing at all. Maverick rounds the door into the Community Villa, his footsteps echoing just like the last time I was here, and it makes my skin crawl.

"It doesn't sound like anyone's here," I say, glancing around.

Maverick breathes in slowly. "They might not be."

"Not even the Reanimates?"

He bites his lip.

"Maverick?"

"No, the Reanimates probably aren't here," he admits. "It's, uh... my understanding that there are only dead witches behind the closed doors."

I turn to study the doors lining the hallway and blink, unable to process what I'm seeing. *All* the doors are closed. "They're... *here?* In the building? Why haven't they been buried?"

"Do you really think Willow had the time?"

"Good point." I purse my lips. "Which one is Ambrossi in?"

He doesn't need to say anything as he moves purposefully down the hall. It makes me wonder how much time he actually spent in the Wilderness and how many times he came back during those few days to visit. When we make it to Ambrossi's door, the reality of what we'll find behind it hits me, and I freeze. I don't want to go inside. Picturing what I've already seen, I *can't* go inside.

"He's... he's not *decomposing*, is he?" I clutch Maverick a little tighter. I don't know when Ambrossi died, but I know it wasn't recently. That thought cuts me in ways I haven't been hurt yet.

Maverick shakes his head. "The Healers cast spells to preserve the bodies until things settle down enough for us to properly bury them all."

That's some relief.

"I don't think I can go in there," I admit.

Maverick frowns. "With everything you've been through, I don't believe that. You're stronger than you give yourself credit for."

"He was like my brother... as weird as that sounds. The thought that he's actually gone... I mean, seeing is believing, you know? If I don't go in there, if I don't see him like that, maybe I can just pretend he's still…" I swallow, the words sticking in my throat, and look down at the floor.

Maverick purses his lips. "I could say something, but I honestly doubt it would make you feel better."

"Say it anyway." There's no possible way I could feel worse.

"He died as he lived, Lilith. He wanted to help witches so badly, he gave his life for his cause. There's nothing nobler than that."

Tears well in my eyes, but I don't want to admit it. Damn him for being right.

"Ready to go in now?" he asks.

"As ready as I can be."

Maverick slowly opens the door, as if he thinks I'm going to change my mind at any moment. Somehow, I don't, and then we're in the room, beside the bed—the bed where Ambrossi's dead body lies. Contrary to popular belief, he doesn't look like he's sleeping; he looks like the Sickness that killed him. His cheeks are sunken in, there are bags under his eyes, and his skin looks leathery.

It's like a being made to look like him rather than Ambrossi himself.

"I can give you a minute alone, if you'd like," Maverick offers.

I cling to his arm. "No, don't go. Please, don't go."

"Okay." He holds me a little tighter to comfort me.

I look at Ambrossi again, studying him from his head to his feet. There are probably hundreds upon thousands of things I could say to him, that I *should* say to him, but none of them come to mind.

"I love you, and…" I stare at the body that once belonged to my favorite Healer. I want to say something else like that, something sweet, something that shows just how much he meant to me. Instead, when I look at him, all I can say is the one thing I think every time I've let someone down. "And I'm sorry."

Maverick frowns. "Hey… what—"

"Don't," I say, reading his mind—that he thinks I have nothing to apologize for.

But an apology is all I have. If I'd done something, or *tried,* maybe I could've helped him. Maybe I could've kept him away from whoever passed him the Sickness. If I'd ever tried to explore healing, maybe I could've made the cure.

A tear rolls down my cheek and lands on the white sheet beside Ambrossi's stiff arm. It soaks into the fabric, a splash of darkness against the light. No matter what I think, it's all just speculation now, because I'll never know the answers. I can't turn back time.

"Let's go, please," I say, and more tears break free, dripping onto my arm and Maverick's.

He hesitates.

"Please." It barely comes out in a breathy whisper.

Finally, he takes us from the room, and when he closes the door behind us, I still don't want to breathe. My chest feels like someone has stabbed me with a white-hot poker. If the mind really has power over the body, a simple command should have been enough to make the pain disappear. If I tell myself I'm not sad, shouldn't it be so? But I still *feel* it, sharp and hot like a blast of magic passing through my brain, destroying every rational thought in my head.

I don't want to do it, but I fall apart. Every piece of me crumbles until there's nothing left to break.

Chapter Thirty-Five
Mourning

AVERICK IS UNCOMFORTABLE with my raw display of emotion. I see it on his face, but I also can't blame him. If someone started crying in my arms, I would feel the same way. Maverick didn't know Ambrossi as well as I did. Still, it upsets me that he isn't as broken as I am over the Healer's fate. I want Maverick to feel my pain—every ounce of it. Feeling something this heavy by myself is a punishment I'm sure I don't deserve.

I'm a blubbering mess by the time the crying fit passes. I gasp for breath, trying to regain control, and I'm not sure if this is better or worse than the previous ten minutes of crying. Maverick pats my back gently, most likely hoping I'm finished so we can resume our lives.

My pain fades into a heavy numbness, a deep nothing in the pit of my stomach, and I embrace it. For a few minutes, it's nice to let myself succumb, to feel nothing at all. If it meant never feeling pain like that again, I could live with this numbness for the rest of my life. As Maverick weaves through the halls of the Community Villa and I see just how many doors are closed, I grow to despise this numbness. No, the absence of emotion is so much worse than the stronger wave of anger and despair. It's like my heart has died and can never be brought back to life.

I wish I could sleep for a month or two.

"I hate to say this, to be the bearer of bad news—"

"Could've fooled me."

"—but there's one more stop on this floor."

"Please take me back to Willow. I don't think I can take another minute of this place." I hope he has sympathy somewhere in him.

"But Clio wants to see you."

That's all he has to say to change my mind. If Clio wants to see me, that means he's still alive. And with life comes hope. It breaks its way through the numbness in my chest, a tiny light in the blackness, and I hold onto it like a lifeline. If it goes out, I'll plunge back into the darkness, and I most likely won't come back out.

Clio is in the same room he shared with Ambrossi, though now that second bed is empty. I hold my breath as we pass it, imagining what Clio must look like today. All I can see is Ambrossi's withered flesh, and I try to imagine Clio with the same pallor. The sight frees a few more tears. If Maverick notices, he doesn't say anything.

When we reach Clio's bedside, Thorn and Callista are hovering around, various herbs in their tiny hands. Maverick freezes instantly, and I remember that he didn't know they were here.

"Wh—"

"It's okay. They're doing me a favor," I tell him.

"Does Willow—"

"No."

Thorn watches us with dark eyes, uncertainty flitting across her face. She looks ready to fly away at a moment's notice.

Conflicted emotions tear across Maverick's face. "Lilith, how could you—"

"Please don't say anything else." I glance sharply at him.

"I'll tell her when I get a chance, but they're trying to help."

He says nothing, but I'm relieved. That's as close to acceptance as he'll get. I'll take it. At last, I turn my attention to Clio. He looks about how I imagined—more like Ambrossi than I would like to admit. He's lying on his back in the bed, his eyes closed, his face turned toward the wall.

"Clio," I whisper.

He opens his eyes with what looks like great effort and smiles up at me. "Hello, beautiful." His voice is so rough, it sounds like he swallowed a bowl full of glass.

My heart melts to pieces, and I look at Maverick. "Put me down next to him, please."

"Lilith—"

"Now!" Why is he hesitating? Wasn't it his idea to bring me here in the first place?

Maverick grimaces and sets me down on the mattress. "I'll be back in a minute," he promises, but I wave him off.

He's worried about contamination, but I'm not. If I haven't gotten sick by now, I mostly likely won't. Even if I do, what does it really matter? I try to curl closer to Clio, but it's hard. The smell of vomit is overwhelming, couple with the reeking Sickness. He's lost so much weight that his bones nearly protrude through his skin, making it almost impossible to cuddle with him.

"We'll give you a minute alone," Callista says before she and Thorn follow Maverick into the hall.

"How are you doing?" I ask, reaching up with shaking fingers to swipe a thin lock of his black hair off his clammy forehead. It's the one loving gesture I can still manage. I'm not used to seeing his hair in his face. When he's well, it's almost always slicked back.

"I've been better." Clio nuzzles closer to me, pressing a kiss to my forehead. His lips are so dry and warm, it doesn't feel nearly as tender as it should. "Seeing you again makes it easier."

I frown. "Makes *what* easier?"

"Li, I'm sick, not stupid. I know what my future is now that I have this."

"That's not going to be you." Now I'm angry, blaming him for breaking the moment, for making me face the reality I want nothing more than to ignore.

"We lost *Ambrossi*," he says and breaks into a coughing fit.

With trembling lips, I pat his back until it stops. A glob of blood lands onto his blanket. He doesn't seem to notice it, but I can't tear my eyes away.

"If this can kill him, it can kill anyone," Clio says.

"No, Clio. No." I grab his chin to look him right in the eyes. "Because now we have a weapon we didn't have when Ambrossi was sick. We have Lynx."

"Lynx?" His voice is soft. "As in *Councilmember Lynx*?"

I nod. "He's here, and he's alive. He's going to make you better."

Clio smiles at me but says nothing.

"What?"

He shakes his head.

"What is it?"

"It's like you said about your legs. There *is* no making anything better."

My heart breaks all over again.

"Come on, Lilith. Time's up." Maverick strolls into the room.

"No. I want to stay." I push myself even closer to Clio.

"We need to go." Maverick slips his arms under my back.

"I said no!" I roar, grasping the metal bedframe as he tries to pick me up.

Clio's eyes are glazed over. "It's okay, Lilith."

My mouth falls open at this acceptance of his that only feels like a betrayal. Finally, my fingers slip loose, but I'm kicking and screaming the entire time Maverick drags me across the room. I don't want to go. I've never seen Clio so vulnerable in my entire life, and I don't know what to do. Leaving won't help me figure it out. We almost make it out the door when Callista and Thorn return. I reach out and capture Callista between my hands. She stares at me with wide eyes, and Maverick stops in disbelief.

"Did you find out anything about the Sickness?" I demand.

She shakes her head. "It's powerful magic. That's all I know. I've done what I can to alleviate the pain and vomiting for Clio, but the Sickness is winning. My magic will not work much longer, I'm afraid."

I translate that to mean that if Lynx doesn't regain his abilities soon, I'll lose Clio forever.

Chapter Thirty-Six
Prisoners of War

SILENT TEARS RUN down my face when we make it back to Willow's room. I'm tired of crying, truth be told, but I can't stop. It's embarrassing, this open display of humanity. Callista gave me the most sympathetic look I've received in a while on the way out of Clio's room, and for the briefest moment, I assumed she would say something useful— that she had a spell or a treatment for the sadness.

But there is no cure for a broken heart. Except for time … maybe.

When Maverick returns to Lynx's room, Willow wipes at her face and looks up, watching us. "Where did you go?" Maverick doesn't answer, so she looks at me and sees my tears. How could she not? "Never mind."

I take a few deep breaths, wishing I was somewhere else. Even though what happened in this room was the most important thing half an hour ago, I can't focus on it now. I want to be alone, *need* to be alone, but I can't do a thing about it. I sniffle again, and Maverick holds me a little tighter—a hug?— before relaxing his grip.

I wipe my tears away once more and turn my attention to Lynx. He's sitting straight up in bed, but by the way his cloudy

227

eyes don't move off the wall, I'm assuming he still can't see. That's just as well. I don't want him to see me like this, either. The conversation we're about to have with him would be hard if he knew I was here.

Willow pulls Maverick to the corner of the room, away from Lazarus and Lynx, and I look up at her in curiosity. Whatever she has to say isn't good news, but when is it, anymore?

"Zane sent Katrina with a message," she says, tapping her silver ring.

"What did she say?" I ask, wondering if the battle is finally over.

"The fight has ended, and they're... saying there *are* casualties." Willow's face twitches. The news isn't a surprise to any of us, but it still hurts her to say it. "Katrina says they've got hostages."

"How many?" I ask, my jaw hanging slightly open. I didn't know the Elemental Coven were the type to take hostages. Live and learn.

"I don't know," Willow replies. "She didn't tell me more than that, but I think that's your cue to go. You've been here long enough."

"You're sure you don't need anything else?" Maverick asks with a little hesitation. He isn't one to disobey direct orders, but like me, he doesn't want to leave this place or these witches. Having to do it again and again should make it easier, but it doesn't. Every time we have to do this, we can *anticipate* the exact pain it'll cause one more time.

I want to tell Willow my suspicions, to argue that we can't leave just yet, but when I see the look in her eyes as she gazes at Maverick, I can't do it. I understand her concern all too well.

***

MAVERICK AND I exchange looks as we cross toward the

portal. "Sucks to do this again," he admits.

I nod. "Who do you think they captured?"

Maverick shrugs. "Your guess is as good as mine."

"I didn't know we were the kind of witches who do that thing."

"We're the kind of witches who do what we have to do in order to make it through the war."

"Fair enough."

"How is it on the other side?" Maverick calls to Zane, his eyes narrowing the slightest bit.

Zane breathes in slowly, his lips pressed together as he looks at Maverick and then at me. With that expression, I don't want to hear his words. Maverick looks away from the other witch to stare at where the portal usually opens.

Zane lifts his massive, dark hand, fingers tearing through the very air itself, and in its wake, the shimmering entrance of the portal emerges. Maverick looks down at me, adjusting me on his hip, then steps forward.

Zane rests a hand on Maverick's shoulder. "Watch yourselves out there."

"I always do." Maverick steps toward the portal, then looks at the Reanimate. "Thank you, Zane."

"Thank you," I echo. Then the portal swallows us up and spits us out on the other side, away from the purple plants and bright sky. Away from Clio. On this side, sunlight peers over the horizon. We've been gone for hours.

I want to say *something* to Maverick as he walks, anything, but I can't think of a word. I study the way he blinks and breathes out, carefully conserving each breath as much as he can. My heart thumps with the dread of what's coming, the dead we'll see, and the witches who survived.

Who are the prisoners?

By the time we make it back to the Wilderness, my heart feels ready to explode with anticipation. No one greets us this time. It's empty and silent except for the crunching of

Maverick's feet on the underbrush. Branches are scattered across the ground, charred gashes in the trees. A metallic smell fills the clearing—the lingering odor of spilled blood. When I breathe deeply enough, the scent is accompanied by ash and burned leaves. While it's obvious that something big occurred here, it's not as bad as some of the other battles I've experienced.

Months after the Battle in Ignis, there are still signs of the struggle there—lost houses and blood baked into the sand. Here? The proof of battle will be gone by the time night falls. I fully believe that until Maverick weaves us deeper into the Coven, and then I see exactly what I'd hoped to never see—a line of white blankets, each one covering a witch who didn't make it through the battle.

They won't be so easy to clean away.

My body tenses, and Maverick feels it. "Don't look at them," he says and moves faster to hurry us through the madness.

It's impossible to look at anything else. I want to know, I *have* to know, who is under those tarps, which of those witches are our own and which are the enemies.

I want to know everything. I squirm against him, trying to break free. "Maverick, let me go!"

He only takes a sharp turn through the trees, pushing through the dense foliage and out onto the other side to finally put the macabre scene behind us. I can still see the line of corpses when I blink, but it's easier to handle than seeing it all right in front of me.

I'm grateful to Maverick for that.

Katrina meets us at the heart of the Wilderness, and I'm so glad to see she's okay, to see she's *alive*. I reach out and demand a hug before we move right into our conversation.

"Glad you're back," she says as we break apart. Then she frowns. "So it's true about Ambrossi?"

Maverick nods grimly. "Yeah, it is."

"And Clio?"

"He's still alive for now."

"We'll save him," Maverick says tersely.

Katrina's brows pull together as she stares at Maverick, waiting for an explanation.

"Willow rescued Lynx," I explain.

"He's in the Land of New Life?"

"Lazarus and Willow are with him," Maverick says.

Katrina's sudden silence is more than unnerving—for Maverick as much as for me.

"How many dead?" he asks.

She still doesn't say a word.

"Did we know any of them?" I add, looking away.

"Willow said there are prisoners," Maverick says. I look up at him sharply.

Katrina blinks a few times. "Yes. There are prisoners."

"Do I know them?" I repeat, wondering if Maverick will try to derail this line of questioning too.

Katrina shakes her head. "I doubt it. Their names are Colby and Reggie."

They don't sound familiar, and I'm relieved. If they were witches I knew, it would've made things harder. Then again, I'd be overjoyed to see Hyacinth a prisoner of war.

"Is that *all* you have?" Maverick asks, tilting his head.

Redness blossoms across Katrina's cheeks, and she reaches up to adjust her bun. She's lying. Why didn't I catch onto that sooner?

"Um... well... the third isn't really a prisoner. He's more of a... personal project."

"Who is it?" Maverick demands.

"Crowe's brother. But we got him for Crowe's benefit. He's not really part of the Council. He won't know anything."

I understand that much, but Maverick, apparently, does not.

"I don't care what you think he may or may not know. We won't be certain until he's questioned just as thoroughly as

231

his counterparts. Bottom line, he came in with our enemy, and he's on our soil. That makes him as much of a prisoner as the others."

Katrina's lips draw into a tight, thin line in an attempt to contain her rage. When she speaks, her voice is just a little too calm. "For now."

"Take us to them," Maverick says, clearly aware of the fact that he won't win that fight. I have to wonder what'll happen the moment he steps into the room with Kieran.

"To be honest, Colby is the only one who's conscious right now," Katrina says.

I frown. "What did you do to the others?"

Her smile looks innocent enough, but it's false.

"Well, okay."

"Colby's first, then," Maverick says.

Katrina nods and leads us through the trees.

"How'd you capture him?" I ask her.

"I didn't. One of the Wilderness witches did. He was injured." She shrugs.

"Who is he?" I try to remember if I've ever heard of him before.

"He lived in Ignis before becoming a Council witch. He's older than us." Katrina shrugs again. She doesn't know much about him, either.

When we reach the right tree, Katrina leads us in the climb. Maverick lifts me toward the rope, letting me follow behind her. We shimmy our way up into one of the larger houses, and Katrina pauses at the top to help me onto the threshold.

Then Maverick picks me up again, and we stand on the wooden ledge, waiting for Katrina's direction. "He's in here. We have him subdued with magic-suppressing restraints, but there's no way to guess what he'll say. He isn't pleasant."

The last bit is a warning, but seeing as I'm also unpleasant, it doesn't carry much weight. Whatever he says, I'm sure I'll be able to counter it, anyway. Maverick enters without hesitation, itching for a fight—especially since we left the battle early. He passes me to Katrina before circling the prisoner. A man with long black hair hanging in his eyes is bound to the chair. There's an empty seat across from him, and Maverick sits in it after his initial examination, no emotion on his face as he studies the witch from head to toe.

Colby looks at him, his lips curling into a sneer. Then his eyes drift toward Katrina and eventually land on me. His upper lip twitches, revealing teeth stained red with blood. Apparently, Katrina's gentle care doesn't extend to *all* the prisoners.

"Are you going to tell me what you know about the Sickness plaguing my people, or am I going to have to beat you in front of these lovely ladies?" Maverick's tone carries a sick sweetness as he leans forward to rest his elbows on his knees.

Colby looks at him before glancing at me again. "Beat me. It won't change a thing. I've told you freaks what I know. There *is* no cure. Everyone who catches it dies. That's it."

Except the Reanimates.

"Every illness has a cure," I find myself growling at him.

"You really think so? Things are that simple to you, huh?" He laughs as pleasantly as if I just told him a joke. "Wait a minute. I've seen you before. You're the Sage's little pet, right? You should know better than anyone what magical damage can do." He nods at my devasted legs and laughs again, spitting a mouthful of blood onto the floor.

"So we were right to assume you were behind it." One of Maverick's hands clenches into a fist and opens again, over and over.

"Well, not me personally, but…" Colby winks.

Maverick stands slowly, carefully, as if he's getting up for a snack. His clenched fist hurtles up into Colby's jaw, bringing a sharp click when the prisoner's teeth smash together. When Maverick pulls his fist back again, Colby's head falls toward his chest, and he's out.

KAYLA KRANTZ

Chapter Thirty-Seven
Hope

"**W**ELL, THAT WENT about as well as can be expected," Katrina says dully.

I nod, watching a single drop of Colby's blood fall to the wooden floorboards.

"Confirmed what we know," Maverick says, rubbing his knuckles. "That's as good as anything. Now, let's see what our other prisoners have to say for themselves."

Katrina nods, and we move on to the next room with Reggie. He's older and tied to a chair as well. The only difference here is that a pair of Caleb's handcuffs are also around his wrists. The man's eyes are still closed, and I take that as my opportunity to study him from head to toe. He doesn't look like much. I wonder what Katrina saw in him when she decided to take him from the battlefield.

"From what I've gathered, this is the witch directly responsible for the Sickness," Katrina says. "Molly brought him in herself."

"*Him?*" Maverick studies the man in the chair, as if he expects a different witch to burst out of hiding and reveal the big joke.

"Yes, him."

"Why would they send him out into the fight?" I ask.

Katrina shrugs. "I don't know. There's no telling the extent of his magic."

"They probably wanted him to take out the Wilderness," Maverick says.

Anger flares in my stomach, not because of Maverick's words but because I know he's right. The Council wanted to punish the Wilderness for helping us—punish them by making them suffer the same fate as the Elemental Coven.

"I want to talk to him," I say.

"Lilith…" Maverick sounds way too condescending.

"You had your fun," I tell him. "This one's mine." Before he can protest again, I use my powers to lift the prisoner's chin. His head rolls to the side, but I shake him back and forth, nearly slapping him with my powers.

Finally, his eyes crack open, and he groans. "Wha's place?" he slurs.

"You'll have to speak louder than that." I sound surprisingly confident, considering how broken I am.

"What is this place?" he repeats, but still, it seems he isn't fully conscious yet. His eyes drift around the room.

"You are a prisoner. You don't get to ask questions," Maverick replies coolly, folding his arms. The knuckles of his right hand are still red, slicked with blood where Colby's tooth broke the skin.

"Our information says you're responsible for the Sickness in our Coven," Katrina says.

Reggie smiles in the same way Colby just laughed at me. Maverick's hands ball into fists again. "And if I am?" Reggie lifts an eyebrow.

"Then you know how to stop it," I say.

The witch clicks his tongue. "Could. Possibly. But why would I do that?"

"Because we're telling you to," Maverick says.

Reggie shrugs. "Make me an offer that actually means

something to me."

"You don't get to make demands," Maverick says, taking a step forward. The urge to punch this witch too is clearly wearing on him.

"You can't be mad at *me* for what happened. This? The Sickness? You drove us to it. All your dead Covenmates are *your* fault. And they will *all* die. You too, in time."

"No, Sir." Maverick offers a wicked half grin. "Because you're going to reverse your magic. Or we'll kill you."

Reggie shrugs. "That'll stop the spread, sure. But everyone who's already sick? They'll succumb to it anyway." He laughs.

The pain, the rage, the *humiliation*—all of it overwhelms me, and I let everything out in a gust of air that smacks Reggie with such force, it leaves a trail of painful marks across the side of his face and neck.

He howls in agony, and Maverick's smile grows. "You think that hurts? Just wait until your execution."

Reggie doesn't seem quite so confident. "I already told you what you want to know."

"And also refused to help us," Katrina points, cocking her head with a glance at Maverick. "Work your magic."

"Gladly." Maverick grins, and his eyes glow with their eerie, metallic glint.

Reggie blinks and pulls against the handcuffs, but it's no good. Maverick's magic takes over, tightening its hold. Reggie chokes and gasps for air, but none of us feel bad for him. For all the pain he's put our Coven through, he deserves every minute of this. If it were possible, I'd subject him to a century of it.

Finally, the choking stops, and Reggie's head slumps forward.

"Is he dead?" I ask.

Maverick shakes his head. "No, unfortunately. We'll deal with that later. We have one more prisoner to interrogate, don't we?"

Katrina freezes. "Well, I mean, we found out what we set out to learn… We don't really *need* to talk to Kieran. Crowe and I have him handled."

"Katrina," Maverick says, reaching up to touch his temples. "He's one of them. What do you think you're going to do by defending him?"

"Earn a change of heart. Crowe is so miserable in this place, being with us, and I know his mind is split. This would give him a chance to fix things."

Maverick looks at me, as if he expects me to jump to her defense, but I look away. I can really feel the predicament Katrina is in, and my heart goes out to her. All she wants to do is help her love adjust, and I'm sure that while she's known Crowe, she come to care for his brother as well. I don't want to be caught in their fight, but now Katrina's looking at me, and I realize I don't have a choice.

"If anyone can do it, Katrina can," I say at last.

She gives me a grateful smile, but I barely see it because I'm so focused on Maverick. He doesn't know what to think or do, so he gives in.

"Fine. I'll give you a chance, but if *anything* goes wrong with him, he's going with Reggie and Colby."

Katrina's eyes widen again. Is that *fear?*

"What happens with him and Colby?" I ask, gesturing to Reggie's still form in the chair.

"We take them back to the Land of New Life and execute them," Katrina says.

Sometimes, irony is a beautiful thing.

***

MAVERICK AND CROWE blindfold Reggie and Colby and lead them out of their respective prisons and down to the grass of the Wilderness. Making two grown male witches climb down a rope ladder is a struggle, and I watch the handful of Elemental witches fighting with them, doing their best to get the men to move. If I were them, I would've been tempted to just push these prisoners off the threshold and save the trip to the Land of New Life.

Katrina helps me down, then we make another trip to the portal. I study the backs of Colby and Reggie as they walk ahead of us, thinking of their futures. When the Council executes someone, they go with the traditional burning at the stake, but I don't think that's what Willow's people do. Until today, I didn't know they performed executions at all. I'm learning a lot about my people.

When we cross into the Land of New Life, Maverick and Crowe take the prisoners to the Community Villa, and Katrina takes me to Willow's mansion. I don't protest, because either way, I'd rather avoid both places. I stare at the roof of the Community Villa in the distance, thinking of Clio somewhere inside, and sigh.

When we get into Lynx's room, Willow is still at his bedside. It's only been a few hours since we left, but Lynx looks better. His eyes are glassy still, but he sits with a relaxed, natural posture instead of his previous stiffness upon coming back to life. At the sound of Katrina's footsteps, he looks toward us, caught off guard by the idea of company.

"Who is it?" he demands.

He's recovering well, and I don't know whether to be glad or worried. I look to Lazarus for help, wondering if I should tell him the truth.

"It's Lilith," Lazarus says. "She's here to check up on you."

Lynx's eerie, empty, aquamarine-lined eyes swivel back in my direction. I know he can't see me, but the look still chills me through to the bone. "Why... would you do that after everything?"

I don't know how to respond. When I was on the Council, Lynx was probably the witch I spoke to the least. He kept to himself; the only real conversation we had was after Callista was poisoned. He's suspicious of me, and I understand that. I think how much Lynx cared about the tiny fairy and what Lazarus said he'd done for Flora. He's a good witch with a kind heart, even if he doesn't particularly care for me.

"You're a good person," I say. "I've never had a thing against you."

He's silent, and I can tell he doesn't know what to think of my words.

"I'm glad you're here," I continue.

"Why?"

"You'll be better here. Safer."

"Says who?"

"Says me. Says Lazarus. Says Willow, the girl who literally could've left you for dead and chose not to."

Lynx's lips press together.

"Now that she's done a favor for you, we need a favor *from* you."

"That's really why you brought me back, huh?" Lynx shakes his massive head.

"No. I told you why we did what we did. Incidentally, we really could use your help."

"I know."

I hear all the pain that comes with being a Healer, the pain that comes with the idea that no matter how good someone's intentions, they can't save everyone. "The Sickness."

"You told him about it?" I ask Lazarus.

"Of course," the elderly Reanimate replies.

"If anyone can help, it's you," I tell Lynx. "You won't be alone if you decide to help us find the cure."

Lazarus and Willow both stare at me too now, and my face flushes under so much attention. Here goes nothing. "Thorn and Callista are more than happy to help."

Willow is the only one who looks shocked. "*Who?*"

She heard me, but she's going to give me a chance to

change my answer, to mold it into something that's more acceptable.

"Thorn and Callista," I reiterate. "They've been living here, doing what they can to help keep the sick witches alive. Clio in particular. Fern brought them here, because they were hurt after the

Battle at the Grove. Now they're better, and now they're helping us, Willow. They can stave off the Sickness, but only for so long."

Her lips purse sideways; she isn't angry by what I've said. She's *hurt*. Malcolm was like her very own child, and for the first time, he's neglected to tell her something important. He's left her on the outside.

"They're still alive?" Lynx asks, and Willow turns to look at him.

"You didn't know?"

He shakes his head. "They disappeared after Headquarters was destroyed. I thought... we *all* thought..."

"What? That we killed them?" I ask softly.

He doesn't move, as if he's afraid to answer that question truthfully.

"We aren't savages, Lynx. We save witches. Or we *did,* anyway."

"I know that now," he admits and glances at Lazarus. "And all I can tell you is that I'll try to help any way I can. But I don't know what'll come of my magic now that I'm..."

He breathes in but doesn't say the word. None of us push him; it's something he'll have to come to terms with on his own. Lazarus puts a comforting hand on his apprentice's shoulder—a tiny gesture to remind Lynx that he won't be alone in his battle.

"Thank you, Lynx," I say, letting the tiniest blossom of hope fill my chest.

Chapter Thirty-Eight
Executions...Tiger Style

I DON'T KNOW why I assumed the conversation with Lynx would be hard. It actually went pretty well, all things considered. Now that that's finished, I have to have another tough chat with Willow.

I'm grateful to be in my chair again, which gives me the ability to pull her out into the hall before Katrina tells her anything. I find myself studying her from her long, curly brown hair to the way she stands on her toes like some sort of ballerina.

She's not my sister. The pain of that knowledge spears through me again. "I, um... I've learned a lot... in the other Coven."

Willow's eyebrows draw together at my concern. "What is it?"

"We... we're not..."

"We're not what, Lilith?" Her black eyes stretch wide.

"We're not sisters." I say it so quietly that she may not have even heard me.

Willow's lip quirks up at the corner. It's a slight tick, the kind that comes with uncertainty—the assumption that I'm pranking her. "Of course we are."

I look up at her through haunted eyes. That uncertain smile still plays on her lips, but her eyes betray her true emotions. She's confused. "According to Molly, you're my cousin."

"Who's Molly?" Now her smile's gone. "What does she know?"

"She's Ivy's sister. My... mother."

Willow flinches as if I've slapped her. "You're certain of this? What does Ivy have to say about it?"

I shrug. "I haven't seen her."

"So Molly could be lying."

I stare at the floor.

"She *could* be lying... right?" Willow bends low to bring our faces together, desperate to make eye contact.

I look back up at her slowly, my head feeling like it weighs a thousand pounds. "I don't think she was."

"But... I actually *remember* the day Mom brought you home. She never... she never said anything..."

"I know. Molly said Ivy did that to protect her. To protect the Wilderness."

"I can't believe this." Willow lifts a hand to her forehead. Her eyes take on that glittery, watering look, like she's about to bawl her eyes out.

For everything that I could say, that I *should* say, I can think of nothing.

She reaches out and pulls me into her arms, holding me to her with her strong grip. A cold hand strokes my hair, and she says softly in my ear, "I don't care what they say. What they believe. You'll always be my sister."

I can't stop my own tears as I hug her back. She's right, after all. Sisters are all we've ever been to each other, and that's not about to change today.

The door creaks open, and we pull apart, staring at Katrina.

Her blue eyes are wide. "Sorry to interrupt."

Willow sniffles, and the emotions she bared to me a minute before are gone. "That's all right. What's happening with the prisoners?"

Katrina's spine is rigid as her eyes move between Willow and me. "I can come back…"

"Nonsense," Willow says.

"Okay. Well, um, from what Maverick and I gathered, one of the prisoners, he's, uh…"

Willow narrows her eyes in impatience. "Yes?"

"Well, he's the one directly responsible for the Sickness."

Willow glances at me, then back at Katrina in disbelief. "You're sure?" she asks with a frown. "You've confirmed it?"

Katrina nods. "As much as we can. Based on information from the other prisoners and the witch himself, that's correct. We didn't want to remove the magic suppressors."

"That's not worth the risk," Willow says, her eyes distant. Slowly, she shakes her head, confused. I'm right there with her. Why would the Council would send a witch like that into battle when he could inflict damage from miles away?

"Maybe they didn't think we'd find him," I offer. "Or catch him."

"Something doesn't feel right about it," Willow says. "It was too easy to find him."

"Who knows why the Council does anything?" Katrina asks with a shrug.

Willow doesn't look so sure. She looks unnaturally pale, even for sure, like she's going to be sick.

"The witch… he said there's no way to reverse the Sickness. That once it's out there, it'll continue to affect whoever's already contracted it. Maybe that's why the Council sent him out to fight. He's served his purpose."

"No one in the Wilderness is sick?"

I shake my head. "As far as I know, they are all fine."

Willow's frown deepens. "Where are the prisoners

now?"

"In the Community Villa, ready for their executions." Katrina's voice is the most professional-sounding I've ever heard it.

"Three of them, right?" Willow asks.

Katrina shakes her head and looks at the ground, her cheeks flaming with a blush.

"Two for execution," I say. "The third is a work in progress."

"Okay." There's no anger in Willow's voice. "Let's go pay them a visit."

Katrina and I follow her. For a witch heading toward an execution, Willow's footsteps are surprisingly light. I don't know how she manages it. Despite all this new information, she moves through the purple plants with grace, like she's dancing, and I just watch her in admiration. Her words float through my head again, and I can't hold back a small smile. *You'll always be my sister.*

The hallway in which Crowe and Maverick locked up their prisoners is on the opposite side of the building from Clio's room, but that doesn't stop me from making excuses to escape, to see him for just a little while.

It doesn't work. Willow's onto me as much as Maverick, and in a group, we all travel outside. Colby and Reggie are blindfolded, one led by Maverick and the other led by Crowe. Willow walks at my side, and Katrina follows a few steps behind, ready to help me with my chair if it happens to sink into the mud. Between us Elementals, there's very little in the way of conversation. The trip through the purple plants leads to a few pleas and sobs from Colby, but Reggie doesn't make a sound. It's odd just how much their roles have changed since their interrogations.

We just let Colby scream and cry until Maverick gets so tired of it, he silences the witch with his magic. As we pass through Willow's mansion, we gather a crowd of witches; everyone seems to know without being told what's happening.

Two or three tigers bring up the rear, fascinated by the new smells.

By the time we reach Willow's throne room, just about every Reanimate in the Coven has gathered. Now I realize how the Elemental Coven means to execute these prisoners—the pit and the group of snarling tigers inside it. I fell in there once and came out with nothing more than a scratch and bruise. I didn't realize how dangerous these tigers could be until now.

Willow smiles as she approaches the pit. Maverick holds Colby by the back of his shirt, close enough to the pit that the witch's toes dangle over the edge. Crowe does the same with Reggie.

"For crimes against your fellow witch, this Coven hereby sentences you to death," Willow says. "Do you have any last words?"

Colby shakes his head, grinning, and Reggie still says nothing. Maverick and Crowe exchange a glance and a nod before releasing their grips on the prisoners. With a quick push, the two Council witches fall into the pit. The tigers erupt into a frenzy of snarls, and the awful sound of ripping flesh rises with the screams of the condemned. I look away, but the other witches cluster closer, trying to see as much of the gore as they possibly can.

A few minutes later, it's over. I stare at the bloody pieces of cloth scattered across the bottom of the pit, thinking about how fragile life really is.

Chapter Thirty-Nine
Through Thick and Thin

THE REANIMATES ARE in a better mood after the executions. Even Lazarus attended the show, which surprises me. The good cheer is an odd reaction to something so brutal, but I understand it. They really feel free, as if a weight has been lifted, but I can't bring myself to feel the same. Things aren't over yet.

There are still sick witches. We still need a cure.

Gradually, the Elementals lose interest in the scene and leave the room one by one until Willow, Katrina, and I are the only ones left.

"Now that that's out of the way, how many witches did we lose in the battle?" Willow asks Katrina.

"A handful." Her nose twitches. I wonder how many that is, exactly.

Willow nods. "They're still in the Wilderness?"

Katrina nods.

I picture the scene again with the witches laid out under white tarps. If those were only *our* fallen witches, it seems like more than just a handful.

"I'll see who I can bring back," Willow says and moves to leave the room.

I grab her arm. "Wait. What about Lynx and the cure?"

"That's something he will have to do on his own," Willow says. "I've done all that I can for him."

I frown, not wanting to admit she's right. But really, Lynx's magic falls on him.

"It's late, Lilith," Katrina says.

"Some rest will do us all good." Willow scratches the back of her neck.

I want to argue—I want to *make* Lynx work on his magic as soon as possible—but I know I won't win. They've already decided what we're going to do. My protests won't change a damn thing.

Clio, please hold on just a little longer.

***

WHEN WE RETURN to the Wilderness, it's pouring rain. The sky nearly shakes with thunder, and a bolt of lightning tears across the sky. As we move through the tall trees, the streaks of light make me more and more nervous. What happens if the lightning were to strike one of them?

I can still picture the dead witches, soaked through with mud and rain as they lie on the ground. If it floods, they'll float. I shiver and glance at Katrina, knowing the reason behind the storm.

My brother can shapeshift, and all I can do is make it rain, Kieran said to me during our only encounter in Aquais.

The rain doesn't seem to bother Willow, either. As the rain pelts us, soaking our hair and our clothes, she walks a line down the row of bodies. Her dress is plastered to her skin, but she shows no discomfort, moving from witch to witch, silently pulling the sheet back to see who she's lost. I recognize Quinn in the lineup, and the irony is not lost on me that he died in the same battle as his sister. I wonder who killed him after his triumph over Rayna. When Willow reaches the last body, she pulls the sheet and freezes.

Her face is expressionless, water running off her and through her soaked hair as she stares at the unmoving witch before her. Slowly, I glance down at the body. It's Ivy. Willow comes back to the moment with a deep gasp. Without a word, she reaches out to pull the sheet back over Ivy's face.

"Wait. What are you doing?" I ask.

"Moving on." Willow's clutch on the sheet tightens.

"We can't just leave her."

"Why not?" Willow snaps, anger surging through her. "She left us." Her voice breaks, and I know what's going through her head—everything I told her, everything Ivy's done. No matter who I am to Willow, Ivy is still her mother.

"Because she came back, Willow," I say softly. "Because she saved us. Because she didn't give up on us when she probably should have. Because she's your *mother*."

Willow closes her eyes, like she's trying to block me out. When she opens them again, she looks so devastated that it hurts. "Okay." She throws the sheet aside before dropping to her knees beside Ivy.

That reveals all the injuries that killed the woman. I wasn't exactly close to Ivy, but the sight brings tears to my eyes. Willow sets a hand on Ivy's shoulder and drops her head. A purple glow connects the two of them.

When Willow's magic is finished, she collapses, and Maverick is right by her side.

Ivy sucks in a raw, desperate gasp and struggles to sit up. Then she turns her hazy gaze toward Willow.

Chapter Forty

The Cure

WHEN WE RETURN to the cabin, we're all muddy, bloody, and exhausted, both mentally and physically. I thought the day would never end. But when we enter the main room, it's clearly not time to rest just yet.

Kieran sits in the living room, the magic-suppressing handcuffs binding his wrists and a thin chain tying his ankle to the leg of the couch—Katrina's attempt to calm the storm. He looks up at us, and I glance at Crowe and Katrina.

"Long time no see," Kieran says cheerfully, smiling at me.

"Yeah." I try not to look as awkward as this feels.

"Lilith is on her way to bed," Crowe says. Without skipping a beat, Katrina takes me from Maverick and heads toward my room.

I know when I'm being snubbed, and of course I'm irritated. Why are they always so quick to remove me from the situation?

"Are you really gonna keep him on lockdown?" I ask.

"You saw what happened to Colby and Reggie," Katrina

replies stiffly.

I try to picture Kieran sharing their fate, and it turns my stomach. He hasn't done anything other than being in the wrong place at the wrong time. It wouldn't be a fitting end for him, and it wouldn't be fair.

"I understand your concern, Katrina, but how long do you think you can keep him here like this?"

"However long it takes," she blurts.

It's dumb hope, pointless optimism, and I don't try to argue with it. I can't if she doesn't want to see the reality of our situation.

Katrina sets me on my bed and without another word, leaves, and shuts the doors behind her. It's been a long day for everyone.

***

I'M THE FIRST one awake in the morning. I'm so excited to get back to the Land of New Life, to get to Lynx and Clio's side, that I barely slept. I wheel myself to the bathroom to clean off the worst of the dirt. My telekinesis helps me put on some fresh clothes, wrap clean bandages around my legs, and make my way to the living room.

Kieran is asleep on the couch, his ankle chained to one of the legs. I move slowly, hoping to not wake him. An awkward conversation with Crowe's brother is *not* how I want to start the day. On the other couch, Maverick's still passed out too. This is the most vulnerable I've ever seen him, and it leaves me with an odd feeling.

Like I'm looking at something that could get me hurt.

"Maverick," I whisper sharply.

His head pops up. I wonder what it's like to be that light of a sleeper.

"Everything okay?" he asks, his voice cracking with fatigue.

"No. I'm ready to go see Lynx."

He yawns and sits up before glancing across the room toward Kieran and then down the hall. We both consider waking Crowe and Katrina before we go, but Kieran won't manage to escape with or without a babysitter. So we don't bother.

"Let's go." Maverick stands and lifts me out of my chair.

Through the entire trip to the portal, I'm buzzing with energy. This is the day we find out just what Lynx can do. As a Reanimate, he doesn't need to sleep, and I hope he's dedicated some of his time to working on his magic.

At the Community Villa, we find him in his room. Lazarus sits in a chair in the corner, catching up on sleep that he doesn't really need.

"You're here early," Lynx says, staring at the ball of energy trapped between his hands.

"I'm ready to see what you can do," I tell him.

Lynx nods. "I had a feeling." He looks at Maverick. "Can you set her on my bed, please?"

Maverick and I stare at him in wonder. "Why?" Maverick asks finally.

"We need to see if my ability is still intact, right? Honestly, I'm worried about treating something life-threatening like the Sickness without some practice first."

"What's the plan?" I ask.

"You're the perfect specimen, Lilith." Lynx's hazy eyes drift toward my legs. "I'm going to try to fix you… like you wanted me to when we first met."

My heart skips a beat. "You want to *what?*"

"*Fix* you." His eyes are still cloudy, but the aquamarine shines through like a cloud's silver lining. "Please trust me."

I look down at my legs and back at him. Oddly enough, I do trust him; I just don't trust the idea that he *can* fix me. I've come to terms with never walking again. Knowing the story of Flora and her permanent death, I'm not sure I want his magic to touch me at all.

But if I won't do this for myself, I can at least do it for Clio.

The minute I realize this, all my reservations disappear. "Okay. It's worth a try."

"You don't have to do this," Maverick says.

"I know." I turn to look up at him. I don't *have* to do anything, but if testing this means giving Clio another chance at life, I'd even cut off my legs to make it happen.

"Okay." Maverick bends over to gently set me on the mattress beside Lynx.

Up close, Lynx is much bigger, his frame dwarfing mine as we sit hip-to-hip on the bed. I shift a little, trying to put some distance between us, but the bed's not big enough.

"You ready?" Lynx looks down at me. I nod, and he takes a breath, reaching across my body to set his hands on my ankles. Now I'm staring at his back as he squeezes my ankles. The jolt of pain shooting up my spine makes me wince. For one heart-stopping moment, I get the sickening feeling that this is all a trick, that he's still with the Council and is now destroying my body any way he can. Maverick stares back at me, frowning in concern. He takes one hesitant step forward, but I shake my head, trying to convince us both that for once, everything will be okay. Maverick doesn't quite believe it, but he stays puts, watching for the slightest cue that I need him to step in.

Slowly, Lynx's hands inch up my calves, working harder into my skin. He pushes and prods the bruises in my legs, injuring the already devasted skin in ways I didn't think were possible anymore. By the time he's halfway to my knees, I don't know how much more I can take. I want to scream. I've experienced a lot of pain in my life, but this has its own category. My vision blurs and darkens as I fight back the dizziness.

"Stay with me, Lilith," Lynx says. "I need you to focus."

I try to focus on *him*, but it's hard. I'm ready to succumb to the pain, to give in and accept that I never had a chance anyway. Then Lynx removes his hands. The pain stops a few seconds later, and now we're both staring at my legs like we expect them to start talking.

"Well?" Maverick takes one more step toward us.

Lynx grabs the edge of one bandage and unwraps the cloth, moving through each rotation with agonizing slowness. Then he throws both bandages aside with an extravagant flick of his wrist. I'm almost afraid to see what's become of my useless legs. I'm so used to seeing my left calf covered in pink scar tissue that the sight of the normal, supple flesh makes me faint.

Chapter Forty-One
Blessings and Curses

"LILITH. LILITH, CAN you hear me?" Katrina's voice cuts through the blackness.

Groaning, I struggle to open my eyes. "What happened?" I reach up to cradle the worst of the pain in my forehead.

"You fainted," Lynx says.

I push myself up when I realize I'm still in his bed.

Embarrassed now, I try to move away from him again. Then I remember and look at my legs—at the perfect, porcelain skin encircling my left calf.

Lynx watches me with wide eyes, studying my reaction. Does he think I'll be angry? Should I be? I slowly poke at my leg, not sure what to do when my fingertips brush soft, healthy skin. This has to be a dream. It's the only way this makes sense.

Crowe steps toward the bed, his green eyes calm as he offers his arm. Those eyes ask me one question. Am I ready? I nod and grab his arm. His other arm slips around my waist as he gradually eases me toward the edge of the bed.

Katrina's in the room now too, watching me. I must

have passed out for a while if she and Crowe managed to return to the Land of New Life before I woke up again. Whatever the case, I'm glad they're here now. No one speaks as Crowe scoots me forward just enough that I slip off the bed. I'm terrified of the pain I've grown so used to feeling when my feet hit the ground. There's no pain at all. My knees don't buckle. I don't collapse. With stinging eyes, I blink back the tears and take a step. After another, Crowe lowers both his arms, and I cry out, grabbing at him and knowing that I'll fall. But he steps away from me, and I'm still standing. On my own two feet. No limp, no pain.

Through her fingers over her mouth, Katrina mutters, "That's incredible."

I turn back to Lynx with shining eyes. He lifts an eyebrow and studies my legs, probably looking for a sign that something went wrong. Finally, he meets my gaze and offers a small smile. I want to scream 'thank you' a thousand times in a hundred languages, but it doesn't seem enough to express this overwhelming gratitude. So I turn and leap back toward the bed to wrap my arms around his neck. I kiss his cheek and pull this stranger closer to me than most of my friends have ever come.

"I can never thank you enough," I whisper in his ear.

Lynx's massive arms swallow me when he hugs me back. We break apart, and Crowe puts a hand on my shoulder, grinning. This is a special event for him too, I realize. As my mentor, he's earned a certain pride in this too.

The bed creaks beneath Lynx, and I look at him again, still surprised by how massive he is. His body glows with a new, ethereal light, mesmerizing me, and he smiles. "Now, let's tackle that Sickness."

"What's happening?" Willow's voice echoes in the hallway, then she bursts into the room. All the color drains from her face.

Lynx stands from the bed that just yesterday was his literal deathbed. Willow's mouth drops open, and she searches for Maverick but finds me first.

"Lily, I… Your legs." Even in a whisper, her voice shakes.

I laugh. Not because the situation is by any means hilarious but because it's such a relief that I can do this—that I can be a *good* surprise for once. "I know. His magic definitely works." There's still a future for this Coven; we can save so many witches now with this turn of events. I'm ready to smile and dance if it'd cheer her up, but Willow looks horrified. "What's wrong?"

"Tell me it wasn't Lynx," she says, closing her eyes.

Lynx's cloudy eyes are wide, as if he thinks he's in trouble now for doing what we've asked of him. I want to grab his hand and tell him everything's all right, that what he did was a wonderful thing, but I don't think it'll help right now. Not when Willow's this upset about it.

"You might not like what I say," I tell her.

Willow's eyes squeeze even tighter, and a choking squeak escapes her. If Willow could still cry, I'm sure she would right now.

Katrina, Crowe, and Maverick all look just as confused. But Katrina goes to Lynx and whispers something in his ear. Then she laces her fingers through his and leads him out into the hall. Crowe follows but stops in the doorway.

I rush toward Willow, surprised and worried that I can't read her. "What's wrong?"

"Oh, sister. I'm happy for you, I am." Her eyes crack open.

I tilt my head, and Maverick takes his place beside her. "*Are* you? You could've fooled me."

"I'm sorry. It's just… his magic…" She leans toward me to whisper, "The whole thing with Flora, remember? I can't…I won't be able to…" She pulls away but holds my gaze. "You know what this means for your future… when you… when you…" She can't finish the sentence.

"When I die?"

She nods, her black eyes so wide, so innocent-looking, that I want to grab her and hold her. Sometimes, it's hard to remember she's a leader, a warrior, that she's survived *death;* seeing her now like this makes her look more like a fragile doll.

Darrius thought the same of me, didn't he?

I smile. "Don't worry about that part."

Willow recoils. "Don't *worry* about it?" she snarls. "How can I not?"

"Willow, if I'm really going to kill the Sage and take her place, I *should* be able to die. No one should have that much power forever."

Folding her arms, she stares past me.

"Willow?" Maverick prompts, giving me a concerned, sideways glance.

She swallows and looks down at her hands. "Maybe you're right."

"No, Willow," I say, realizing she took my words personally, as the leader of the Elemental Coven. "You were born for this role. *You* should always lead your people." Just to make a point, I glance at the witches still silently watching us. "They admire you so much. And they respect the Hell out of you."

"Do they? I failed them so badly with the Sickness. If I—"

"Don't do that." Maverick places a hand on the small of her back. She looks up at him. "Don't do that," he says again.

I nod. "Don't ever tell yourself that. There was nothing any of us could've done. Even Reggie said the Sickness couldn't be undone, and he blamed the magic."

"Doesn't mean he was telling the truth."

I tap my temple. "Trust me, he was." Then I pull her into a hug. "You're the best leader I've ever met."

She smiles and leans away. "That's high praise from the future Sage."

"So accept it. The Sage knows all."

Laughing, she gives me a gentle push. "Whatever you say, cousin."

Maverick frowns and blinks at us. "Uh... what?"

Willow smiles wide enough to fully reveal the gap in her front teeth and gently grabs his arm. "You've got a lot to catch up on." She laughs again.

The sound of her laughter wipes away all the worries of the past few moments. I glance into the hall at Crowe and the other witches standing there. "Clio first," I say and bolt out of the room, racing past Crowe and Katrina and Lynx.

Running on my own two legs brings I joy I just can't put into words. I stumble over my feet a few times but quickly catch myself. Moving like this, without depending on others, is so freeing, I throw my head back and laugh down the hall. Kado hears me and comes bounding out of our room to run beside me.

Our group pours into the Community Villa, our footsteps thundering down the hall. When we reach the last door, I fling it open, both terrified and eager to see what's waiting for me.

Callista and Thorn hover over a bowl of water in the corner, and Clio still lies in bed. At first, he doesn't move, and I have the horrible thought that we're too late. Then he slowly lifts his head and coughs. Even through the Sickness, I can see the surprise in his eyes. "Li, you're..."

"Walking." I step right up to his bedside, grinning.

"How—" He stops dead when Lynx appears by my side.

"All is possible in love and war," I reply.

Lynx nods and approaches Clio. "My name is Lynx. Hopefully, I'll be the one who saves your life."

Clio's eyes ask a hundred questions, but he reaches out to brush his fingers against my hand before he grips the bedrail and looks up at the massive Reanimate.

"Are you ready?" Lynx asks.

"Will it hurt?" Clio asks, eyeing me.

"No more than you've already been hurt," Lynx replies.

Nodding, Clio takes in a deep breath, and Lynx rubs his hands together. In what seems the quickest and the slowest moment of my life, he reaches his fingers toward Clio's chest. But Clio's bone-thin hand snatches out to grab Lynx, both of them uncomfortable with the contact. "Even if you can't save me, just know I will always be grateful for what you've done for her."

Lynx nods, and Clio lies back against the mattress. Lynx finally brings his fingers down onto Clio's chest, and I shift anxiously from foot to foot. Lynx mutters under his breath and stumbles once, reminding me of Willow in the midst of her own magic.

Willow steps forward in silent concern. When Lynx stumbles again, his hip collides with the railing of Clio's bed, sending a loud clang echoing through the room. He catches himself and sits down.

"Are you okay?" Willow calls.

Lynx does not answer. A minute later, his fingers fall away from Clio's chest, and he slumps over across Clio's legs. Willow and I rush toward him. She lays a hand gently on his back. "Lynx?" Her other hand cups his cheek.

I glance at Clio and the flush of color in his cheeks. Slowly, he sits up, returning to the Clio I know with every passing second, as if the Sickness never existed. His eyes clear of the sickly gleam, and he blinks, studying me from head to toe before hopping out of bed and pulling me into a hug that crushes all the air from my lungs.

"Damn it, Lynx!" Willow cries, willing to shake him fiercely now in her panic. We turn back to her just as she looks, her black eyes glassy. "I think we lost him."

Chapter Forty-Two
It Feels Good to Laugh

THE NEWS IS like a punch to the gut. It doesn't hurt as bad as it might if Clio hadn't recovered first. But after what I've seen, I've learned to believe in the impossible. I dart out of the room, leaving a confused Willow and Clio behind me.

For perhaps the first time in my life, my mind is clear. I run through the Community Villa and all the way back to Willow's mansion. Lazarus is still asleep in his chair, the way old men sleep, and I drop to my knees beside him. "Lazarus. Lazarus!" I shake his arm.

He's hard to rouse, but at last his eyes open. "Lilith? What are you doing here?"

There's no time for words, so I touch his forehead right between his eyebrows and pour all my thoughts into his third eye. He's on his feet at once, moving fast for an elderly Reanimate.

We return to Clio's room to find Clio still beside Lynx, trying to revive him. Willow stands in the corner, her face buried in her hands.

She's lost hope again—the most dangerous thing she could do.

Lazarus goes to Clio, and I go to my cousin.

"He's going to be okay," I tell her and pull her into a hug.

She doesn't resist and leans into me. "How can you be so sure?"

"Because Lazarus is here."

She shoots a startled glance across the room. Lazarus has already pushed Clio out of the way, and together, they roll Lynx over onto his back. Lazarus grabs the massive witch's head with one hand and Lynx's shoulder with the other. Lazarus is *looking* for something.

Lynx gasps, though his eyes remain closed.

"Oh, my God," Willow mutters. "Is he going to—"

"Be okay?" Lazarus nods. "What he did was a great feat for any witch." He looks from Clio to me. "He just needs to rest."

A snore erupts from Lynx's open mouth; the sound is so unexpected, so welcome, and so sudden that Willow laughs. The chiming sound of it is the icing on the cake—the release of so many weeks spent in pain and fear. Now that I can see light at the end of the tunnel, I laugh with her.

Chapter Forty-Three
Warm Goodbyes

WE AGREE TO let Lynx rest. Thorn and Callista work overtime, pouring their magic into sustaining the few witches still afflicted with the Sickness. Lazarus stays by Lynx's side, and I walk beside Willow down the hall. This is the first time I've felt like her equal, and the thought makes me want to cry all over again.

Clio walks behind us. After all the days of being bedridden, he's just as glad to be on his feet as I am.

"So where's... Mom?" I ask Willow, glancing over my shoulder at Clio. He doesn't sense anything out of the ordinary. I'll have the conversation with him one day, but now is definitely not the time.

"She's getting on," Willow says with something close to pride. She turns into her throne room, where Ivy sits in her cat form, surrounded by the undead tigers. The scars and marks of her death are even more prominent against her silvery fur, but the tigers don't seem to care. When we enter, they form a circle around her, watching her every move.

The tigers have bonded with Ivy. They *like* her.

"She's their new caretaker." Willow's voice cracks a bit.

That used to be Grief's job, but he's among those who fell to the Sickness before we could help them.

"There's a place for her after all," I muse.

Willow sighs and scratches the back of her head. "There always has been. I just had a hard time realizing that for a while."

The smallest smiles graces my lips. "Me too. I still have my concerns, but at the end of the day, she'll always be your mother."

Willow slings her cold arm over my shoulders and pulls me into a sideways hug. "And nothing is more important than family."

***

LYNX WAKES LATER that night and cures one more witch. Despite his dedication and willingness to do himself harm, Lazarus has limited him to healing one witch a day. Any more than that may push Lynx past capacity; he may even lose his gift forever.

Those are terms to which we can all agree.

Willow has regained her confidence. I see it in the way she moves. There are still a handful of sick witches, but she knows they will all pull through. So do I. She is so determined in her decisions that she tags along with us to the portal on or way to the Wilderness. There, she tells her witches to pack their bags and prepare to come home.

Before we leave the Wilderness again, Molly finds us. The woman is a blurry shape in the shadows, watching us through pleased eyes. "Your Coven will survive," she says as soon as we approach her. "You are all strong witches who have been through things no one should have to face."

"Thank you for taking us in," Willow says and grasps the woman's hand with both of her own. The truth seeps in, making this a little strange—aunt and niece. My cousin and my mother. "If there is ever anything my people can do for you, let me know. I will be honored to fulfill it."

Molly bows her head and looks at me, her eyes glittering with pride and sadness. "May we meet again, Willow. Lilith." She turns toward the shadows.

"Wait!" I dash after her.

Molly turns just as I wrap my arms around her. "You'll be seeing a lot more of me, Mom," I promise her.

She hugs me back, then pulls away and smiles, her scars pinched on the side of her face. Then she disappears into the darkness.

"I see the resemblance," Willow tells me when I rejoin her. "You should be honored."

"I am."

She smiles and hooks her arm through mine as we lead what's left of our Coven away from the trees and the thick undergrowth, toward the strange place we've all come to know as home. Before we hit the boundary of the Wilderness, Hazel stops us.

"Leaving?" she asks, pulling me into a hug.

I nod. "Thank you for all your help, Hazel."

"Goddess bless." When I walk away, I hear her calling after me, "I'll always believe in you!"

Chapter Forty-Four
Never Broken

*T*HE NEXT FEW days are spent settling the returned witches back into the Land of New Life. Lynx cleans up the last trails of the Sickness, and the Community Villa is open again. All five witches who were cured pledge their gratitude to Callista, Thorn, and Lynx. As a gift, they build a burrow for Thorn and Callista, so the fairies no longer have to live with Fern. They're happier this way. So is Lynx when he emerges from his own Den and is promoted to fill Ambrossi's place in the hospital wing.

Things are looking up for the most part, but there's still Ambrossi. His body remains in one of these rooms, waiting for burial. There are *a lot* of dead bodies still waiting. After the Coven settles back in, Willow decides to get on that next. We bury two witches a day, starting with those who died first.

As the last of them to fall, Ambrossi is the only one buried alone. I take my time getting ready for his funeral this morning. Helena and I both sew our own dresses. We hold each other for hours, talking through our memories of Ignis and crying. Clio stays nearby but doesn't say a word. He's mourning

266

in his own way by pretending he's not sad. Usually, I do the same. But if I choose to do that today, I think the grief would drive me insane.

Crowe and Clio carry Ambrossi's body to the patch of grass that was once undisturbed but is now studded with dozens of graves. Maverick finishes digging the hole and climbs out as the entire Coven gathers together. There is no separation of Reanimates and living witches this time. After everything, our differences are forgotten so we can mourn the Elemental Coven's most dependable Healer.

Clio, Helena, and I are the first ones to throw handfuls of dirt over Ambrossi as he's lowered into the grave. I stand beside the hole in the ground, clenching each handful of upturned earth, and imagine my hands filled with goodness, with love and peace—the kind that will find him wherever he goes.

After everything he's done for our witches, he deserves it.

Willow is the last to throw her own handful of dirt. Despite our mourning, the Coven takes the time to huddle together, hugging as a group. The message is quite clear. We may be hurt, but we will never be broken.

Chapter Forty-Five
Realization

BY NATURE, I am not a cheery or optimistic person; these warm, positive emotions will vanish eventually. The only problem is, I don't know what will replace them. I spend the afternoon in the tiny graveyard, imagining that I'm spending time with Ambrossi. I'm not quite ready to say goodbye, though I can't let Helena or Clio know that. For once, they're currently not worried about me, and I love that; I'm well enough to be left completely alone.

As I wander through the graveyard, I read the tiny, hand-carved plaques created for each grave. I catch Dawn's name on one—a tiny silver square closest to the trees—and I pause. My eyes fill with tears. It seems so unfair that all the effort we put into saving her meant nothing when the Sickness came for her. We gave her hope by pulling her out of the Council's bunkers, but we couldn't deliver on our promise to keep her safe. They killed her anyway.

I turn away from the stone, wondering now why I thought it would be such a good idea to stay here. Seeing exactly who survived and who didn't certainly doesn't make me feel any better. With these plaques, they're no longer a faceless group of witches who fell to the Sickness.

When I turn away, I see Sabre's name among them. He was with us when we went to the Wilderness, so he may have died in the battle and not from the Sickness. If that's the case, though, why didn't Willow revived him?

The strange feeling of not knowing the answer makes me think of my astral trip to Aquais. For all my snooping, I wasn't able to find the Sage there. She wasn't in the bunker, either. That means the Council is keeping her somewhere else, and Aens is the only place unaffected by either the battles or the Sickness. That would certainly explain why I didn't see Hyacinth in Aquais.

***

I HUG CLIO in my room. Kado bows over his front paws, staring at me with his tiny stump of a tail wagging back and forth. I kneel to hug him too, so happy that I can maneuver my body without any help.

"You're glowing," Clio says.

I look up at Kado, feeling myself blush.

"I don't think I've ever seen you so happy before."

"Things are as close to perfect as they can be," I reply, though the thought of Ambrossi makes me frown. "Things were never perfect before, but I... I know who I am. And that's all I ever really wanted."

Clio smiles. "I can appreciate that."

I smile and pull him close. He holds me like a precious gem, and when I lift my face toward him, our lips meet. No, things aren't perfect. But right now, it's very close.

An hour later, Clio snores beside me on my bed.

"Hey, are you asleep?" I ask, poking him in the ribs.

No response.

I look at Kado, but the dog is spread out across my legs, his eyes closed. I reach out to pet the fluffy fur between his eyes, and he doesn't stir. This is my happy place, right here and right now. Even with Clio and Kado asleep, the fact that they're with me, comfortable and safe, makes me breathe easy.

I lie awake, still thinking of the graveyard. Things might be better for me, for now, but until this war is over, the darkness will always return. It won't be finished until the Sage dies, and as the second most powerful witch in the Land of Five, I've already come to the realization that it's my duty to kill her.

I close my eyes, steady my breath, and slip into my astral form. Then I make my way to Aens, surveying the eerie moors illuminated by the moon's silver light. Even less homes have lit fires and candles, and I wonder if that's because there are less witches here or if they're all just asleep.

I move toward the home Hyacinth shares with her mother Papra. They're both sleeping in their rooms, but there's no sign of the Sage here, either.

Now, I'm completely at a loss. I drift toward the Coven altar, envisioning the moment I met the Aens Adept, Leo.

He must live close by, so I decide to seek him out. Halfway down the hill, I stop at the familiar witches pacing outside one of the homes—big, hulking shapes. Witches from the bunker. If they're guarding this house, the Sage *must* be inside. I slip right past them in my astral form to find Leo sitting in the living room, whispering as he practices his magic.

I watch him for a moment before moving farther into the house. Another guard stands outside another door. On the other side of it is the Sage, right here in the open lands of Aens.

Tabitha's voice floats through my head. *She's waiting for you.*

I breathe myself back into my body and frown at the ceiling. There aren't any panicky tremors or tears when I return this time. Now, I'm filled only with purpose.

I know what I have to do.

Chapter Forty-Six

For Better or For Worse

EVERYONE IS STILL asleep, which makes this easier for me. This is something I have to do alone. Clio would never let me leave if he suspected I was going to do something so reckless, which is why I let him sleep. If anyone follows me, it'll be the last time they follow anyone. The Sage set this up from the beginning; she decided a long time ago that in the end, I'd be the one to face her. I appreciate that decision. In the old days, before the Covens, a new king could only rise after his predecessor's death.

For better or for worse, no one will know a thing until it's over.

I expect Kado to wake up at the very least—his undead ears hear everything—but he doesn't stir. I pause in the doorway, gazing at them both with love and appreciation. There's a chance I won't come back. I know that. So I close my eyes, blow them a kiss, and force myself to turn into the hall.

Before I leave Willow's mansion, one of her tigers follows me just beyond the door, interested in in my plans until I stop briefly to pet its head. With an irritated twitch of its tail, it turns and leaves me for something else. Then I head for Zane

271

and the portal. This part will prove more difficult. He'll be suspicious of me traveling on my own, despite the fact that I never could before. I rack my brain for an alternative route out of the Land of New Life, but Zane is the only way I know.

So I steel myself and wipe all emotion from my face when I approach him, hoping not to give anything away.

"I heard the news," he calls and eyes my legs. "That's wonderful."

"Thank you." I smile, but he doesn't open the portal. "I'm headed to the Wilderness. I didn't get to tell Hazel the good news."

"Of course. I'll be sure to let Miss Willow know where you've gone if she asks." Zane opens the portal.

I smile, but it just doesn't feel right. I feel awful for lying to such a kind witch, especially if he's going to involve Willow. She's the last person I want to know about me leaving.

I'll either be back home or dead before she knows where I've gone. That only makes me feel worse.

"Sounds good." I practically throw myself through the void just to put an end to the conversation.

On the other side, the opening closes with a pop. I'm on the border of Aens, just like the first time the Elemental refugees came to the Wilderness. I take a breath and do what I've dreamed of doing for so long. I run across the moors, streaking through the moonlight as the cold night air fills my lungs.

In real life, this trip is far more exhausting than in my astral journeys. I'm out of breath before I even pass Hyacinth's house, but I don't slow down until I'm well past it. Out of all the Council's abilities, Hyacinth's insane mind-reading has been the most worrisome, especially now.

At the Coven altar, I sit in the shadows and pull my knees up to my chest, trying to settle my breath and my thoughts. I haven't seen any other witches yet, but I also haven't closed in on Leo's house.

This all seemed so much easier in my head.

THE SAGE

When I'm ready to move again, I stick to the shadows. I reach Leo's house fairly quickly but find only one witch kneeling outside. It's Leo. The group of guards from the bunker may have been an illusion for my sake, but it makes me wonder just how many witches are left on the Council's side.

I'm close enough now to see Leo's bowed head, his hands clasped together as he whispers into the night.

He's praying. I never would've taken him for the spiritual type, but in times of crisis, no one can be blamed for changing their ways.

Lurking behind the next house over, I'm glad Maverick convinced me to test my divination, because this is the real test. I need to know exactly how many witches are in Leo's house. The last thing I need is to run into one of the Sage's lackeys before I ever get the chance to find her.

I close my eyes, breathe, and feel the energy in the air around me. There's the pull of Leo's aura in front of the house. I reach out a little farther, paying attention to anything and everything I feel inside the tiny dwelling.

Sweat trickles down my forehead, but I don't stop. Then I find what I need; there are three witches inside. I let the connection drop, and the bubble of energy snaps back toward me like an elastic band. I clap my hands over my mouth to keep from uttering my surprise.

I came all this way, knowing the challenges I would most likely face, but I didn't have a plan for getting past anyone. Of course, I could charge in and recklessly try to take them all, but even three—plus Leo—is too many, regardless of how many powers I possess.

Thinking, I gaze up at the top of the hill and the Coven alter—a hulking stone covered in yellow words and images. It's as good of a distraction as any, so I reach out with my mind.

I imagine my telekinesis as a hand. Gently, I brush two invisible fingers across the side of the stone. A yellow light glows upon the altar. In minutes, the Aens witches pour from their houses, murmuring groggily and wondering why a Coven meeting would be called so early in the morning.

Leo stands and runs toward the glowing altar. He can sense that something isn't right, but I hope to be in and out of that house before he figures out what that is. The three witches inside stay where they are, so I run toward the house with everyone else distracted and peer into the window.

Two huge men sit at the kitchen table, one of them with a cup of tea and the other staring sightlessly across the room at the wall. They look frozen, and I realize immediately that I've been holding them like this with my powers.

I breathe out slowly, feeling the quiver run along the net of my telekinesis, and my confidence soars. I stand up straight and barge into the house. When the door slams shut, the men cry out, but they still can't move.

One of them tries to utter a spell, but his limited movement provides nothing more than spark that quickly disappears. I move straight through the tiny house, no longer worried about the Sage's guards. Then I find the witch I've spent countless nights thinking about. I find the Sage herself.

Chapter Forty-Seven
Final Confrontation

"**L**ILITH. THIS IS a pleasant surprise." The sage sets down her mug and stands, like she's greeting an old friend instead of an enemy.

I hadn't exactly expected her to be asleep, but I hadn't expected such a welcome, either. But Tabitha did say she was waiting for me. "Let's not pretend this is a surprise for anyone," I say. "You knew I would be here. You knew it would come to this. Just you and me. You planned it, right? And you've been waiting for it ever since. This whole time... you've been playing all of us. The puppeteer behind this entire war."

The Sage nods without shame or fear.

"Why?" I demand, balling my hands into fists. How can anyone sit through such a damning accusation? "I don't understand why you would do this. You dedicated your life to destroying us instead of accepting what we've become. Instead of finding a way to heal this mess and improve the Land of Five. So many witches have *died* because of you. Good witches who didn't deserve any of it. You can't sit there with your infinite knowledge and tell me I'm wrong."

The Sage blinks and slowly eyes the room. "This place,

the Land of Five, is flawed in ways that cannot be mended so easily. The UnEquipped will soon outnumber the Equipped. Can you imagine what would happen if witches lost their powers altogether? If witches were born without any abilities at all, because the magic was so suppressed in the blood it could not be expressed?"

"We would survive," I tell her. "The UnEquipped are some of the best people I know." My dead adopted mother had no powers. Neither did Helena before she was slain in battle and revived. All the UnEquipped who fought hand and foot in the Battle of the Wilderness were good people too. "I used to think the UnEquipped kept our Covens running while the Equipped kept them strong. It's the other way around, don't you see that? Without them, we would be nothing."

"No, Lilith. Their presence endangers us every day. This war was to clear out the weakest witches among us. Those who survive will flourish. Create a new, stronger generation of witches."

"You're a fool if you think mass genocide was ever a solution." My foot stomps the ground in anger. "That's always been your problem, though. You use people up, and when they're too exhausted to continue, you throw them away. The only flaw in the Land of Five was the corrupt woman in charge of it. I *believed* you when you said you wanted what was best for me. You only want what's best for you."

"I've lived a long time, Lilith. I have seen things most witches could never imagine. Have you ever gone without food for so long that your body stops feeling the hunger? I have. I know what it means to see everyone playing their part. For this world to function, there cannot be room for those who can't fully care for themselves."

I scoff. "Like me. I couldn't walk, so I was expendable like everyone else, is that it?"

The Sage looks at my legs and smiles. "Don't worry, child. I was never dishonest in that aspect. Look at who you've become. You are a strong, beautiful witch, but this woman standing before me would never have emerged without this war. You would have remained hidden, forgotten within the net of safety your parents created for you in Ignis. You would have forsaken your powers, given it *all* away, just like that."

"And you couldn't stand the thought that I would *choose* to be UnEquipped?" I shake my head, unable to look away from her. "You really believe you've done the right thing, don't you?"

"I didn't get this far in life by guessing," she says. "I've made a lot of difficult decisions in my time. All of them were for survival, because life is never easy. From the day we are born until the day we died, we must fight for it."

"Not like this. We could've helped each other, but you chose to damn us all."

"You may think that now. But you're young. One day, years from now, you'll appreciate the world this war created for you. Yes, I started it with a purpose. And now I must finish it. This is how it ends, Lilith. Here and now."

Frowning, I shoot her a sideways glance. "What are you talking about?"

Smiling like a sweet grandmother, she reaches into her pocket and pulls out a boline knife. The blade is sharp, the polished surface glinting in the firelight. "With this," she says.

I look from her face to the knife and back again. I knew the end of this war wouldn't come without one of us dying, but I never imagined she would willingly offer her life, especially in such a gruesome manner. Part of me feels uneasy, that all this is only an effort to keep me at bay until her witches come to her rescue. I extend the reach of my divination and don't feel anyone else around us.

It's just the Sage and me.

And she's serious.

"You *want* me to kill you?"

"You have a strength most witches dream of attaining. It is why I chose you as my apprentice. It is why I've shared with you what no one else in the Land of Five knows. You have what it takes to dispose of those who cannot live up to their own potential. You will make them right, and under your lead, the survivors will rise from the ashes and build a new world in ways I never could."

I eye the blade warily. "This isn't right." There are a hundred things that the Sage might deserve, like a trial or an execution. She might even deserve a quick death now if she attacked me first. But I can't just murder her.

Can I?

People do terrible things for the ones they love.

"We don't have much longer, Lilith. We both know that." The Sage extends the knife toward me again. "This war has seen you through your entire life. It's fitting that you're the one to end it, and you have the power to do it. If you don't, nothing will change. The war will continue, and more witches will die."

"That's not the only option," I say. "You could step down. If you won't fight me, step aside and let me take your place."

The Sage shakes her head, eyes glittering with tears. "Your energy is pure and good, Lilith, dear. But you know that even the best Healer can't save everyone. Why do you believe you are any different?"

I open my mouth and close it again. She's right. Why am I dragging this out when it could all be over in the next five minutes? "You have the grace of the Elementals and the remaining Councilmembers. You can unite them all. Once I am gone, there will be no one to stop you. You will become the new Sage, and I have no doubt you will use that responsibility for the greater good."

Trembling with the knowledge that she's absolutely right, I step toward her and take the boline. It's much lighter than I thought it would be. It really wouldn't be hard to sink the blade into her neck. She'd bleed out in minutes, and if I couldn't work up the nerve to do it with my own hands, my telekinesis would take care of the rest.

She blinks at me and smiles, sorting through all the thoughts at the front of my mind. "It's okay, Lilith. Do us all a favor."

I stare into her eyes, and the longer I do, the less I actually see her. I see Regina, Howard, Ambrossi, all the witches who died in vain for a pointless war that never had to be fought. This fate is *better* than she deserves, and maybe she's already come to that conclusion.

I need to be the one who does this.

I take a deep breath, and my body struggles to comply.

Do it.

I take a step toward her and lift the blade. It feels like the right choice when the blade comes slashing down into the soft skin of the old woman's throat. Blood pours from her body, and I feel like I'm watching the whole thing from somewhere around the ceiling. The knife drops from my hand before I collapse to my knees, watching the growing puddle of crimson surrounding her, doubling in size to soak through my dress. I don't look away until I hear the Sage's dying breath.

A rush of pressure floods from my chest and into my limbs. I clench my fists, gritting my teeth against the force with the hope that it'll fade. Instead, it only grows until my hearts feels like it may explode and kill me too.

I shout escapes me, and the pressure recedes. It leaves behind a prickling feeling of strength. I blink, but the power exists everywhere, even in my eyes. I stare at the bloody body before me with an entirely new level of respect.

The Sage wasn't just powerful. She was *godly*.

Chapter Forty-Eight
The New Sage

MY CONSCIENCE IS clean as I stare at the Sage, searching for movement I don't find. I don't know why I hope she survived this. Part of me—the part still mourning Ambrossi—thinks this was all too easy for her, that somehow, she got away with every wretched thing she's done to the witches in the Land of Five.

That may be so, but it's over now.

That doesn't quiet the voices, so I take a breath. Mechanically, I slide forward, my knees slipping through her blood, and pick up the knife again. I turn to the Sage's body, knowing what I'm going to do without any hesitation as I lower the blade. I close my eyes, but a minute later, I'm holding her severed head by the white wisps of her hair. Her death may have been better than she deserved, but she *is* dead. I just made sure she stays that way forever.

Fighting back the urge to vomit, I carry the head out into the hall. Leo enters the house just as I step into the front room. The two witches in my net are freed from their hold, and all three of them rush toward me, ready to fight. But when they see the gruesome trophy in my hand, they stop.

THE SAGE

"The Sage is dead," I tell them. My new powers flare behind my eyes, reflecting in each of theirs.

I haven't proven it, of course, but I know that one swipe of my hand could kill all three of them. Apparently, they know this too.

"All hail the Sage!" Leo says and drops to his knees. The two others follow quickly.

I let them play this out for as long as they want, studying the mix of uncertainty, hope, and fear dotting their faces. There was a time as the Sage's apprentice that I hated to receive treatment like this, but now, I've earned it—this recognition and validation that came from all the blood, sweat, and tears.

"Well, let's share the news with the Land of Five," I tell Leo and walk past him with dignity, the Sage's bloody head swinging from my hand.

"O-of course." He stands, dips his head, and travels toward the front door.

The other two witches rise slowly from their knees, but they don't move. Two more witches from the bunker meet us at the door. Leo gestures toward me, and they realize what's happened.

"Welcome, Sage," one of them says.

I ignore them and turn to Leo. "Gather your Coven."

He takes off for the Coven altar at once, gathering most of the witches already milling about from the false meeting call. They converge around their Adept.

"What is it?"

"A new Sage has risen," he tells them.

Absolute silence can be the loudest sound in the world without a way to interpret it, but the Aens witches don't let it last long. Excited voices blast out across the moors.

"Who?"

Leo gestures toward me, and when the Aens witches catch sight of me, they drop to their knees, swearing their allegiance, murmuring praises and blessings. When Hyacinth reaches the altar, she and Papra stand out amongst the group reaction.

Their eyes are wide, and mouths agape in surprise. I stand there, tall and straight without a word, basking in the recognition of the witches who less than an hour ago all wanted me dead.

***

I'M A BLOODY, muddy mess when I make it through the portal. Zane's eyes grow wide when he sees me.

"I-is that…"

I nod.

"All hail the Sage!" he cries.

Smiling, I make my way toward Willow's mansion.

Fern meets me halfway there. "Something's changed," she says at once. Then she blinks, and her eyes widen too. "You did it," she whispers. "I knew you could do it." She flutters close to me, resting her forehead against mine. I feel her powers tugging at my own, testing their strength. "I'm so proud of you."

Willow runs toward us. "What happened?" She pants for breath and slows down, looking frazzled. "Zane told me to come at once—" Then she studies me from head to toe, seeing the blood on my dress and the lump of flesh in my hand. "You did it," she whispers. Her hands fly up to her mouth, then she shouts, "You did it!" Willow drops to her knees, laughing so hard that she starts coughing. "We've got to call a Coven meeting at once."

"Okay. I'll get Clio. And we'll—"

"No." Willow stands again. "Not with *our* people. The entire Land of Five needs to hear this."

Chapter Forty-Nine
Actions

WILLOW HANDLES ALL the logistics, going so far as to take the Sage's remains from me, for which I will be eternally grateful. Clio and Helena walk beside me toward the Ceremony Grounds. It's easy to imagine that we've returned to my Arcane Ceremony and that everything we've been through was just a dream. It's not.

Clio smiles at me and squeezes my hand. Helena hooks her arm through mine. Willow walks behind us. Everything feels so right as we climb the rise and look down on so many faces, the survivors of an unnecessary war, the witches who deserve to enjoy the rest of their lives.

The eyes of the old Councilmembers shine up at us in fear, but as I take my place, I smile down on all of them. The thing that hurt us was the same thing the Council depended on—division. That's what I'm here to undo, to take away the boundaries between the Covens and urge our people to live as one. Just as they do in the Wilderness.

Of course, not everyone welcomes me with open arms, but I never expected them to.

Hyacinth and Grail are on their knees, side by side at the

front of the crowd. The other witches have given them a wide berth. Maverick and Crowe rest their hands on each of the condemned witches' shoulders, holding them in place. Hyacinth glances up at Crowe once, possibly seeking pity or sensing betrayal. But she quickly realizes Crowe won't change his mind, and her purple eyes grow wide.

And Grail? I don't even want to see his face after the harm he's caused, so I don't. I stand at the top of the hill, staring down at everyone. When I glance sideways at Willow, she only offers an encouraging smile.

It's my time to shine.

An older witch hobbles forward from the crowd. His movements are slow, his body ancient, but he makes steady progress across the Grove to take his place in front of the kneeling witches. Grail's eyes close when he realizes who stands before him, and I can't help a small smile. Before them stands a witch I never officially met, a witch I've only heard stories about—Caleb, the witch with the ability to strip others of their magic. Hyacinth, Grail, and the first few rows of witches stare at him. Not very many know what he's capable of, but they will soon.

Caleb takes a breath, lets it out in prayer, and asks Hyacinth and Grail if they'd like to do the same. They shake their heads, Hyacinth almost despondent. Caleb relents, pulls off his black gloves, and tosses them to the grass with a heavy thud. The crowd gasps as he sets two fingers on each of the condemned witches' foreheads.

"Please, Lilith," Hyacinth pleads through shaky breaths. "I'll be good."

I see the venom running through the front of her mind. She's lying. This is the right thing to do. Evil witches do *not* deserve access to magic. So they won't have it.

Caleb's eyes glow with a red hue, first filling his irises then blossoming out to the whites of his eyes. Tiny lines, red rivers of light, stream across his face, almost like his skin weeps blood. The lines multiply and grow, streaming down his neck and running across his collarbone, steadily making their way down his arms.

Hyacinth tries to plead one more time as the magic hits Caleb's wrists, but as soon as it passes to his fingers and touches her and Grail, they're quiet. Their eyes grow wide, neither of them able to move, like they've been struck by lightning and the jolt hasn't yet left their bodies. The red lines travel across Hyacinth and Grail's faces, their irises shining like Caleb's before he pulls his hand away. As soon he breaks contact, their eyes flutter and close before their heads drop forward.

Caleb glances between them but says nothing. He bends down in a regal manner, scoops up his gloves, and puts them on. The he walks away as slowly as arrived, taking his place at the bottom of the hill.

Maverick and Crowe pull the condemned to their feet, but it's as if Grail and Hyacinth are waking from a deep sleep. Hyacinth struggles to regain her footing, and although Grail stands with ease, his eyes don't stay open very long. Maverick slaps him awake a few times. I focus on Hyacinth's thoughts. Immediately upon coming back to the world, she tries to reach out, to read Grail's mind, and is baffled by the sudden silence. She blinks and picks a different target, only for the same result. Frantically, she turns to Crowe but can't read him, either.

"No!" she screams, and though I don't want to smile, I do when I hear the pure anguish in her voice.

Impressed murmurs travel through the witches, and I raise my hands into the air to stop the noise. Everyone but Hyacinth, Grail, Maverick, and Crowe drops to their knees. Almost everyone. A few more hold out, which I expected, especially after what they just witnessed. I let my arms fall, and light fills my eyes, shining like Maverick's do before he uses his magic. The light is so bright, so intense, that the witches who refused now kneel as well.

With them all gazing up at me, wonder and uncertainty

in their eyes, I feel inclined to make a grand speech about how much better things will be now that I'm the Sage. They don't *need* pretty words. They need strong decisions made to better their lives. And that's exactly what I plan to give them.

I don't know what Willow was hoping I'd say to them, but I've chosen something that's honest, transparent, and sums up everything they need to know about me.

"I'm glad to be your Sage."

Excited screams and cheers rise from the mass of witches. Tears well in my eyes. All the Covens shout their loyalty, but the surviving Ignis witches call out the loudest—my old boss Angel; Tarj, the original Ignis Councilmember; and Helena's parents. When my gaze turns to them and I see Helena finally in her place beside them, I know I'll do these people right.

Witches who didn't even know one another turn to their neighbors and embrace them. The joy and relief is overpowering. I let myself cry, but for the first time in my life, they're not tears of sorrow.

For the first time in my life, I can say with confidence that everything is going to be okay.

THE SAGE

About the Author

Kayla Krantz is fascinated by the dark and macabre. Stephen King is her all-time inspiration mixed in with a little bit of Eminem and some faint remnants of the works of Edgar Allen Poe. When she began writing, she started in horror but somehow drifted into thriller. She loves the 1988 movie Heathers. Kayla was born and raised in Michigan but traveled across the country to where she currently resides in Texas.

She has ideas for books in many genres which she hopes to write and publish in the future.

http://www.facebook.com/kaylakrantzwriter/
https://twitter.com/kaylathewriter9
https://authorkaylakrantz.com/

Other Works by This Author

The Moon Warriors: A Novella

A Coven of witches and a group of demons have been at war for centuries and now live in peace under an agreement. The terms are simple—members of either side are not permitted to cross the boundary. When Talia's beloved is killed, she immediately suspects a demon is behind it and crosses the border to search for the culprit. On the other side, however, she meets her first demon, named Marcus, and her entire belief system is turned upside down. With the help of Marcus and Talia's familiar, Mushroom, she gets to the bottom of her sweetheart's death and learns the importance of keeping your friends close and your enemies closer.

The OCD Games: A Christmas Romance Novella

Erica struggles with her obsessions, to the point where her life is ruled by them. After losing her job, she seeks out a new one with the aid of her best friend, Kara, by her side. Change has always been tricky but between support group and art classes, Erica finds herself in the right state of mind...until she meets the mysterious Blaine. As she gets to know him, she learns that everything happens for a reason.

CPSIA information can be obtained
at www.ICGtesting.com
Printed in the USA
LVHW050917020720
659500LV00003B/100